Together in Lilacwell

Sasha Morgan lives in a village by the coast in Lancashire with her husband and has one grown up son. She writes mainly contemporary fiction, her previous series having a touch of 'spice', probably due to all the Jilly Cooper novels she read as a teenager! Besides writing, Sasha loves drinking wine, country walks and curling up with a good book.

Also by Sasha Morgan

Lilacwell Village

Escape to Lilacwell
Return to Lilacwell
Together in Lilacwell

Sasha Morgan

Together in Lilacwell

CANELO

First published in the United Kingdom in 2023 by

Canelo
Unit 9, 5th Floor
Cargo Works, 1–2 Hatfields
London SE1 9PG
United Kingdom

A CIP catalogue record for this book is available from the British Library.

Print ISBN 978 1 80032 963 8
Ebook ISBN 978 1 80032 962 1

This book is a work of fiction. Names, characters, businesses, organizations, places and events are either the product of the author's imagination or are used fictitiously. Any resemblance to actual persons, living or dead, events or locales is entirely coincidental.

Content warning: This story contains themes of miscarriage.

Cover design by Diane Meacham

Cover images © Shutterstock, iStock

Look for more great books at www.canelo.co

Printed and bound in Great Britain by Clays Ltd, Elcograf S.p.A.

MIX
Paper from
responsible sources
FSC® C018072
FSC
www.fsc.org

For Aunty Mary, who always encouraged and took an interest in my writing.

Chapter 1

Eva stared into space. Her mind was frozen, she couldn't focus on the screen in front of her. A warm hand rested on her shoulders.

'You OK, love?' Startled, her head turned sharply to see the office manager's face etched with concern. Eva just blinked and looked blankly at her. 'I think you need to go home,' she spoke in hushed tones, then gently patted her back.

Maybe she was right, reflected Eva. The past fortnight had been pretty traumatic. She quietly collected her things and slipped away.

On autopilot, Eva drove through the crowded streets of Manchester, observing everyone scurrying about their business. How could everything be so normal when her world had been turned upside down? It seemed absurd how people could chat, laugh... even smile when her heart was breaking.

Eventually she pulled into the car park then made her way into the block of flats. Hers was on the top floor, with panoramic views of the city skyline and the canal, where she'd often watch the swans glide past. It was in a scenic and quiet city centre location, with close access to the train station. Only a year ago Eva had been so pleased with her new home. Now it felt like a prison. Luckily, Simon hadn't quite moved in fully, just a few of his possessions lay scattered about the flat; his muddy football kit for one, dumped on the tiled floor, she noticed on entering the kitchen. Obviously, his life went on as normal too, she thought resentfully, throwing his kit into the washer. How could he even think about playing football when she was struggling to get out of bed in the morning? Then, inevitably, the tears came, spilling out, pouring down her cheeks until great, racking sobs took over, shaking her whole body. Would she ever be the same?

Six weeks ago, Eva had held the white plastic stick containing life changing information. She was pregnant. It had come as a complete shock at the time, but as the knowledge seeped in, so had the anticipation. As each hour passed, the more adjusted she became, until by the end of the day the confidence she'd grown matched her newfound excitement. A mother; she was about to become a mum! Her mind swirled with eagerness. Would it be a girl or a boy? What would he or she be called? She couldn't keep the flat, they'd need to move to a proper house with a garden. The enormity of the situation had swamped her mind.

It had been a Friday, and Simon usually stayed over for the weekend. Eva decided to cook a special meal to celebrate. She imagined his face, overjoyed when she told him the good news. She'd wear the slinky, black dress he'd bought her for Christmas, not to mention the black, lacy underwear. Eva had shaken her chestnut hair free from its clasp and left it tousled to rest on her shoulders. Using only the minimum of make-up, she brushed a touch of mascara to highlight her green eyes and a pale shade of gloss across her full lips.

However, the evening hadn't quite panned out the way Eva envisaged. Granted, Simon's face had lit up, but only when seeing her looking slim and sexy, giving him the eye – that, and catching a whiff of the casserole in the oven. He'd smiled and raised a seductive eyebrow at the candlelit table with champagne chilling in an ice bucket.

'What's the occasion?'

'We're celebrating,' she'd told him.

'Really?' he frowned, not quite knowing where this was leading, worried he'd forgotten some anniversary.

She went to wrap her arms around him. 'I'm pregnant, Simon,' she whispered into his ear. He froze. Eva pulled back to examine his face. Nothing. It was devoid of any emotion. A still silence hung between them. 'Say something, Simon.'

'How? We've always been so careful.' He almost sounded accusing.

'I know… but it must have been when I was ill.'

Eva had been sick several times a few weeks ago with a bug she'd picked up, and retrospectively assumed her pill hadn't been effective for a few days afterward. 'Simon?' Her voice quivered.

'This is a shock, Eva.' He ran a hand through his hair and sat down. He'd turned ashen. The notion that he was going to be a dad, and all the responsibility that entailed, didn't fill him with glee – more like dread. Eva saw it written all over his face. It was at that point she knew. This wasn't right. It was untimely, for him anyway. When she voiced this, he gave a huge sigh.

'It's…'

'A shock, yes, I know,' stated Eva flatly, beginning to feel insecure and unsettled. They had been seeing each other for two years, after all, and he'd often declared his love for her. He took her hands and looked into her eyes.

'Eva, just let me get used to the idea, OK?' He leaned over and kissed her.

—

The trouble was, Simon couldn't 'get used to the idea.' Try as he might, the thought of giving up his flat, his nights out, his football and his freedom to be saddled with a full-on, live-in relationship and baby didn't fit in with his plans. He liked living alone and spending the weekend with Eva; it was a perfect compromise – the right balance for him. Whilst he didn't want to completely move in with Eva, he equally didn't want to be without her either. He thoroughly enjoyed her company. She was fun, laid back and accepted him for who he was. Eva didn't nag him about seeing his mates, playing footie, or drinking too much. She never gave him ultimatums about their relationship but was happy to go with the flow. All his friends liked her, and she them. Eventually, yes, he conceded, things would change, he'd be more committed in time, but this news had hit him like a thunderbolt. His hand was forced, the tide had changed. He'd no doubt it was a genuine accident – Eva would never pull a stunt to trap him, but even so, trapped he was. Then, in equal measures, came the guilt. He didn't like feeling this way, and in many respects, he wished he could whip up some enthusiasm. But he simply couldn't. Nor could he pretend.

A quietness between the two had developed. Simon, more out of a sense of duty, put his flat on the market and they started to look at houses for sale. Something inside him wanted only his name on the mortgage, but he soon realised that was impossible. Buying a house in the part of Manchester they wanted needed two wages poured into it. *Goodbye Switzerland, no more ski trips for me.* In fact, no more holidays at all for the foreseeable future, he dully reflected. Instead, he had to get his head around prams, cots, baby seats and all the other paraphernalia having a baby encompassed. The one thing he point blank refused to give up was his Audi TT convertible. That was a bridge too far. Eva didn't press the issue but could hardly see the practicalities of keeping it. Still, if it meant appeasing him, he knew she wouldn't complain.

–

Eva never complained. She quietly tried to make the best of the situation, until it was taken out of her hands.

She'd woken with acute pain in her abdomen one Saturday morning. Simon had gone to football practice. Doubling over, she made it to the bathroom only to see blood oozing from her. Her heart stopped. The baby. She was losing her baby. Instincts told her to ring for help, but her legs gave way, and she was forced to stay sat on the toilet. After what seemed an eternity, she managed to get to her phone in the hallway. Eva knew it was pointless ringing Simon, he'd be on the football pitch away from his mobile. She rang her parents, hoping they'd be in. Her mum answered the phone.

'Mum, I need you to come quick,' she gulped.

'Whatever's the matter Eva?' The urgency in her mother's voice was evident.

'I think I'm having a miscarriage.' She started crying hysterically.

'I'm on my way, love. Just …sit tight.'

Eva lay on the hospital bed. She'd been examined and the doctor had confirmed the worst. Her mum gripped her hand tightly.

'You'll get through this love, me and Dad are here to support you.' Eva just stared at the ceiling, feeling numb. It suddenly occurred to her that Simon hadn't been contacted.

'Simon, I need to ring him,' she murmured.

'I take it he's playing football?' her mum asked in a condemning voice. She'd never disguised her disapproval of Simon. The opposite in fact; blatantly criticising him at every opportunity. Unfortunately, it seemed Simon had provided her plenty of opportunities of late. Both her parents had picked up on the vibes he'd put out regarding the baby and their dislike of him had intensified. An awkward moment hung in the air. Her mum shifted uncomfortably, then spoke very quietly. 'Listen Eva, maybe this happened for the best.' Eva turned to face her.

'How can you say that?' she asked incredulously.

'I mean… you hadn't exactly planned it, had you, love?' She tried to reason, then added dryly, 'Simon certainly hadn't anyway.' Tears swelled up in Eva's eyes. The words cut deep because Eva knew them to be true.

–

Simon further confirmed this by taking his flat off the market that same day. Whilst he had genuinely been saddened, there was no mistaking the way his life seemed to return to normal. After the initial few days of upset and comforting Eva the best way he knew how, he'd reverted to just staying at her apartment at weekends again and going on nights out with his mates.

For Eva, it was the polar opposite. She struggled coming to terms with the whole scenario – the shock of the pregnancy, the plans they'd made, the complete loss. All in such a small space of time. It had left Eva in turmoil. She couldn't function. More than anything, she couldn't get over the lack of compassion shown, not only by Simon, but also her parents. How could anyone say her miscarriage was for the best?

It hurt like hell that Simon had lapsed back to his easy-going lifestyle so swiftly, reflected Eva, as she slammed the washing machine door shut. Probably because he was relieved, she admitted to herself. And it was at that moment she'd made her decision. They were over.

The size of a raspberry. Her baby had been the size of a raspberry, with its ears, eyes and nose shaping, and its arms and legs forming, before exiting her body and leaving her empty. Void. Eva turned her laptop off. She couldn't keep doing this, torturing herself by looking up the stages of pregnancy, checking at which point hers had ended. It was pointless and, more than anything, painful. Instead, she forced herself to focus on more pleasant things, like what had made her happy before all this. Eva brought her mind to holidays, walks in the country, cosy nights in, films she'd watched, books she'd read, music she loved playing. Anything to take her mind off the miscarriage. She couldn't even think about work, having to face everyone again in the estate agent's office, watching the pity in their eyes and all those awkward moments of silence. There was only so much one could say, and it had all been said, none of it having the slightest effect on her. So, Eva had arrived at her second decision – she had handed in her notice and quit. Typing the email to the office manager had been easy, even though her future felt so uncertain. Luckily, under the circumstances, her manager had waived the months' notice she should officially work. Secretly, she suspected they were relieved, she'd hardly been able to concentrate on her short return to the office after all.

Her parents had been amazing, offering to support her until she found her feet. Although her mum's words in the hospital had cut deep, Eva knew they were more clumsy than malicious. The way her parents had rallied round, showing her so much love, had helped, and encouraged her to come back home and live with them temporarily, gave her the push she needed to rent her flat out, which provided some income while she recovered and worked out her next steps.

Sighing, she made a coffee and sat down in her parents' lounge. There was only so much daytime TV one could handle, and she snapped it off before throwing the remote control across the settee. Putting her head in her hands, she tried to figure out exactly what she was going to do with her life. Then, her phone burst into life, interrupting her thoughts. It was Beth, her oldest friend.

'How are you, Eva?' She heard the concern in her voice, but it wasn't overloaded with sympathy, like most.

'I'm bored. I need to sort myself out.' She sighed again.

'Right,' Beth's voice had changed to assertive, 'what you need is a good night out.' Did she have any idea? Eva thought bleakly.

'Not at the moment, Beth. I just couldn't,' she answered flatly. There was a pause. She imagined her friend racking her brains for a magic solution.

'When were you last truly happy?' Beth suddenly asked quietly. The question surprised Eva. After giving it some consideration, she replied.

'At college. We had a blast, didn't we?' She smiled, remembering the antics they'd got themselves into. Ever since downing a bottle of cider together in the common room and giggling all through the afternoon's lessons, they'd been inseparable. Together they would egg each other on and having a sneaky drink or cheeky fag behind the caretaker's cabin became a regular event, as did bunking off. Now and again both girls were partial to a bit of retail therapy.

'We sure did,' agreed Beth laughing, then added, 'get back into it.'

'What?'

'Your ceramics. You were brilliant.'

Eva's eyes glanced about the room, filled with the pottery she had proudly brought back from college; the large terracotta urn, the colourful glazed bowls, the little woodland animals, to the delicate, intricate rose; each petal she had painstakingly moulded and crafted. Beth was right, she did have a talent, but had chosen not to pursue it at university, to her father's dismay. Often, he would remind her of what she was capable of achieving, but she'd never really taken him seriously, not seeing a career in what she considered a hobby. She played around sometimes when she visited her parents and could potter about in the shed where she'd practised or done homework for college but had let the hobby fall away when she moved to Manchester. Now, though…

'Hmm, you've given me something to think about,' mused Eva.

'Listen, gotta go,' Beth hissed. 'Stage director's calling me. Speak soon.'

Eva pictured her in the hustle and bustle of the theatre, doing what she loved. Beth *had* chosen to pursue her talent. She was a costume designer for a production company, frequently calling Eva on set from all sorts of exciting locations.

For the first time, Eva felt a stab of jealousy. Why had she allowed herself to just dawdle along in a job that hadn't really inspired her? Working at the estate agents had been nice enough, but she was now beginning to realise what she'd been missing out on, the opportunities she had given up. Again, she compared herself to Beth and a sinking sensation began to creep inside. *It's not too late*, she heard her father's voice tell her. It wasn't. She was only in her mid-twenties.

A kernel of an idea began to take root. A spark had ignited within, and Eva reached out for her laptop, this time with the intention of researching something positive.

Chapter 2

Fitz closed the cottage door, not bothering to lock it. Without any neighbours here in the dense woods there was no need. In fact, not many people even knew of its existence, tucked safely away from prying eyes – just the way he liked it. Fitz had built the cottage himself, using his talent and craft as a woodsman. His home really could have been lifted from a children's fairy tale, with its arched windows, a creaky oak door with large, cast-iron hinges, low slated roof with stove flues poking out puffing smoke, and a decked veranda where his hammock gently rocked in the breeze rustling through the trees. It was magical. It was tranquil. It was exactly Fitz.

He was at his happiest in the peace and quiet left to carve, saw, chisel, sand, whittle, hammer, and stain his wood. He made bespoke pieces, whether it be furniture, outdoor structures, delicate ornaments, toys, or life-size statues, they were all masterpieces. Fitz had the patience and time to be fastidious with his work, which was why he was well sought after, having a long waiting list of customers eager to buy his wares.

As well as his workshop next to the cottage, he also rented a business unit in the nearby village where he showcased his work. The Cobbled Courtyard contained a small complex of craft shops, including a blacksmith, pottery studio, florists, and a sweet little cafe. The complex had recently been taken over by Jasper Hendricks, whom Fitz particularly liked, being a down to earth landlord and of similar age to him. He'd attended Jasper's Christmas wedding not so long ago, along with the other tenants of The Cobbled Courtyard.

A quaint village in the north-west of Lancashire, Lilacwell was popular amongst the more discerning traveller who didn't want to endure the crowds and queues of the popular Lake District, not too far away. Boasting old stone cottages and humped-backed bridges stretching over bubbling streams that wound through verdant forests, the village had a timeless, peaceful quality to it, which meant very few of its inhabitants ever left. Those who were lucky to stumble across it always returned. So had been the case with Fitz. Once visiting Lilacwell, he had been captured with the serenity immediately surrounding him.

It was as though the place was hugging him, protecting him. And protection was what he had desperately been seeking. Some might say he'd been running away, but Fitz had had no choice; for his own sanity he needed to start a new life, and so had settled in this beautiful village. Here he could be himself, without being scrutinised or judged. He doubted those that had condemned him once would even recognise him now with his beard, long dark hair, and weather-beaten complexion. His physique had certainly changed, too, from pen-pushing in the city to hard manual work. Here he could do what he liked best, working with his hands, which had given him a new-found great skill of such exquisite craftsmanship. Here he could walk along the country footpaths, or across the green, velvet fields with his bare feet, under a starry sky.

He'd never known calmness like it. After an application process, he'd been given permission to buy a plot in the woods and build his cottage, in order to upkeep the surrounding area. As well as carpentry, he provided a forestry service and maintained the forest he lived in. It had been ideal for him, the perfect solution.

As he walked through the trees and out onto the dirt track leading to The Cobbled Courtyard, he noticed the 'To Let' sign in the pottery window. It seemed Jasper had finished renovating Jessie's old studio and the flat above, ready to put it on the market to rent. It saddened him that Jessie had left. He'd grown fond of the old lady who had more life and vitality than anyone he knew, with her twinkly eyes in a kind, creased face. She had entertained him no end, regaling him with stories from her rather eventful past. The courtyard wouldn't be the same without her. Still, there was always the rest of the clan: Max, the blacksmith, forever filthy, covered in black soot – with a dirty mind to match, reflected Fitz with a wry smile; James, the florist, who was the polar opposite with his gentlemanly ways and impeccable manners; not to mention Tom and Tess, the young couple who ran the Courtyard Cafe whilst being parents to baby Chloe. Theirs was a happy bunch and now with Jessie going, they were all slightly concerned of the impact this would have; how the dynamics would change once a newcomer arrived.

Fitz wandered over to his little studio and opened up. The smell of wood hit him and, as always, offered comfort, making him feel completely at home. He went over to his desk, throwing his keys on the table, and played the answer machine for any missed calls or messages. He emphatically refused to carry his mobile phone everywhere. The last thing Fitz wanted was to be available 24/7, not for anyone.

'Hi Fitz, just wondering how the tree house is coming along. It'll definitely be ready for his birthday next week, won't it? Anyway, get back to us when you get this. Thanks.'

Fitz rolled his eyes. Of course, the tree house was ready. Did Alex really think he'd disappoint his own godson on his fifth birthday?

'It's Pru here, can you give me a call back please?'

Ah, the sensible, no-nonsense Prudence Tomkin-Jones: a local councillor, until her Dunkirk spirit and ability to get things done saw her hand-picked to spearhead a charity organisation. Pru was energised, pragmatic and proactive, far wiser than her thirty years; all the things her celebrity artist husband was not. Although almost a decade older than his wife, he didn't always act his age. Kit Tomkin-Jones was lazy, a tad selfish and most certainly didn't get things done, well, not very often anyway. However, when he did decide to shift himself into gear, his paintings were phenomenal, selling like hot cakes for extremely hot prices to A-list celebrities, sheikhs, lottery winners, successful entrepreneurs, or anyone else with substantially deep pockets. Which was fortunate, really, considering the upkeep of the rambling, ancient manor house they lived in.

'Yo, Fitz, how's it going? Time we had a piss up. Friday, at the usual?'

And that was Kit. The complete contrast to his long-suffering Pru. Fitz chuckled to himself. It most definitely had to be a case of opposites attracting. How else had Pru and Kit ended up together? Maybe she'd seen what a lost cause he was, and in true Pru nature had decided to save him. At least someone had, Fitz reflected sadly. Who would save him? *Could* he be saved?

Chapter 3

'Well, Mrs Molloy, we did it.'

Rory turned momentarily to his brand-new wife and smiled. They were driving home, back to the Lancashire village of Lilacwell, nestled in the Forest of Bowland.

To say they had had a whirlwind romance was an understatement. Having only met the previous summer through a mutual friend, Cassie and Rory had fallen for each other the moment their eyes had met. The attraction had been instantaneous and mutual, leading to Rory leaving his barrister's chambers in London to set up a smallholding with Cassie in her home village.

He'd been no stranger to Lilacwell as his friend and former colleague, Adira Hendricks, lived there. She and her husband, Jasper, owned The Laurels, a large country house on its own estate and it was on this land that Rory had bought and renovated a barn, making them neighbours. Now the barn was almost complete. Rory and Cassie had named it The Harvest Barn, which was very apt, considering the crops they grew. Together they had put their sweat, blood and tears working the land and growing their smallholding. They had planted fruit trees, sowed fields, built polytunnels and raised vegetable beds. They had built a chicken coop and kept a goat, all while overseeing the barn conversion.

But it had been worth the slog; their hard work had paid off. Cassie, in her wisdom and never one to miss an opportunity, had marketed their progress, contacting a local country magazine who had written an article on the young, eco-entrepreneurs. They had also signed a book deal with a big publishing house and appeared on local TV. Cassie had also plugged Rory's infamous title – The Eco Warrior – from his days representing an activist group to further pursue their business. Local people and hostelries were happy to be supplied with the produce from The Harvest Barn, which doubled up as a business name as well as their house name.

Amongst all this, it had become a running joke that they would elope. At first it was said in jest, with them not having a spare moment to arrange a wedding; the conversion of the barn and getting the smallholding up and running had taken up all their time and energy. But, in true Rory and Cassie style, they took the plunge and actually did it. They eloped, in secret – well, almost. Someone had to look after their hens and goat. That had been Adira's job, which, being three months pregnant, hadn't been ideal. Still, once the morning sickness was out of the way, off she had trundled, together with Jasper, down the fields where their land met Rory and Cassie's, to feed their clucking hens, Kevin – their very loud cockerel – and Belinda, the bleating goat.

Adira and Jasper had been the only people to know of their elopement. Truth be told, because it had been a well-known joke within their families, Rory and Cassie doubted either sets of parents would be too surprised when they found out. Nobody more than they knew how impulsive and impetuous their offspring were. And Rory and Cassie truly were spontaneous. But look at what they had achieved – a beautiful, converted barn and a thriving smallholding. They were proud of their accomplishment and rightly so. It only seemed natural to want to be husband and wife, and as of five days ago, that's exactly what they were – a married couple. Only Lilacwell didn't know it yet.

This only added to their excitement, knowing they'd done it all clandestinely. Like two naughty children they giggled as Rory parked the Range Rover outside their home. On cue, Kevin let out a piercing, 'Cock-a-doodle-doo!' as if welcoming them home, which then set the chickens off, clucking away, which then prompted Belinda to bleat repeatedly.

'Do you think they've missed us?' laughed Cassie.

'I'm sure they have,' grinned Rory. 'Come on Mrs M, let's face the music.'

Chapter 4

Adira sat at the breakfast bar sipping green tea. Usually, she would have enjoyed a cappuccino made from their rather complicated looking coffee machine, but not these days. The very thought of coffee made her retch and want to vomit. Again. It was fast becoming a ritual, all this morning sickness, and she would be glad to eventually see the back of it.

Her husband rubbed her back in sympathy.

'OK now?' he soothed, after having heard her throwing up in the bathroom moments before. He was sat at the kitchen bar on his laptop.

'Yeah,' she sighed, and took another gulp of tea, desperate to get rid of the metallic taste lingering in her mouth. 'I'll be all right, it'll wear off soon.'

'At least we don't have to feed the chickens,' he grinned in an attempt to cheer her up.

'Or Kevin and Belinda,' she smiled back. Despite feeling a touch delicate, Adira was looking forward to seeing her friends again. She'd known Rory since working in the same London chambers as him, but she was probably closer to Cassie, after having worked alongside her, too, at The Inn at Lilacwell, when she had first arrived at the village. It was only last July that she and Jasper had hosted The Laurel's summer ball, where Rory and Cassie had first met.

It seemed a long time ago, so much had happened since. Now she was pregnant, about to be a mother. Besides Jasper, nobody was more excited about the baby than Fletcher, Jasper's uncle. It was Fletcher who had kept the family estate running, until Jasper, his only heir, had stepped in and taken over, though Fletcher had stayed living with them at The Laurels.

Only recently had Fletcher disclosed to Jasper a family secret – but it didn't take Hercule Poirot to see the striking resemblance between the two of them, more than one would expect between an uncle and nephew.

Although all three lived in harmony together under one roof, Adira and Jasper were currently valuing their time alone while Fletcher was holidaying on a river cruise. He and his long-term friend and companion, Lilly, had set sail and were enjoying the delights of the Danube.

'It seems so quiet without Fletcher here,' remarked Adira, looking round the kitchen. Normally he'd be here, cursing the coffee machine he'd never quite mastered properly, or burning the toast. It was now all so calm and tranquil.

'You should enjoy the peace while you can,' laughed Jasper, although he too was pining for Fletcher inside. He'd missed the old boy terribly, always a father figure to him, in every sense. Knowing this, Adira placed her hand over his.

'Not long before he's back,' she comforted.

'I know, he'll soon be here, spreading his bonhomie,' he replied, making them both chuckle. Then Adira noticed the screen he was working on. She squinted to read it.

'Any takers yet?' she asked, pointing to the advert on the page seeking out a new tenant for the vacant pottery unit in The Cobbled Courtyard.

'Hmm, yes, just one,' replied Jasper. 'I think she sounds ideal.'

Chapter 5

Making his way to The Inn at Lilacwell after a long day of physical work, Fitz couldn't wait to sink a pint. He loved the place, with its rustic character and stone floors, inglenook fires and antique furniture. It still held an intrinsic down to earth charm, albeit being an award-winning hotel, which Fitz appreciated. It welcomed visitors donning either dressy heels or muddy walking boots, and of course, dogs were always made a fuss of.

Kit was propped up by the bar on his third malt whisky when Fitz joined him.

'There you are, about time,' the artist remarked before ordering him a pint.

'Cheers, mate. Sorry I'm late, got chatting to Max.'

On hearing this Kit gave a low chuckle. He had warmed to the blacksmith and his rather satirical outlook on life. They'd shared many a drunken night at The Inn at Lilacwell, putting the world to rights with their outlandish opinions, which often included mock and ridicule at the expense of others. Not to mention Max's dirty humour that could make a grown man blush.

'Ah, how is Maxy boy?' Kit threw back his drink.

'Same old, you know Max,' replied Fitz with a wry grin. He took a long swig of beer. 'That's good.' He'd been more than ready for a pint after working all day in his workshop.

'I see Jessie's unit's been let already,' said Kit. Indeed, the sign had now been taken down and they had all been notified of a new tenant.

'Yeah, another potter apparently. Jessie left the kiln.' Thank God he hadn't had to try and cart that out of the shop when he had helped the old lady move out. Then, as an afterthought he added, 'I thought you might have wanted the studio?'

Kit shrugged. The thought had crossed his mind, or rather his wife's, but typically he hadn't acted upon it. 'I'll probably need somewhere a bit bigger.'

Fitz smirked. 'You mean, to store the many pictures you haven't painted yet?'

'I've made a start,' Kit objected, making Fitz laugh.

'Hmm, it's in the finishing though, isn't it?'

Kit sighed. 'I'm just not feeling it, you know?' He searched Fitz's face for some kind of understanding, from one craftsman to another.

'Not really,' he replied flatly. Fitz was way too pragmatic to appreciate Kit's 'arty-farty' ways. Fitz was a doer, not a procrastinator like his friend. He often thought Kit played on being the eccentric celebrity artist, tucked away in his country house, waiting for inspiration. Why couldn't he simply get on with it? The man had talent, yet here he was languishing away letting it all go to waste. He'd seen Kit's paintings – well everybody had – and they were notoriously good, often mistaken for photographs such was the fine attention to detail. Kit had a real flair for capturing the spirit of his subject, whether it be a person or animal, and it was while he had been commissioned to paint the daughter of an aristocratic family that he'd met and completely fallen for his wife, Pru. Prudence

Tomkin-Jones had turned twenty-one and her portrait was to hang proudly at Wolven Hall.

–

Originally called Lilacwell Manor, the locals knew it as 'Wolven Hall' owing to a legend that the last wolf in England was slain on its grounds. To add to this, there was a coat of arms above the studded front door showing a wolf with the Latin inscription, '*homo homini lupas est*' which translated to 'man is wolf to man,' the motto of the Tomkin-Jones family. The magnificent house, along with its history and legends had gripped Kit from the moment his brogues had stepped foot on the marble tiles. *Now this is what I call style*, he'd thought as his eyes took in the sweeping staircase, high ceilings with ornate carvings, huge chandeliers and family portraits hanging down. They seemed to be glaring at him. He had hoped his painting would be just as impressive. For the first time in his career, he had begun to feel a touch daunted. Kit's anxiety was soon calmed when he met Pru. Her smiling face and warm charm instantly soothed him. It was as if she sensed his apprehension. Being the only child of Cyril and Patricia Tomkin-Jones, Pru had always known her position, and what was expected of her; she was the next custodian of Wolven Hall and with that duty came inherent responsibility.

Pru was good with people. Her intuition made it easy to grasp a situation and act accordingly, and when she had seen the flicker of trepidation in Kit's eyes, she immediately tried to pacify him. Pru was used to seeing how people reacted to her home, how awestruck they could be. So, she did her best to make them feel welcome. As Kit set up his easel and paints in the library, Pru had chatted and offered him tea. She'd shown a genuine interest in his work, asking who else he had painted. Kit had felt himself relax in her company. She made him smile with her posh accent, but down to earth ways. Pru was a natural beauty and a pleasure to paint with her fresh complexion, huge eyes and dark hair piled up neatly with a diamond tiara; she reminded Kit of Audrey Hepburn. He'd almost suggested she hold a cigarette lighter, emulating the iconic *Breakfast at Tiffany's* photograph, but then thought it a little crass on reflection.

Pru, in turn, had also been captured by this quirky, handsome artist. She loved the way his golden locks flopped carefree over his face, his bohemian style and dress, how his paint-stained smock shirt hung over faded, ripped jeans. Of course, she had read of his reputation in the tabloids, everybody had. Kit Flanders had been dubbed 'Philandering Flanders' due to his antics and womanising ways. The nation had lost count as to how many beauties had been photographed on his arm. The archetypal story of rags to riches had caught the press, for Kit had humble beginnings. Coming from a working–class family, he had obtained a scholarship to study at a top art college in London. From there, he had grown from strength to strength, his first big break coming when an aged star of the silver screen had spotted him.

So, when the hottest artist in the country had landed at Wolven Hall, Pru was more than excited to meet him. She hadn't been disappointed. Neither had Kit, until his painting was completed and his work at Wolven Hall was done. Pru, always the lady, had waited and waited for Kit to make the first move, but as the days turned to weeks, her impatience festered, until she saw him in the newspapers again, with yet another woman on his arm.

Enough was enough. She might be ten years younger than him, but she still knew her own mind and better still, knew what was good for him. Kit needed stability. He needed attention. He needed love. And she was going to give it to him. On impulse, she emailed him, inviting him for dinner.

Somewhat surprised by the sudden invitation, Kit accepted out of curiosity. What was her game? Pru was far too good for him. He knew it, she knew it, and, more importantly, her family knew it. But that didn't stop Cyril Tomkin-Jones marching his beloved only daughter and heir down the church aisle to the scrubbed-up artist waiting for her. In true Pru fashion, she had fought hard, against her own parents and all the other opposition, to marry Kit Flanders. She had gone and stuck her neck on the line, waving two fingers to the snooty attitudes and judgmental toffs. It only seemed manners that Kit took the family name. At least that way he couldn't be referred to as Philandering Flanders any longer.

Unfortunately, for the past year, he hadn't been referred to at all. He had potential clients waiting, those who had asked for portraits months ago, but had yet to respond. He really did need to whip up some enthusiasm and start painting again.

Fitz looked at him quizzically. 'You OK?' he asked, slightly concerned and beginning to feel guilty. Had he been too off-hand?

'Yeah.' Kit slowly nodded his head. 'I just need that incentive, something to set the creative juices flowing again.'

'Hmm,' replied Fitz and took another gulp of beer. 'You'll soon get back into it,' he appeased.

Chapter 6

Eva slowed her car down as she entered the village of Lilacwell. The views were breath-taking, from the patchwork of green, lush fields to verdant forests, clear bubbling streams, and little stone bridges. The place radiated a calmness of its own. Eva wound down her window and inhaled the fresh, clean air, instantly knowing she had made the right move. This was where she needed to be, every sense in her body told her so. For the first time in a long, long while, Eva felt herself slowly unwinding. Her shoulders relaxed and at last her troubled mind started to ease.

Internally, she thanked Beth for sowing the seed. If it hadn't been for her friend's encouragement and relentless coaxing, she might never have made it here, to this small piece of paradise. Eva parked up and took out her phone to text her.

> Made it. It's perfect. Thanks for everything
> xxx

This was soon answered with: *Go girl!*

Typical Beth, she thought with a smile full of beans and enthusiasm, always willing her on. Eva hoped Beth would be able to visit her soon. She could just about accommodate one visitor. Living above the shop was going to be a tight squeeze, only having one bedroom, a bathroom, and a kitchen-living area, but Eva had been adamant this was going to be her future home, because whilst it was pretty cramped upstairs, the downstairs studio was absolutely ideal. The ceramic shop had a large, wide bay window letting in all the light she would need while working, plenty of storage with its thick, wooden shelves running across the walls, a practical stone floor and a kiln, discreetly placed in a recess at the back. It even had a tiny tea point and a downstairs loo. Her parents, whilst delighted by Eva's decision, were also a tad reluctant to see her set off alone again so soon. Her dad had volunteered to dig out her potter's wheel from the garage and bring it to Lilacwell at the weekend but, although Eva was grateful, she also knew it had been an opportunity to suss out her new abode. She hoped they'd be impressed, the last thing she needed at the moment were any negative vibes. Eva had had enough of them to last her a lifetime.

Facing Simon and telling him she was moving had been emotionally exhausting. Initially, he'd been shocked when she had told him of her decision to rent out her flat and relocate to Lilacwell.

'But…you've never even been there,' he'd frowned, perplexed by her news. 'How do you know you'll like it?'

'I don't know, Simon. I'm taking a leap of faith,' she'd stoutly replied, a touch irritated. Who was he to question her? It's not as if he'd been a reliable shoulder to cry on. Once again, she was reminded of how well he'd been able to bounce back to his normal life. At least he had had the grace to look slightly crestfallen at her going away, although Eva couldn't help but suspect it was tinged with relief. Was she just a reminder of how guilty he should be feeling? The thing with Simon, she had now deduced, was that he'd wanted to have his cake and eat it too. He cared for her but wasn't prepared to make any sacrifices. As long as Eva was happy to go along seeing him when he wasn't busy playing football, or drinking with his friends, then all was swell. But not anymore. Simon's selfishness had been well and truly exposed by his unsupportive actions, behaviour, and his complete lack of empathy. Even now, by showing surprise at her announcement to start afresh, he showed Eva how little he understood her.

'We'll keep in touch, won't we?' he'd asked, searching her face, still dumbfounded.

Taking a deep breath she replied, 'No, Simon, I don't think we will.' And with that she'd turned and never looked back.

So, the peaceful, uplifting effect she was experiencing on entering Lilacwell was the best sensation in the world, instilling the belief that deep down, it had been the right decision to make.

Eva followed the directions she'd been given to The Cobbled Courtyard and soon found the entrance to the charming set of craft shops. It was as pretty as the website had presented, with its appealing stone buildings and brightly coloured wooden doors, each with its own sign depicting what the unit was. Her eyes gravitated towards her studio marked The Potter's Bolthole. Eva had loved the name the previous owner had given it. Glancing around, she read the other shops' signs. There was The Fresh Bouquet with its wooden flower box bursting with red geraniums under the window, The Hot Spot which she presumed to be the blacksmiths, judging from the smoke puffing out of the chimney and the sound of hammering metal from the open doorway. Next to hers was Crafty Carpentry where a wooden carved statue of a Green Man stood solemnly at the door. Finally, there was the Courtyard Cafe which looked warm and inviting with its pastel-coloured bunting swooping across the outdoor decking area with sweet bistro sets. It was all so picturesque, with an old-world charm. Eva so hoped she would fit in.

It hadn't taken Eva long to load her belongings into the small flat above the shop; the bulk of her stuff was coming with her parents shortly.

As Eva opened the studio door, she'd noticed an envelope with her name on the windowsill. Eva opened it and smiled. It was a welcome card from the owners of The Cobbled Courtyard.

> *Wishing you much happiness living here at The Potter's Bolthole.*
> *Very best,*
>
> *Jasper and Adira Hendricks*

What a thoughtful gesture, thought Eva, leaving her with a tender, tingling feeling inside.

—

Fitz was knackered. After a night's drinking session with Kit and a full morning installing his godson's tree house in readiness for his birthday party, he decided to take a rest and head to the Courtyard Cafe.

'Hi Fitz!' called Tom, busy behind the counter. 'Your usual?'

'Yes, thanks mate.' With the bright sunshine pouring through the window, he decided it was too nice to stay indoors. 'I'll be outside Tom.' Fitz sat on the decking facing his shop and noticed movement coming from the pottery studio next door. Squinting, he made out a figure putting pieces of ceramic on the shelves. So, this was his new neighbour.

His black coffee soon arrived via Tess who usually worked the tables. 'Thanks, Tess,' smiled Fitz.

Tess pointed towards The Potter's Bolthole. 'The new lady seems nice enough. We went round this morning and introduced ourselves.'

'Ah, right.'

'Yeah, she's called Eva, from Manchester apparently.'

'I see,' said Fitz, looking over again. Eva was right by the window now and he got a better view. He was surprised at how young she looked with her off the shoulder top, skinny jeans and hair scooped up in a messy bun. She suddenly turned and caught his stare. For a moment they locked eyes before she smiled and waved. He nodded his head, feeling a little awkward that she'd caught him looking. He'd hate to come across as being nosey when he was usually the exact opposite. Just then, James came out of his florist shop with a bunch of lilies and made his way over to The Potter's Bolthole. Eva had opened her door and invited him in. Fitz saw them interacting with each other. Maybe he should go and introduce himself too before the day was up, he was her next-door neighbour, after all.

Once he had finished his coffee, he went back into his workshop and looked around for something suitable to give as a welcome present. He opted for a mug tree, which he'd carved in the shape of a real tree with lifelike branches. Jessie had made the cups which hung from them, making it an ideal gesture. After giving it an hour, in time for James to leave, he went round and tapped gently on the door.

'Come in!' He heard a voice call.

Inside, he was faced with several wooden crates scattered across the floor and Eva's back, standing on a ladder putting ornaments on the very top shelf. The last thing he expected was this pert bottom staring him full in the face. He coughed.

'Err... hi, I'm Fitz,' he said. She turned to greet him. What a beautiful smile she had, reaching her deep-green eyes. They reminded him of the sea on a cool, still day. Her chestnut brown hair shone deep and glossy, like his favourite wood stain.

'Pleased to meet you. I'm Eva.' She climbed down the ladder and held out her hand. It felt warm and soft.

'Here you are.' He handed over the mug tree. 'Just a little something to say welcome.'

'Oh, how kind!' Eva carefully took the tree and inspected the delicate, intricate carving. 'It's amazing, thanks Fitz.' Then added, 'Is Fitz short for something?'

'Just Fitz,' he answered simply with a tight smile, obviously not willing to offer more information.

'Right... err, well let's christen it, shall we. Fancy a cuppa?'

'A coffee would be great, thanks. No milk or sugar please.' He watched her as she made them both a drink.

'These cups are gorgeous.' Eva examined them as she poured the kettle.

'Jessie made them, the lady who lived here before you.'

'Did she?'

'Yeah, we both sold the mug trees,' he explained. 'A bit of a cross-studio collaboration.'

'How lovely. Did Jessie live here long?' Eva handed him his coffee.

'Thanks. Yes, Jessie lived here the longest, we're all going to miss her.' Then, realising how offensive that may sound quickly added, 'But I'm sure you'll like it here too. Welcome to The Cobbled Courtyard.' He raised his cup in salute.

Eva raised hers. 'Cheers.' She smiled again, lighting up her pretty face. Her skin was pale and smooth, like porcelain. Those sea-green eyes of hers seemed to be assessing him too, he couldn't help but notice. A charged pause hung in the air for a moment before Fitz spoke.

'All settled in then?'

'Yes, thanks.' she answered, still looking at him rather intensely. Fitz was beginning to feel uncomfortable. As if reading his mind, Eva quickly turned her gaze away, blushing slightly. He noticed her flushed cheeks and found it rather endearing. People rarely blushed these days.

Another pause hung in the air.

'Have you met Max, the blacksmith yet?' Fitz asked, wanting a distraction.

'No. He's the only one who hasn't called. Does he keep himself to himself?'

Fitz spluttered into his coffee.

'No… not exactly.' He tried hard to keep his face straight. Eva picked up on the vibes.

'I take it he's quite a character then?' she laughed.

'You could say that,' he grinned, his eyes sparkling with amusement.

'Hmm, that might explain why his forge is called The Hot Spot,' she said, still half laughing. Then she commented, 'I was admiring the carved statue at your door. It's the Green Man, isn't it?'

'It is.'

'Isn't that a sign for—'

'Fresh beginnings,' he finished, looking directly at her. 'Well, I'd better let you get on.'

–

Fitz finished his coffee and put the empty cup on a shelf.

'Thanks for the present, it's very thoughtful,' Eva said.

'You're welcome. Bye.'

Eva weighed him up with a sense of déjà vu. She was sure she'd seen his face before, though couldn't place him. A strange awareness filled her, but she didn't know why. He smiled and left, leaving Eva wondering why his face resonated with her. And what a face it was, she thought, watching him enter his workshop through the window. All swarthy and compelling, with a strong jawline, and how his blue eyes twinkled when he smiled. As for those biceps, my goodness, she fanned herself, getting quite flushed again. He did have an air of mystery about him though, which only added to Eva's attraction. Then she giggled to herself, what would Beth make of him?

Chapter 7

Fitz shut the door behind him and lent on it for a few seconds with his eyes closed. Eva recognised him, he was sure she did. Well, she *was* from Manchester, it was feasible. His worst fear, his ultimate dread, was on the verge of unfolding, he could sense it. A heavy, nauseating sensation began to surge up from his stomach, making his legs weak. He stumbled and reached out for a stool to steady his shaking body. Forcing himself to take deep, steady breaths, he waited for his heart rate to slow back down to normal. He'd assumed that surely here he'd be safe, away from prying, accusing people. But no, it appeared Lilacwell was not going to be his safe haven after all. He'd worked so hard to accomplish his business, his home, his new lifestyle – was it all about to vanish? And what about the friends he'd made, was he going to have to say goodbye to them too? A cold sweat broke out over him. A drink. He needed a whisky to calm himself, he thought, walking back out of his studio and home through the woods. He'd get the wood burner going and finish off that bottle of Jack Daniels.

As he entered Woodsman Cottage, hidden away in the trees, the familiar, cosy surroundings helped Fitz to feel safe and secure. Soon he was snug by the warm fire, sipping his drink. The hot fluid burned his throat, but he slung it back anyway, wanting that reassurance and comfort alcohol initially brought. Eventually the steady voice of reason kicked in. Thinking about it sensibly, Fitz went through the facts. Eva may not have recognised him, and even if she did, who was to say how she'd react in any event? Would she blow his cover, or could she be persuaded to keep it a secret? This left him in a quandary. How was he to play it? If she did know who he was, he could pre-empt any difficulties and talk to her, appeal to her better nature. But what if he was imagining the whole thing and Eva had no idea who he was, or about his past? Would he be making things worse? He needed to spend time with her, suss out what the situation was.

As the whisky took effect, Fitz stared into the flames and allowed the memories to come flooding back…

Theo Fitzgerald had been born the much beloved son of Major Miles Fitzgerald and his beautiful Greek wife, Dimitra. Miles had met and fallen completely under the spell of the young, dark-haired beauty whilst holidaying on the island of Patmos. As an older gentleman, he had worshipped Dimitra from the moment he'd clapped eyes on her, showing nothing but respect and the willing-ness to love and look after her. Dimitra too, was taken by the handsome soldier, with his impeccable manners and caring ways. She'd felt special, protected, and, as her parents often reminded her, he had the means to make her – and their – life extremely comfortable. So, with the whole family's blessing, Miles and Dimitra had married within six months of meeting in the small, white chapel overlooking the turquoise sea in Patmos. The attraction had never faded, for either of them. Their marriage had been a fairy tale, with their love growing day by day.

When Dimitra had given birth to their first son, Miles was overjoyed. Having married later in life, he had almost given up on ever becoming a parent. When gazing into his firstborn's adorable face, he knew he could deny him nothing. And he hadn't. Theo had been given everything; endless love and attention, a little brother, Lucas, who idolised him, a good education, a healthy allowance, a Mercedes for his eighteenth birthday, a flat in central London for his twenty-first and all the support any parent could possibly give. It had all paid off. Theo hadn't squandered his upbringing and privileges – he'd taken advantage of them. He was proud to boast of his qualifications gained at one of England's top public schools. He didn't mind name dropping when asked for referees' contacts. His family knew many influential people, his own godfather was a Lord. Theo flourished with his connections and background; he milked them to the full. When he'd landed his first job at the London Stock Exchange, Miles had been more than proud. Theo had been the Golden Boy, and everything he touched seemed to turn to gold. So much so, Theo had been encouraged to invest more and more, to see the shares rocket into orbit and give the stakeholders the returns they craved. And for a while, he did just that. Theo saw promotion after promotion. It seemed his career was soaring to ever-lofty heights, heading in the same direction as the shares he poured money into. Theo was making millions and it was at this point, at the height of his career, that he decided it was time *he* felt the benefit, as much as the shareholders. Sure, he was earning a tidy sum, but that wasn't enough for Theo. He wanted to make a real fortune – just like those he was advising. So, he convinced his father to lend him a serious amount of money. Two million pounds, in fact. Miles had had slight reservations, who wouldn't? But ultimately, he had faith in his son. He re-mortgaged the enormous country house in Cheshire and handed over the cheque.

Theo was to plough it into a new up-and-coming aviation company. Aerospace Plus made planes for budget airlines and was making a big name for itself. The business was growing rapidly, employing thousands with a huge turnover. Theo had been studying the market for a while and he'd noticed Aerospace Plus's steady increase in performance. He was at pains to time it just right, but that's what he was notorious for, storming in at the exact crucial moment.

Only this time, Theo had got it disastrously wrong. The same day he had sunk his two million into Aerospace Plus, one of its planes had sunk into the Indian Ocean. Not long after the plane's catastrophic crash, the company's shares followed suit and also plummeted. The business was bust. The money was gone. Theo couldn't believe it when he saw the news. His world froze. How could this have happened to him? He never got over the pain and anguish he had caused his family, and even though they tried to console him, Theo was no fool. He knew what his actions had cost them.

In the end he'd run away, no longer able to stomach the look of despair in his mother's eyes and regret in his father's. Even his little brother avoided him, resenting the fact his hero had lost them their home. Theo had been distraught, not knowing who to turn to or where to go. His 'friends' at work sneered him, no longer the Golden Boy now, as he clearly couldn't be trusted with anyone's money. Theo was to be avoided like the plague, kept away from any important project.

One day, he simply packed a rucksack and got on the first train out of London. He sold his flat and transferred the money to his father's bank account; it seemed a pitiful gesture really, considering he'd paid for it in the first place. After travelling through the night, the train finally pulled into Lancaster station. Theo, in a daze, got off and plonked himself on the opposite train on the platform, standing waiting to depart. It took him to Clitheroe. From there he just walked and walked, for miles, without any planning or forethought until eventually he had staggered into Lilacwell. Theo had inadvertently found his salvation. Or at least, he thought he had.

It had been Kit who had first spotted him in the pub, sitting lonesome and defeated in a corner. He'd taken pity on the sad looking stranger and brought a pint over to him. Theo had enjoyed the company. For once it was good to relax and listen to a fresh voice, who asked very few questions of him, and was happy to talk about himself. Before long, Theo found himself smiling, actually laughing as Kit regaled humorous stories about the people in the village he had stumbled across. The one thing Theo had divulged was that he'd been looking for accommodation, pretty obvious judging by the large rucksack sat at his feet.

'Come home with me,' shrugged Kit. 'We've plenty of room.' And so, it was that Theo, or Fitz, as he'd called himself on impulse, settled in Lilacwell. He'd chosen his childhood nickname. He didn't want to be Theo anymore.

Only once had he texted his parents. He told them he was fine, that he needed space and time to work things out. Then, he'd thrown his phone out into the river and bought another cheap one. He didn't want contact.

His stay at Wolven Hall with Kit and Pru had proved most fruitful. He decided to set up his own carpentry business. At school he'd always loved woodwork and he had had an intrinsic knack for it. Having once built a den with his father in the garden, and seeing his son's enthusiasm and talent, Miles had installed a workshop for him, where Fitz designed and made garden furniture. Back then it had been a mere hobby, but it had always de-stressed him. Fitz had needed a steady income and a place to live while getting his business off the ground, and Pru had gone into overdrive to assist him. He'd be eternally grateful for her help, especially managing to persuade the local council to not only give him his forestry job, but permission to build his own home in the woodland.

Since then, Crafty Carpentry had gone from strength to strength. He'd actually surprised himself at its early success, especially as all the while his name had been splashed across his home's local newspapers, depicting his humongous financial disaster and the sorrow he'd brought the Fitzgerald family. Photos of him had been published, thankfully all of him looking clean shaven, with short hair, wearing a suit. He was hardly recognisable in a small village in Lancashire. But two years later, maybe someone finally *had* recognised him.

Chapter 8

Cassie and Rory stood amongst the piles of cardboard boxes. Their new kitchen had arrived and was ready to be installed. It was the last major job to be completed in the converted barn; up until now they had managed with a camp stove and microwave oven. Apart from having the new kitchen units installed, the bedrooms upstairs needed to be decorated, but they didn't consider that as urgent, more cosmetic.

No, it was the kitchen that Rory and Cassie were both keen to see finished. It would be the heart of the home and they were eager to get it just right. Cassie had bought a huge farmhouse table from a house clearance which was to be the centrepiece. The mismatched wooden chairs they'd also sourced, second hand on eBay, would accompany it well.

Although the kitchen units were new, Rory wanted to keep with the rustic vibe and the oak doors had been distressed, to give an old, lived-in look. The white Butler sink added to the farmhouse feel, but their absolute pride and joy was the cream AGA oven with shiny, brass knobs.

All the plumbing and wiring had been completed, so it was just a case of fitting the cupboard carcasses and worktops now. As ever, the two of them were prepared to tackle the job themselves. As Cassie had said, 'We're two intelligent people, of course we can fit a kitchen.'

Famous last words, as the two were getting to grips with the assembly instructions.

'Just think, this time last week…' smirked Rory, seeing his wife in work overalls, splattered with mud and God knows what else from the hens and goat. Her pixie cut hair was still slightly damp from this morning's rain when she'd fed the livestock. It was hard to imagine her as his stunning – clean – bride from a few short days ago.

'I know,' Cassie sighed. 'We were exchanging vows in our glad rags.'

It had been the most magical time for them, following in the footsteps of over two hundred and sixty years of couples, drawn to the Blacksmith's anvil to forge their love in marriage.

In true Rory and Cassie style, they had chosen the most renowned of historic places to elope, Gretna Green. Since 1754, the old Blacksmith's Shop had been the home of runaway lovers, pledging their promises in a romantic, enchanting, and spine-tingling way. Utterly the right setting for Rory and Cassie, they only wished they could have enjoyed their honeymoon slightly longer in Scotland, but as ever, the smallholding came first.

At least they were together, working alongside each other. Gone were the days when Rory had to say goodbye to a fretful Cassie and head home for London. Never once did he regret jacking in his career as a barrister and city life. He'd never felt happier than being here in Lilacwell, where the air was fresh, the rivers ran clean, and the green countryside stretched out for miles. A far cry from the busy, polluted, traffic jammed streets he'd been accustomed to in London. And of course, Lilacwell was much nearer to his family, who were also based in Lancaster.

They had summoned up the courage to tell their parents about running away to tie the knot. As predicted, they hadn't been too surprised, almost expecting to hear it, from Rory's mum at least. 'Typical Rory,' she'd said, half laughing, but deep down was relieved her madcap boy had at last settled down. Cassie was his ideal match and both she and Rory's dad were more than pleased he was living so much closer to them.

Cassie's parents, whilst also happy for the newlyweds, couldn't hide their slight disappointment not to have seen their daughter marry. This had made Rory and Cassie feel a tad guilty.

'We'll hold a celebratory dinner,' Rory had suggested, to make amends. 'Invite family over, once the kitchen's finished.'

'Yes,' agreed Cassie, 'and friends!' She was of course thinking of Adira and Jasper.

For now, though, getting the kitchen finished was proving easier said than done.

Chapter 9

Max had spent all day hammering red hot iron and dipping it to hiss in the cooling water. The forge was quite literally boiling inside, and he stood outside to take in a moment of fresh air. On doing so, he noticed movement coming from the pottery studio. His gaze followed the new woman out of her unit as she made her way towards the cafe. *Hmm, very interesting*, he thought, admiring the svelte figure. His eyes gravitated towards the bare flesh of her shoulders. Without a second thought, he followed her into the cafe. She was chatting to Tess and cooing over baby Chloe as she bent over her pram. Max took in the view.

'Oh Max, come and meet Eva,' called Tess. Eva turned to face him.

'Well, hello, Eva.' He gave a grin as he looked her up and down, obviously taking every aspect of her in. Eva's lips twitched. His reputation had clearly preceded him, knowing he looked a bit of a rogue with soot smeared over his face and hands. 'I won't shake your hand,' he said, guessing what Eva was thinking. 'I'll get cleaned up first,' he winked, making Tess laugh.

-

It was hard to guess his age, being caked up in muck and dust. Judging from his slightly greying temples, she'd guess early forties. He definitely had a playful charisma about him and obviously found it easy talking to the ladies.

'You'll soon get used to Max,' said Tess to Eva. Tom then joined them, carrying a brown paper bag.

'There you go, Eva, one baked potato and chilli.'

'Ah, lovely thanks.' Eva took it. 'Tonight's tea. Too tired to cook,' she explained to Max.

'If only I'd known. You could have come to mine for supper.' He gave her a lazy smile and raised an eyebrow. Eva didn't reply and just returned his smile politely. 'Maybe a drink at The Inn?' he continued.

Eva stalled momentarily. 'Erm…'

'Just the one, to get to know the locals?' he gently persisted while Tom and Tess exchanged knowing looks.

'Why not?' Eva answered.

'Great. I'll call at eight then,' and with that he turned and vacated the cafe.

'Typical Max,' he overheard Tom laughing.

'Oh, he's harmless,' butted in Tess. 'You'll enjoy yourself, really.'

She wasn't disappointed. As soon as she entered The Inn at Lilacwell with Max, all the occupants turned and gave a cheery smile.

'Meet our new neighbour, Eva,' he announced, approaching the bar. Kit was on his usual stool and leaned back to get a good view.

'Ah, hello Eva, I'm Kit.' He held out a hand which she shook.

'Hi.' No introduction was necessary. Eva only just managed to stop her jaw from dropping. The last thing she expected was the celebrity artist, Kit Tomkin-Jones, to be present.

'Hello, I'm Pru,' said a stunning, dark-haired lady, 'Kit's wife.' Again, Eva recognised the face, but wouldn't have remembered her name. 'So, Max hasn't wasted any time in bringing you here,' she teased.

'No, although he was the last person I met in The Cobbled Courtyard,' replied Eva.

'Ah, so you've met Fitz then?' Pru gave a mischievous grin. 'Easy on the eye, hmm?' Eva just provided a non-committal shrug 'Talking of which...' Pru's head turned towards the door, noticing Fitz enter, 'here's the man himself.'

Eva turned to see him. He was looking straight in her direction and, once again, their eyes locked.

'Fitz, what'll it be?' called Kit.

'Just a pint please, thanks.' He only intended to have the one, considering the whisky he'd downed before. After drowning his sorrows – or rather, his insecurities – he'd suddenly craved company. The Dutch courage from those whiskies, though, gave him the confidence to look Eva fully in the face. He stared into those sea-green eyes of hers, which were beginning to mesmerise him. Could he see any flicker of recognition in them? It was hard to tell.

Eva was transfixed. There was something about him which demanded interest; it was a strange, yet persuasive feeling, almost drawing her in. The air between them was charged.

'A drink, Eva?' asked Max dryly.

'Err... oh yes please, gin and tonic, thanks Max.' Eva quickly answered. Whilst Max was busy at the bar, Fitz grinned at Eva.

'So, you've finally met Max.'

'Yes, he persuaded me to come here and meet everyone.'

'Sounds like Max,' he smirked, before taking his pint from Kit, nodding thanks as the man was engrossed in a conversation with his wife. She watched his tanned biceps move as he lifted his pint glass. He wore a fitted black T-shirt and black jeans which emphasised his firm thighs. Eva hadn't had time to change, so still had her skinny jeans and off the shoulder top on.

'I didn't know Kit Tomkin-Jones was a local,' Eva hissed under her breath, still a touch star-struck. Fitz chuckled.

'He's very down to earth. Top bloke in fact. So is Pru, she helped me enormously when I first came to Lilacwell.'

'Where do you come from?' Eva asked.

-

Fitz sharply eyed her. The question seemed innocent enough, judging by her expression.

'Cheshire,' he said, examining her reaction.

'Oh, I'm from Manchester.'

'Yes, I know.' They stared again at each other, until Max interrupted them.

'There you go, one gin and tonic.' Instead of staying, Max turned to join Kit and Pru, which surprised Fitz, yet was glad of the opportunity, and decided to seize the moment.

'It's my godson's birthday party tomorrow. Would you like to come? Meet the rest of us?'

Down from earlier, her hair was sitting silkily on her shoulders. Fitz resisted the urge to touch it.

'That would be nice, thanks Fitz.'

-

'Well, they seem to be getting on.' Kit raised an eyebrow. 'Looks like you've been pipped at the post, Maxy boy,' he joked, nudging his pal.

Max shrugged. 'You win some, you lose some.' He was no fool, he'd picked up on the chemistry between Fitz and Eva. It was one thing being a Casanova, but he knew when he was beat.

Chapter 10

'Happy birthday, dear Ed, happy birthday to you!' chorused the small family gathering, as an excited little boy blew out the five candles on his cake. Fitz had been so pleased with his godson's reaction to the treehouse. Watching Ed as he was led with his eyes closed into the garden, to open them and find his very own wooden den, hidden amongst the trees, had been a joy. Everyone gathered had been amazed with Fitz's creation, resembling something from *The Hobbit* with its curved structure and arched door. He'd even made a sign saying, 'Ed's Hideaway' and hung it from a branch.

Eva was particularly impressed, not only with the treehouse, but the way Ed obviously idolised his godfather, throwing himself into his arms as soon as he saw him.

'Thanks, Uncle Fitz!' Ed hugged him hard.

'You like it then?' he laughed, tufting his hair.

'Yes! Yes!' roared the little boy.

Eva stood slightly back from the crowd, watching how Fitz easily interacted with everyone. Although she'd been welcomed heartily, Eva still felt a bit of an outsider, being new to the group. She noticed a few of the women make a beeline for Fitz. Hardly surprising, given how tall and handsome he looked in his checked shirt and jeans, a true lumberjack, she'd thought to herself. Suddenly he caught her eye and beckoned her over. Eva wove through the guests to get to him.

'Eva's the lady taking over the pottery studio,' Fitz explained to an attractive lady with red hair cut sharply into a bob.

'Ah, I see,' she gave a rigid smile. 'I'm Janey, the village doctor,' she supplied and held out her hand. Eva barely touched it before Janey placed it back in her trouser pocket and turned back to Fitz. 'Are Kit and Pru coming?'

Feeling in the way, Eva edged back, bumping into Anna, Ed's mum.

'Oh sorry!' Eva said, spilling her drink.

'Oops!' Anna backed off, then gave her a quick grin. 'Doctor Mulvaney gave you the brush off then?' She'd seen how aloof Janey had been with Eva.

'Err… well, I've had warmer welcomes,' Eva replied *sotto voce*, making Anna chuckle.

'Hmm, I can imagine.' Then she waved to Kit and Pru who had just entered the garden. Ed went rushing over to them, eager to open the present Kit was carrying.

'There you go buddy, happy birthday.' Kit crouched down and passed him a square shaped parcel. Ed quickly ripped it open to reveal a framed caricature of himself, complete with button nose, big eyes, wide smile, and tufty blond hair. Kit had captured the spirit and mischief of him perfectly.

'It's me!' he cried, showing it off.

'It sure is,' said Pru, picking Kit up and giving him a squeeze.

Eva turned to Fitz who was looking in her direction and smiled. She then watched as Kit tickled Ed, one arm round Pru. Kit wore a loose white shirt and burgundy waistcoat with black jeans and boots. His signature floppy, blond fringe brushed over his eyes. He had a certain bohemian style that, as an artist, one would expect.

'Come on, let's speak to Alex,' Fitz had moved next to her and gently guided Eva towards the back of the garden. Alex was Ed's dad and a very close friend of his. He was a bank manager and had overseen Fitz's business loan in the early stages of setting up Crafty Carpentry. Fitz had immediately warmed to Alex, with his honest, trust-worthy advice. He knew that Alex was a true professional and very discreet; so much so, that he had opened up to him more than anyone else in Lilacwell.

For a start, Alex knew his full name. Obviously, when applying for a bank loan, Fitz had needed to give all the necessary details, outlining the need for anonymity, without going into too much detail. He'd told Alex that he'd had a failed business venture, which was true, but omitted the figures involved. He also stated that it had created a fall out with his family in Cheshire and wanted to keep a low profile. Alex had assured him of his discretion and never probed deeper.

A close bond had been formed when Ed, then only three years old, had fallen off his tricycle and badly sprained his ankle. Fitz had made him a miniature walking frame to help him get about easily, into which his favourite cartoon characters were carved. It was a touching gesture which had made a big impact on Alex and Anna. When they had decided to christen Edwin (named after Alex's dad) which they shortened to Ed (a compromise for Anna) along with his baby sister, Fitz had been honoured to stand as Godfather to him.

'Thanks again for this, mate. It's fantastic.' Alex stood admiring the treehouse.

'No worries. Glad you're pleased with it.'

'So, how are you finding Lilacwell?' Alex asked Eva with a smile.

'So far, so good. Everyone's been really friendly.' *Apart from Janey*, she didn't add.

'Fitz!' called Pru from the far end of the garden.

'Won't be long,' Fitz said before leaving Eva.

'He's a good bloke,' Alex nodded towards the back of Fitz.

'Yes, he's made me feel very welcome,' agreed Eva.

'Where are you from?'

'Manchester.'

'Ah, near Cheshire then.' Alex eyed her carefully. Eva frowned, was there some significance in that?

'Daddy, daddy look!' cried Ed, who had climbed into the treehouse.

Alex rushed forward to him; any further questioning of Eva promptly forgotten in the face of his adventurous son. 'Careful, Ed.'

Eva went to get another drink from the kitchen, and on doing so, saw Janey talking to Kit on a garden bench by the backdoor. Kit was laughing at something she was saying, and she was quite animated with her hands mid-air, smiling. Hmm, a far cry from the icy reception she was given. As she entered the kitchen, Fitz and Pru were deep in conversation. Eva caught the tail end of it.

–

'—so, I was thinking dinner party?'

'If you think—'

'Just a select few,' interrupted Pru, eager to press her idea on Fitz.

'Lovely.' He gave a wan smile in defeat, clearly knowing full well Pru wasn't really interested in his opinion.

'Ah, Eva there you are,' beamed Pru. 'You'll make up the numbers nicely.'

'Sorry?' Eva looked from Pru to Fitz, who was smothering a smile.

'I'll let Fitz fill you in. Now, where's Kit got to?' and off she went.

'A dinner party for Kit's fortieth,' Fitz told her. 'Only I'm not sure that's what he'd actually want.'

Eva grinned. 'I see. And what would Kit want?'

'A piss up at The Inn probably,' he said, laughing.

'Oh dear,' giggled Eva.

'Anyway, looks like you're invited.' With a soft gaze, he looked straight at her.

'Well, someone has to make up the numbers,' Eva replied dryly, making Fitz laugh again.

Chapter 11

Jasper passed the grandfather clock in the hall as it chimed five o'clock. He calculated Fletcher's taxi home would be arriving in about half an hour and he couldn't wait to see the old boy. Adira was right, The Laurels just wasn't the same without him. They were used to Fletcher's noise, whether he was shouting at the TV watching the horse racing, whistling cheerfully as he went about his everyday business, or just simply hearing his voice as he chatted to the two of them in the evenings. Fletcher was a good talker, regaling tales from the past, always exaggerated for optimal entertainment; he had a wicked sense of humour, and often had them in hysterics with one anecdote or another. But he was also a good listener. Fletcher had offered wide-ranging counselling on numerous occasions to Jasper as he grew up, and still did, even though he was a grown man. And Jasper appreciated it, for Fletcher was his anchor; steadfast and reliable. He'd be lost without him. Which was why Jasper was keen to get him home safely.

Fletcher had given them all a scare when collapsing with an angina attack whilst on holiday in the Highlands after having rather enjoyed himself a little too much with all the eating, dancing and, particularly, the whisky bars.

Jasper had had to collect him from the hospital and bring him home safely. Ever since, he'd been at pains to keep an eye on the old boy. Jasper only hoped he'd behaved himself on the river cruise with his lifelong companion, Lilly, and hadn't overexerted himself. He'd given him strict instructions, but he knew Fletcher. He was a law unto himself. Jasper couldn't help but grin at how Fletcher had been on his stag do not so long ago; he had outdrunk them all, then called to the bar staff for a lock in!

Fletcher wasn't the only one who had been a touch too reckless or careless that night. Jasper was convinced that was when Adira had conceived, and he couldn't be more delighted. Having a child to pass the family home on to was important to him, and to Fletcher. Jasper recalled Fletcher's words when he first came back to The Laurels to live: 'It's time to pass the baton on to you now.' Well, one day he'd be saying the same.

Walking into the library, he saw Adira resting on the chesterfield reading a book.

'What's that?' he asked, taking a seat next to her.

'A book on baby names,' she replied, not looking up.

'Oh, any favourites?' He hadn't thought of any names yet, except he'd want the name Fletcher in there somewhere, if their baby was a boy.

'How about Gaia for a girl?'

'Gaia?' Jasper frowned, never having heard that name before.

'Yes, it means mother earth, apparently.'

Jasper laughed. 'Sounds like something Cassie and Rory would pick.'

'I know,' Adira chuckled.

Jasper leant over and looked at the book. 'What about Aden for a boy, meaning handsome? Like your husband,' he teased, then moved forward to kiss her lips. They both jumped on hearing the front door slam shut.

'He's back,' said Jasper with surprise and got up to meet the man in the entryway. Adira followed behind, just as happy to have Jasper's uncle back home.

There he was, the same old Fletcher.

'Hello, hello!' he boomed. 'Jasper, come here my boy.' He gave him a slap on the back, then turned to Adira. 'And you get prettier every time I see you.' His eyes twinkled.

'Oh Fletcher, it's good to see you,' said Adira, moving in for a hug.

'Well, 'owt fresh? Anything happen while I've been away?' Fletcher looked from one to the other expectantly.

'Not really... oh yes, Rory and Cassie eloped!' trilled Adira.

'By the bloody hell!' Fletcher roared. 'Good for them.'

'How was the cruise?' asked Jasper while helping Fletcher to take his coat off.

'Brilliant, absolutely brilliant.'

'You did take it easy, Fletcher, didn't you?' Adira cast a concerned eye over his appearance, as if she would be able to tell from sight if he'd taken any unnecessary risks.

'Yes, yes, don't fuss, lass.'

Jasper hung up Fletcher's coat in the closet, peering back over his shoulder as he did so. 'And Lilly, did she enjoy it?'

'Oh aye, she had a whale of a time,' chuckled Fletcher. Then he clapped his hands together. 'Now, let's get that kettle on and I'll tell you all about it.'

Chapter 12

Eva hummed peacefully to the radio as she put the final touches to the studio. The Potter's Bolthole was looking charming, with its workbench running along the side wall, on which sat her paints, brushes and utensils, plus thick, wooden shelving holding some of the beautiful ceramics she had made over the years. On the stone floor was a huge, multicoloured rag rug and the potter's wheel stood neatly in the corner. She'd taken down the voile in the bay window to really let the light pour in on the whitewashed walls where Eva had hung various black and white framed prints of an art exhibition she'd participated in at college. A friend who was studying photography had taken pictures of her at work, from close-ups of her hands moulding clay to the finished pieces. They were simple but effective, showing the process of the craft.

Eva stood back and admired her work. Not bad. In fact, for the first time in a long while, her spirits began to lift. She'd been in Lilacwell over a week now and was just about settled in. Upstairs her living accommodation was compact, but tasteful. Eva had repainted the white walls to a rich cream, giving a sense of warmth, and after ripping up the brown carpet, she'd been delighted to discover the original floorboards in good condition. She'd gone next door to Crafty Carpentry and asked to buy a tin of varnish from Fitz. He'd looked a little puzzled.

'I've just discovered the floorboards upstairs,' Eva explained, quite excited by her find. 'They'll look amazing once stained.'

'Ah, right,' he smiled. 'Won't they need sanding first?'

'Oh.' Her face dropped, making him laugh.

'I'll do it if you want. It won't take me long.'

'Are you sure?' she asked, not wanting to put on him. But it was tempting to let an expert do the job, given she'd never attempted anything like it before.

'Yeah, no worries. Tomorrow ok? I'll pop round after I've finished here.'

'Thank you, thank you, thank you!' Eva gushed, pleased he could do it so soon.

So, after she had finished the studio, Eva moved what little furniture she had into the bedroom to have the floor clear for Fitz. By next week she intended to open the pottery shop. She had ordered fresh supplies of clay, paint, and glazing, and already her head was bursting with ideas, her hands itching to get to work and feel the cool slab of clay beneath her fingers.

She sensed Fitz felt as passionate about his work too. When she had called yesterday, she'd seen how concentrated and absorbed he'd looked whilst carving a large block of wood. He told her he had been commissioned to make a life-size chess set for a client, who wanted a feature for his garden. Although time-consuming, this particular client had very deep pockets and was prepared to pay an eye-watering amount, and Fitz was glad of the work, knowing it would set him up for the rest of the year. When Eva had interrupted him, he'd been about to take a rest. Like her, he said he often got so engrossed in his work that he forgot to take breaks, totally losing track of time.

So, she appreciated that by late afternoon the following day, he had put down his tools and headed next door.

–

Fitz tapped on the studio door, carrying his sturdy sander.

'Hi, come on in.' Eva opened the door wearing denim dungarees, dotted with aqua blue splodges, and her hair escaping from a high ponytail. 'Just been painting the bathroom,' she grinned. 'Then that's all the walls done.' She led Fitz up the set of stairs to her flat. He glanced around, impressed by her changes. He knew Jasper Hendricks had put in a new boiler and had asked him to make new kitchen units for the flat, but the walls did look better with a fresh lick of paint.

'It's looking good,' he nodded.

'It'll look even better once the floor's done,' she agreed. 'Thanks again for doing this.' She smiled straight at him, and he stared back. She was like a breath of fresh air, full of life and enthusiasm. Whereas he was knackered and stressed. He hadn't been sleeping well, ever since Eva had arrived at The Cobbled Courtyard. Although she hadn't shown any further signs of recognising him, it was still unsettling the way Eva had looked at him on their first meeting. He'd been convinced a flicker of recollection had shown on her face. 'You ok?' Her smile had been replaced with a look of concern. Fitz shook himself.

'Yeah, sorry, just tired.'

'Oh, you should have said. This can wait.'

'No, it's fine, honestly. Right,' he said assertively, 'you open the windows and I'll get started.'

Eva quickly went to each window, pushing them out as far as possible, then closed the doors.

'I'll just be in the studio if you need me.'

Fitz gave her the thumbs up. He had his dust mask on and was raring to go.

–

Downstairs Eva could hear the buzz of the sander while she was lining terracotta plant pots blossoming with greenery along the bay windowsill. The fresh lilies James had brought last week were all fully opened now, their fragrance filling the air. She couldn't help but chuckle, thinking of James and what a kind gentleman he appeared to be with his soft, eloquent voice and country set clothes – a stark contrast to Max. The Cobbled Courtyard was certainly full of characters. Not least of all Fitz, with his dark good looks and air of enigma. She couldn't help but notice those broad shoulders and muscled arms through his open necked shirt and rolled up sleeves. There was definitely something about him though, something she couldn't put her finger on. It was as if they'd met before, but surely one of them would have remembered?

Just under an hour later the buzzing stopped. Eva went back upstairs to see Fitz wrapping up the wire on his sander.

'All done,' he said, taking off his mask.

'It looks brilliant, thanks.' The floor was smooth and even, ready to be stained.

'Just leave it overnight to let all the dust settle, then wipe it down and it'll be ready to varnish.'

'Great, thanks.'

He looked at her for a moment, then said, 'I'd stay out of this room for a few hours, just till the air clears.'

'Ah, right…'

'Do you fancy coming to mine for dinner?'

A thrill shot through her. Did she ever!

'If you're sure you don't mind?' she asked, suddenly uncertain and not wanting to take liberties, especially as he'd just done her a huge favour.

'No. We'll get a takeaway.'

'Actually, no, I've got something we can have,' she insisted, glad she could be of some use. A delivery of fresh produce had arrived the other day in a wooden crate from The Harvest Barn.

When Eva had a flyer posted through her door, she'd been immediately interested in what this enterprising business had to offer. Eva had been further intrigued when learning the company's founder was actually Rory Molloy, the infamous defence barrister of the activists who'd protested against a railway line, otherwise known as 'The Goldgate Tunnellers'. She had made a hotpot with all the vegetables from his Harvest Barn offering, plus an apple crumble and a blackberry pie, so her fridge was pretty full.

As Eva locked the studio behind them, after having grabbed her leftovers to bring to Fitz's cottage, her heart beat a little faster with anticipation.

She found it therapeutic strolling through the woods, chatting to Fitz. In the distance, she saw Woodsman Cottage peeping through the greenery. It looked so quaint nestled in the trees. As they approached the cottage, Eva could fully appreciate the work and skill Fitz must have poured into building his home. She took in the decked balcony where a hammock swayed gently in the breeze. Bird song filled the air along with the fragrance of wild garlic. She sensed this really was a safe haven, especially when Fitz opened the door and she noticed he hadn't even locked it.

'I'll put the wood burner on,' he said, making his way through the open plan kitchen and living area. Eva gasped in awe at the vaulted ceiling, the beautiful bespoke kitchen units, the arched window frames, oak doors with cast iron hinges and polished wooden floor covered with jute rugs. By the wood burner stood a large wicker basket filled with logs and two fireside chairs. It was charming and so cosy; Eva fell in love with it on sight.

Fitz had lit the fire and had turned around to look at her.

'Fitz, this is gorgeous!' she exclaimed, her eyes still darting around, taking everything in. Her head lifted upwards to the mezzanine balcony, which held a double bed. The whole place amazed her.

–

It pleased him that she was obviously impressed with his cottage.

'Glad you like it,' he smiled, loving her zeal and positivism – two traits he'd really learned to value. He suddenly wondered what had brought her to Lilacwell. A broken relationship perhaps? He couldn't imagine she'd been without a boyfriend. She caught him staring at her.

'Sorry, I must seem really nosey, having a good look around your home,' she said self-consciously.

'No, not at all.' He looked at the brown paper bag she was holding. 'What are we eating then?' he grinned.

'Oh yes,' she lifted the bag up, 'my hotpot. It just needs heating up.'

'Sounds good.' Fitz took the bag off her and put the contents in the oven. Then he reached for a bottle of red wine on the kitchen shelf. 'Let's open this.'

Soon they were nicely relaxed by a warm fire, sipping fruity, rich wine, and talking about this and that. Fitz had never felt so peaceful, and it made a welcome change. Would now be a good opportunity to probe further? he wondered. Listening to her chat easily about her childhood and home in Manchester, he decided to dig a little deeper.

'So, what made you decide to up sticks to Lilacwell?' he asked casually, despite knowing what impact that very question would have had on him. She paused, then swallowed. Had he gone too far? He took a sip of wine and waited for the answer, all the time watching her face; the way her glance cast downwards, not making eye contact, and the way she chewed her bottom lip meant something was troubling her. Would she disclose it?

'I... had a miscarriage... and...'

'I'm so sorry, Eva,' he gently interrupted. He hadn't been prepared for that. Suddenly he felt awkward – and intrusive. 'We don't have to talk about it.'

'No, it's all right.' She blinked rapidly, then faced him. 'Simon, my ex-boyfriend, didn't really want a baby. It came as a shock to both of us.'

'I see,' Fitz replied softly, hating that he'd clearly upset her.

'So, when I lost the baby, well... I kind of saw him in a different light.'

Fitz just nodded his head but didn't speak.

'In short, he was relieved, and I was devastated.' Her voice cracked. She gulped back a mouthful of wine before looking directly at him.

Her sea-green eyes were filled with tears. Fitz wanted to touch her, comfort her, but knew he couldn't. This was so personal, such a sensitive issue, and he hadn't known her long enough to wrap his arms around her and offer support. No matter how much he felt compelled to.

'I'm so sorry,' he whispered again, feeling totally inadequate – and humbled. In his quest to discover more about Eva, he had realised that other people had reasons to escape to Lilacwell too, not just himself.

Chapter 13

*You are cordially invited to Kit's 40th birthday
dinner.*

*Please do join us at Wolven Hall on the 21st
June. Pre-dinner drinks on the lawn for 6.30
p.m., dinner to be served at 7.30 p.m.*

Let's celebrate!

R.S.V.P

Max laughed out loud as he read his invitation, knowing
full well who this party was really for. Not Kit, that was for
sure. This was Pru's idea of a jolly good do when in fact
Kit would be content just getting sozzled with his mates
in the local, as usual. Still, it was good of her. Pru was
making an effort, marking the occasion.

His heart suddenly throbbed. Who was making an
effort for him? He'd reflected on his last birthday, spent
alone in the forge, working as usual, to be followed by a
ready meal for one. A lump formed in his throat. Would it
always be this way? Just him, with nobody to share his life
with? The years were starting to creep up on him. Soon,
he'd be forty as well, then what? Who would be organising
his celebration? Would he even have one? The thought of

such a milestone being passed without any recognition depressed him. He might come across as the life and soul of the party, happy-go-lucky-Max with an eye for the ladies, but truth be told, he was lonely. Yes, he'd had relationships, plenty of them, but they never lasted. An outsider might assume it was because Max couldn't be tamed, that he was unable to resist the next pretty face which turned his head, but that wasn't strictly true. He was easily drawn to attractive women, but he needed more than just good looks. He craved *depth*, that deep-down, soulmate stuff he just hadn't found yet. Surely it wasn't asking for too much? Plenty of his mates were happily married, so why couldn't he be?

He tried to analyse why. Didn't people take him seriously? Maybe his behaviour encouraged it, playing the field; perhaps they didn't realise it was all a façade, a veneer hiding his true feelings.

–

Fitz was expecting his invitation, having been told previously by Pru of her plans. His immediate thought was the dress code. Pru hadn't stipulated. Was she assuming everyone would wear dinner suits? Not that he didn't have one; he owned several in fact, but not here. They were hanging pristinely in a wardrobe at his parents' house. His black, pressed suits belonged to another life.

–

Eva was rather pleased to get her invite. Although Pru had bluntly, perhaps tactlessly, expressed she was making up the numbers, it didn't deter Eva from looking forward to an evening at Wolven Hall. She was intrigued to see what lay beyond the ivy-clad stone walls and huge studded door. And as for the 'pre-dinner drinks on the lawn,' she beamed at imagining the clink of champagne flutes, gentle chatter and laughter coming from elegant ladies in cocktail dresses and gentlemen in tuxedos, a quintet merrily playing, dappled sunlight glimmering through the trees streamed with bunting… she clapped her hands in excitement. Wait till she told Beth!

–

Back at The Laurels, the Hendricks were pleased to receive an invitation too, though they thought it was more Cyril and Patricia, Pru's parents, who had instigated it. Fletcher was a long-standing friend of the Tomkin-Jones' and suspected they had ensured everyone at The Laurels had got an invite. Jasper knew Kit to say hello to, but that was all. Meanwhile, Adira was rather excited to see inside Wolven Hall.

'It looks a magnificent place,' she commented after reading the invitation card.

'It is, steeped in history too,' replied Fletcher. Then he chuckled to himself. 'I'm not sure Cyril thinks his son-in-law is up to inheriting it.'

'He's a famous artist, isn't he?' Adira could vaguely recall reading an article on him.

'Kit Flanders, you must have heard of him?' asked Jasper.

'Yes, he rings a bell.' Curiosity filled her. 'How did he meet Cyril's daughter?'

At this, Fletcher laughed again.

'Cyril and Patricia commissioned him to paint her portrait. They've regretted it ever since, I think.'

'Oh dear,' smiled Adira.

–

Even more surprised were Rory and Cassie to receive an invitation. Cassie frowned when showing it to Rory.

'How come they've invited us?' she asked. 'Do you think it's because we supply them?' Although the Tomkin-Jones' were customers of theirs, delivering to Wolven Hall on a weekly basis, they never actually saw any of them there to speak to. They just dropped off the wooden crate packed with fruit and vegetables at the back door.

'No,' replied Rory dryly. 'I think it's more to do with us being somewhat in the limelight at the moment, being on local TV and in *Lancashire Lifestyle* magazine.'

'Really?'

'Yep. That's how that sort work,' said Rory rolling his eyes. He hated any form of snobbery. Truth be told, he hated attention of any kind, least of all from an aristocratic family he didn't even know.

'Hmm, might be good to go though,' replied Cassie thoughtfully.

'You're kidding?'

'No. It could be good for business, all that networking?'

As ever, Cassie had one eye on the opportunity attending a party with rich people could bring.

Rory gave a wry, slow smile.

'You could have a point there.'

–

Fitz was busy in his workshop when he heard footsteps. Turning around, he saw Alex standing inside the doorway, holding a bottle of whisky.

'Just a thank you for Ed's treehouse,' he said.

'Mate, there's no need, really. You paid good money for it.'

'Not nearly enough, and you know it,' Alex gently chided. As a bank manager and financial adviser, he was often telling Fitz to charge more for his carpentry, seriously believing he was underselling himself.

'I love what I do,' Fitz would reply, 'I'm not in it for the money.'

'That's not the point,' Alex always replied adamantly, although he did appreciate Fitz's ethos. He, more than anyone, understood why money meant so little to Fitz. Who knows, perhaps he had the right outlook on life? Especially considering how he lived now, doing what he enjoyed and was good at. At least he wasn't working from dawn till dusk behind a desk.

'Thanks again, Fitz, you made Ed's day.'

'No worries. I'm glad he liked it.' Fitz stopped chiselling. 'Tea or coffee?' At Alex's request for tea, he went to put the kettle on. Once again, he'd lost track of time and needed a break.

'So, I was talking to Eva,' Alex said, taking a stool and sitting down. 'She told me she was from Manchester.' He waited for Fitz's response.

'Yeah, she is.' He handed Alex a mug and sat opposite him.

'Hmm,' replied Alex thoughtfully, taking a sip of his drink.

'I thought she might have recognised me when we first met.'

'Really?'

'Yeah, just the way she looked at me, sort of... like she'd seen me before.'

'And do you think she has?'

Fitz lifted a hand and brushed it over his beard. 'Possibly in the papers, although I did look very different then.'

'Would it matter if she did?' Alex tentatively asked.

'Depends on what her opinion is,' Fitz said with a shrug. 'If she's read the papers, it won't be a good one.'

'*If* she believes all they say,' replied Alex.

Fitz gazed, unseeing, over his friend's shoulder. 'Most do,' he spoke quietly, almost to himself. A few moments passed.

'Have you ever thought of going back? Home, I mean, or at least contacting your family? They must be worried sick.'

Fitz looked downwards. 'I told them I was safe.'

'But mate, that was two years ago,' implored Alex.

'I know… I'm… not ready.'

'I'd come with you, as moral support, if you like?'

Fitz smiled sadly. 'Thanks Alex, but I just can't face them. Not yet.'

Alex nodded his head. He didn't want to push him. Fitz was a grown man and had to make his own decisions.

'So, got an invite to Kit's bash then?' he said, changing the subject.

'Sure have,' grinned Fitz. 'Should be good.'

'I'll say, if Pru's behind it. No expense spared.' He winced at the estimated cost, as only a bank manager would.

'I know,' laughed Fitz, 'and the irony is—'

'It's so not Kit,' interrupted Alex, laughing too.

'Exactly,' agreed Fitz.

-

Eva wasn't laughing. She was stood still, outside by the open window. She'd been about to knock and enter Fitz's studio when hearing her name made her stop short. Eva was rooted to the spot, transfixed. So, her instincts *had* been right. She had cause to believe she'd possibly known him and that feeling of déjà vu had been warranted. But *where* had she seen him before? Obviously, their home ground had plenty to do with it. According to the conversation, Alex had said he hadn't been back there for two years. Why? And what was all that about the papers? What had happened in Cheshire two years ago that she would have known about? Eva's mind boggled. Then, realising she was still standing outside Fitz's shop, she quietly made her way back next door.

For the rest of the day Eva couldn't stop thinking about what she had overheard. In the end, she decided to ask Beth. It was time her best mate called to visit; she missed their chats. More than anything, Eva wanted Beth to meet her new friends, especially Fitz; maybe he would strike a chord with her?

Chapter 14

'Come on, let's open this to celebrate.' Rory pulled a bottle of champagne out of the fridge. Together he and Cassie had finally finished installing their kitchen. It looked amazing with its oak doors, wooden work tops, shiny new appliances, and big, warm AGA. The farmhouse table and chairs blended in beautifully. They had painted the walls in a rich cream colour which added to the cosy country feeling. A multicoloured rag rug covered the centre of the slate floor, giving a splash of colour.

'It's fab-u-lous!' gushed Cassie, hardly believing it was their kitchen. 'It looks like something from a home magazine,' she marvelled, which then caused them to look knowingly at each other. 'Of course, you do know what this means, now that we've finished renovating the barn…'

'Yeah,' sighed Rory. 'It means Julia Partridge will be coming back to interview us,' he conceded wearily.

They had first met the reporter for *Lancashire Lifestyle* magazine at the very beginning of their journey when they first bought the land and barn. Julia had taken photos of the pair working their land and of the dilapidated state the building was in, and they had agreed that before and after shots would make a brilliant follow-up article. Although this was obviously good publicity for The Harvest Barn business, Rory hated the invasion of privacy. Despite being a figure in the public eye, he was deep down quite a private person and it had been Cassie who was the driving force behind the marketing.

'Oh Rory, it'll be fine,' cheered Cassie, hating to see the resigned look on his face.

'I know, I know.' Rory popped the cork and poured the frothy bubbles into flutes. 'But let's not talk about that now.' He handed her a glass. 'Let's enjoy the moment. To our stunning home,' toasted Rory.

'To our stunning home!' echoed Cassie.

They sipped the champagne, savouring its dry fizz, then Cassie was reminded of the birthday invitation from Wolven Hall. 'What about tomorrow evening, are we still up for going?' Again, Cassie knew the reluctance Rory felt about attending the Tomkin-Jones' party.

'I suppose so,' he shrugged. 'Though God knows what I'm going to wear.'

'Or me,' she laughed.

Both their wardrobes consisted of practical jeans, jumpers, and overalls, having little or no time to dress up in glad rags, such was the existence of running a small-holding.

Then an idea came to Cassie. 'We could always wear what we got married in?' she suggested, picturing her bohemian-chic cream silk dress with kimono sleeves and floaty skirt. She could always wear a thin cardigan over it, to make it look less like a wedding outfit. Rory had worn the only pair of smart, navy trousers he owned with a cream shirt and navy tie. When they moved here, he had bagged all his suits he'd worn for work as a barrister up and taken them to the charity shop, with utter satisfaction. He was well rid. It was symbolic for him – living a completely new way of life. Sowing and harvesting fields hardly called for tailored suits. Likewise, Cassie had sifted through her clothes and only kept the functional items which she needed. All the dressy outfits were stored at her parents' house. Now that the barn was fully renovated, storage space would allow her to collect all her belongings.

'Adira and Jasper are going too,' remarked Cassie.

'Good, let's hope we're sitting next to them for dinner then. Don't really fancy having to rub shoulders with the Tomkin-Jones'.'

'They might make a beeline for you, you being a local celeb and all,' Cassie mocked. She was of course referring to his infamous persona of the Climate Warrior, from his days of defending activists as a barrister.

He rolled his eyes. 'Do me a favour, cut the bullshit fame thing, Cass.'

And this was precisely why she loved him because he was so understated, genuine and had real morals. Despite his obvious success as a skilled barrister and having national recognition for his work, he was simply content to be just himself, with her.

Chapter 15

'Happy birthday, darling.' Kit blinked and looked into his wife's face. Hell, she was beautiful. Her soft, creamy complexion was flawless, even at this early hour, and her huge eyes twinkled with mischief. Kit knew that look only too well. He lazily ran a hand up her thigh.

'Hmm, and what have you got planned, my precious Prudence?'

She giggled and bent her head to kiss him. The kiss deepened, then Pru gently pulled away.

'Breakfast in bed?' she asked over her shoulder.

'It gets better and better,' he smiled.

Putting his hands behind his head, he laid back and reflected. He was forty today. Did that sound old? Wasn't forty the new thirty? Then he winced remembering his thirtieth, from what he could, amidst the booze, drugs and hazy memories. Finding Pru, or rather her finding him, had been his salvation. Where would he be without her? Granted, he could do to lose the in-laws, a sentiment he was sure Cyril and Patricia shared.

The thought of them sparked a flare of resentment at how they had, in true Tomkin–Jones style, taken over the arrangements for his party. They had turned what was supposed to be an intimate celebration between family and a few close friends into a circus. People were coming that he didn't even know, they were *their* friends, not his. And even more typical of them, they had to do it bigger and better than anyone else, splashing unlimited amounts of cash. A part of him felt a touch embarrassed at such opulence, especially when considering his modest roots. What would his family think? Living in Wolven Hall could be accepted, after all it was his wife's family home and she shouldn't be expected to leave, so he had levelled that in his mind. But having a lavish, extravagant party in his eyes was excessive, and would be seen as such by his family and close friends too. He closed his eyes in regret. What a waste of money…he then felt immediately guilty at knowing how much effort Pru had put into it. For her sake he would play the part, be the perfect host and convince all his guests that they were welcome, and he was having a ball.

—

Fitz was staring at his wardrobe, still in a quandary over what to wear for that evening's party. In the end he opted for a pair of smart black trousers, plus a pristine white shirt that he'd never worn. He decided against a tie, it may seem a touch too stuffy, but his dark paisley waistcoat would look smart and dapper, he thought.

He pondered over how the evening would pan out. It was the first time his small set of friends, with such contrasting personalities, would meet under formal surroundings. Although Kit was as down to earth as they came, Pru's family most certainly were not. Then there'd be Max, drunk within an hour of landing at Wolven Hall no doubt, bellowing out his risqué jokes; then Eva, hmm, what would she be like? Probably in awe, excited even. He smiled at her shock of having Kit Tomkin-Jones as a neighbour. She hadn't tried to hide the fact she'd been star-struck. Eva was open; what you saw was what you got. Unlike him. Fitz had thought long and hard over his conversation with Alex. A pinprick of guilt was etched inside him, which was beginning to grow. Up until Alex confronted him about his family, he had neatly boxed them off. They belonged to another world, another life. Only in truth, they didn't. And it was futile to pretend otherwise. Fitz knew in his heart of hearts he couldn't continue in this way. Sooner or later, he'd have to face them.

-

Eva was indeed excited. By late afternoon she was at a fever pitch. Having searched the internet and discussed what to wear at great length with Beth, they had both decided upon a turquoise tea dress. It had short tulip sleeves, with a tapered bodice, then a full skirt which hung below her knees. She'd bought a silver shawl to drape over her shoulders and silver jewellery would finish the outfit off nicely. Eva thought she had struck the right balance, not wanting to overdo it. She couldn't imagine everyone in too formal dinner wear, not when Kit was involved.

-

As early evening came, the guests started to arrive at Wolven Hall. Pru was there standing in the huge, marbled hallway to greet them all in her little black dress. To add a touch of fun, she wore a leopard print choker, to match Kit's leopard print waistcoat. Gentle chatter and laughter filled the air as everyone was guided outside onto the lawn where a jazz band played. Staff dressed in black uniforms weaved through the gathering with silver trays of champagne and cocktails. As Fitz predicted, Max was on his fourth glass and in good spirits by the time the others joined him.

'You've scrubbed up well, Max,' teased Fitz with a grin. It was the first time he'd ever seen Max completely clean and in a suit.

'I can make an effort you know,' he replied, helping himself to yet another glass of champagne from a nearby waiter.

'So I see,' Eva laughed, then turned to Fitz. 'You don't look bad either,' she added cheekily with a wink.

'Why thank you.' Fitz gave a small bow. Then he assessed her appearance. She looked stunning in that dress, the colour emphasising her blue-green eyes beautifully. For a moment they both stared at each other.

Max, sensing another 'moment,' rolled his eyes and turned around. On doing so he noticed the village doctor, Janey, across the lawn talking to Kit. For a split second he caught his breath, she stood out head and shoulders above the rest, easily the best dressed woman there.

'Come on, Max, they've rung the gong!' called Fitz over his shoulder as he and Eva made their way indoors with the others.

Luckily, Max, Fitz and Eva were all sat next to each other down the dining table which stretched the full length of the banquet hall. Opposite to them sat Jasper and Adira, along with Rory and Cassie, much to Eva's delight.

'Oh, we've spoken on the phone,' she exclaimed to Rory. 'You deliver to me!'

Rory smiled. 'Yes, The Potter's Bolthole.'

'It's actually me who does the deliveries,' teased Cassie sitting next to him.

'Well, they're most welcome.' Eva nodded back with a grin.

They were then joined by Janey who was placed next to Max.

–

'You look amazing,' he said, moving out her chair. Janey gave a wide smile. It was so nice to be appreciated.

'Thank you, Max. And so do you, by the way.' She turned to him; her head tilted as though she was surprised to hear herself say it. But he did. Max cut quite a handsome figure in his black dinner suit – very swarthy, she concluded.

'Well, like I said to these two,' he thumbed towards Fitz and Eva, 'I do actually make an effort occasionally.'

Janey laughed. 'Maybe you should make an effort more often, if this is the result,' she joked. Then they were interrupted by the sound of cheer as Kit rose and stood at the top of the table.

–

'Ladies and gentlemen, may I just say a few words before we begin.' He turned to Pru sitting next to him. 'Firstly, I must say a big thank you to my wife, who has the kindest, most thoughtful heart and who I'd be completely screwed without.' This brought laughter and claps from all the guests, apart from Cyril and Patricia Tomkin-Jones, who sat rather rigidly, barely tolerating their hapless son-in-law. 'So please, thank you all for sharing my birthday, but let's raise a toast to my darling Pru.' He finished by lifting his champagne flute high in the air.

'To Pru!' they all chorused, raising their glasses.

After the banquet and lots more wine, Pru announced there would be fireworks and asked all to make their way outside onto the terrace. Eva turned to Fitz, her face lit with excitement.

'I love fireworks.' She was practically bouncing on her tiptoes and Fitz smiled endearingly at her. She really was a breath of fresh air.

'Come on, let's get a good space.' He instinctively took her hand; it felt the most natural thing to do.

Eva curled her fingers round his, finding the intimacy quite comforting. She discreetly glanced him over. He looked very suave, a contrast to his usual rugged attire, yet still as masculine. Eva was itching to ask him questions about what she'd overheard the other day but knew better not to. For a start, that conversation hadn't been meant for her to hear. A part of her wished he'd volunteer the information, open up to her, but understood something like that would take time.

'This way,' he ushered them towards the front of the crowd, just in time to see the first firework explode into the inky dark sky. A multitude of colours popped and banged magically, lighting the night with their shimmers and flashes. Fitz looked at Eva's animated face, then, on impulse, he leant forward and kissed her cheek. She blinked, then grinned up at him and squeezed his hand. A gush of warmth overflowed into his soul; something he hadn't experienced in a long time.

Chapter 16

It was the beginning of July, blossom trees and colourful hydrangeas decorated the village, while a faint whiff of lavender filled the warm air, and Lilacwell was gradually recovering from Kit's party over the next few weeks, leaving its residents with plenty to talk about.

Eva had been on cloud nine since Fitz's display of affection. The steady, sensible voice inside her head told her it was only a quick peck on the cheek, brotherly even, but innately it felt like much more, like a real connection. Plus, the way he'd reached to hold hands had all seemed so natural and meant to be. One stubborn feeling blocked her complete happiness, though. It simply refused to disappear. In fact, it had well and truly taken root and was growing by the day. *Who* exactly was Fitz? What was his real name and what was his background, his story? Eva had nothing to go off. Nowadays it wasn't hard to research people, given the internet and social media, but she'd at least need a name to go off. She recalled how he had answered, quite curtly, his name 'just Fitz' when she'd asked if it was short for anything, after he'd introduced himself. A part of her felt a touch snubbed that Alex obviously knew far more about him, but then again, hadn't he helped set up his business? Even so, Eva was determined to get to the bottom of the mystery. She didn't want to appear nosey, but something inside her wouldn't let it go, it was as if she felt compelled to help him somehow, as ridiculous as that may seem. Eva was sensing that Fitz needed support of some kind. She couldn't explain why, but the sensation was very real.

–

After having spent the morning chopping firewood and stacking the logs at the back of his cottage, Fitz was enjoying a soak in his hot bath. Lying in the soapy water, he closed his eyes and relaxed his muscles. Once again, his mind wandered back to Eva and how beautiful she looked at the party. She was so easy to be around, and she did look openly pleased when he'd reached down to kiss her, albeit only on the cheek. It had been some time since such temptations had fled into his mind, but since arriving at Lilacwell, he really hadn't met anyone that had given him that reaction.

Fitz knew he had to act upon it. People like Eva didn't appear in your life every day. He remembered how disappointed he'd been when he'd walked into The Inn and seen her with Max. Then, how his spirits had lifted when it had soon become apparent where Eva's interest lay – with him. Not that he was conceited, but he genuinely felt a true bond. He and Eva seemed drawn to each other, a fact Max had observed, given that he'd soon backed off. So, the ball was well and truly in his court. He needed to make the next move.

So why haven't you?

Because of his past, that's why. If Eva learnt about what he'd done, would her opinion of him go down, just like everyone else's? If his own mother could look at him with such sad, sorrowful eyes, how would Eva look at him? He couldn't bear the thought of her disapproval. He gulped down the panic which had started to rise inside and inhaled steady breaths. He had a choice: he could move forward into a relationship and let nature take its course, or he could remain alone, living like some hermit. If the first, he had to come clean and tell her everything… but how? And more significantly, would it ruin everything before the relationship even had a chance to bloom?

-

As arranged, Beth had come to stay with Eva. By mid-evening, they were well and truly sozzled. Opening their third bottle of wine, they giggled as Eva poured them both yet another generous glass each. Hiccupping, Eva suddenly remembered in her hazy, fuddled brain to run The Potter's Bolthole website past Beth.

'I'll show you my new website,' she said, reaching for her laptop.

Beth was suitably impressed. 'Hey, that looks really good!' She loved the way Eva had kept the design minimal and simple, but very professional, showcasing her true talent through photos of her pieces.

'I'll show you the rest of The Cobbled Courtyard shops.' She clicked on 'The Hot Spot.' Beth whistled at the images of Max, stripped to the waist, hammering red-hot iron.

'He's in good shape, isn't he?' she smirked, raising an eyebrow. Eva grinned, she had to admit, Max did look easy on the eye, showing off his taut torso, and the bandana he wore only added to the 'macho' image. Typical Max, totally exploiting his wares for the best promotional shot. Still, it worked.

'Hmm, wait till you see Crafty Carpentry,' said Eva, tapping into Fitz's website. There he was, but the photographs of him were either his side profile, distant, or had something obscuring his face, whether it be a piece of furniture he was working on, or machinery.

'Can't really get a good view of him,' said Beth, squinting at the screen.

'No, you can't,' agreed Eva, suspecting that was no coincidence.

-

Major Miles Fitzgerald stared out of his study window, sighed, then turned back to his desk. There it was all the evidence telling him of his son's whereabouts. Miles had known pretty much from the start where Theo had disappeared to. Only Theo hadn't 'disappeared' for him; he was merely waiting for his precious son to come home. Both he and Dimitra had understood and respected Theo's plea for 'space,' but now, after two years, they no longer had a choice. Time was of the essence. It really was a life-or-death situation.

Being a Major in the armed forces and having plenty of influential connections, Miles had quite easily made a few calls asking for help. He knew people; people in places and positions that could, and were prepared, to trace his son, whether it be through bank accounts, police CCTV footage, or even in his case, word of mouth. A friend of a friend happened to know the Tomkin-Jones,' which had proved most fruitful. Without knowing it, Theo had been inadvertently updating his parents' knowledge of his new life in Lilacwell. And Miles was happy with the arrangement for now, relieved to know where and how he was – albeit his son was completely oblivious to it.

At first, Miles was just plain relieved to know his son was safe and well. He was proud of the carpentry business Theo had set up. He had even, inadvertently, assisted him with that. On learning how the Tomkin-Jones' daughter had befriended Theo, he asked them to encourage her, in any way possible, to help his son. Obviously, it all had to be done discreetly and Pru hadn't actually known the reason why her parents seemed so keen for her to support Theo, other than they approved of him and how his local business would contribute to the village. Miles had watched Crafty Carpentry grow with pride, always keeping abreast of any news via the blog post on his website.

A part of Miles wondered if Theo knew he'd traced him. Surely, he must realise his family would be frantic to know where he was and *how* he was? It was incredulous to think that he wouldn't know so. Was Theo waiting for him to make the first move? Miles doubted that, judging by his only text. He clearly had wanted time out on his own. Only circumstances had changed. They no longer had the luxury of time – and the clock was well and truly ticking.

He leafed through all the papers on his desk, each documenting the past two years of Theo's life, including printed emails which Miles had managed to intercept. Lucky for him, Theo had used his PC whilst staying with them, so he had successfully logged onto his account, after several attempts at his password. He gulped when guessing correctly, *Hazelgrove29*, the name of the family home he'd been brought up in, followed by his age when he'd taken off.

There was also a report, filed by a private detective he had hired, which filled in all the gaps. He had photographs of Theo's home, Woodsman Cottage, of his carpentry studio in The Cobbled Courtyard, even a few secretly taken pictures of him in the local pub with his friends.

It hurt both Miles and Dimitra that Theo hadn't contacted them since that one and only text. More than anything it was killing his little brother Lucas, both emotionally and literally.

Chapter 17

The Inn at Lilacwell was full as Max pushed the door open, to be greeted by Kit at the bar.

'Maxy boy, over here!' he called, glad to see his friend. Just then he looked over Max's shoulder and noticed Janey follow him in. Max turned.

'Sorry Janey, didn't see you there.' He quickly held the door for her.

'Thanks Max,' she smiled, then went with him to join Kit.

'What are you drinking, Janey?' asked Max, seeing Kit's glass still full.

'A large red please.'

Max discretely looked her up and down, taking in her slim figure. She wore tight fitted jeans and a low neckline top, which emphasised her curves. Did she wear provocative clothing deliberately, he wondered, recalling how sexy he found her in that dress at Kit's party? Or was it just *him* that appreciated her looks? He clocked the way Kit was now talking naturally to her, seemingly oblivious to the stunning woman before him. Max found it hard to tear his eyes off her. Then, realising he must be staring, quickly turned to the bar.

After jostling through the crowd, he managed to get served and before long had drinks in hand. 'There you go,' said Max, passing her glass of wine.

'Thanks Max,' said Janey. 'I see you've scrubbed up well again,' she teased with a wink, then held his gaze, referring to how smart he had looked at Kit's party.

Well, well, thought Max, maybe Janey could be appreciating him too? Judging by the way she was still looking at him, perhaps it was more than just harmless flirting. He raised an eyebrow and grinned.

'I'm glad you've noticed,' he replied, meeting her eye. Then the moment was broken when Kit noticed Eva enter the pub and he called out to her.

They were soon joined by Eva, who introduced Beth. The five of them chatted easily, mainly about Kit's birthday party.

'Oh, the fireworks were brilliant!' gushed Eva, explaining to Beth how the display had ended the party with a bang.

'Sounds amazing,' replied Beth in awe.

'Yes, it was,' agreed Janey, who appeared far more affable tonight in Eva's eyes.

'Good,' nodded Kit. 'I'm pleased Pru's efforts weren't in vain. My darling wife deserves a medal for all she does,' he added.

'Your wife deserves a medal for putting up with you,' retorted Max, making everyone in the group laugh, when in came Fitz.

'That's Fitz, from Crafty Carpentry,' whispered Eva in Beth's ear as he moved towards them. He wore faded jeans and a white close-fitted T-shirt, highlighting his tanned, muscular arms. His dark curls and beard gave him a rugged, handsome look.

'Very nice,' hissed Beth, which Max heard, making him roll his eyes. Bloody hell, did everybody fancy that guy? Then he saw that Janey had overheard the comment too because she gave him a conspiring grin. Personally, she thought Max was the better catch.

'Hi everyone,' Fitz called as he approached them, one eye on the hand pumps, deciding what beer to drink. He was soon distracted by Eva's voice; ever mindful she was close by.

'Hi, meet Beth,' Eva said to him, 'she's my friend from home, visiting for a bit.' Eva wanted her to get a close look at Fitz, hoping she may recognise him.

'Hi, Beth,' he smiled before ordering a pint at the bar. Beth took in the back of him, admiring his broad shoulders.

After an evening of drinks, chat and laughter which was thoroughly enjoyed by all, they each made their way home. Back at the flat above The Potter's Bolthole, Eva was itching to hear Beth's take on the evening.

'They seem a really friendly bunch,' her friend remarked as they both settled down for a decaf coffee before bed.

'They are, even Janey tonight,' replied Eva, she'd observed how much warmer she seemed compared to the first time she'd been introduced to her at Fitz's godson's party. Then glancing at her friend asked, 'What did you think of Fitz?'

'He's nice,' she nodded her head in approval. 'I certainly detected the chemistry between you. Potential boyfriend?' Her eyebrow rose in gentle inquiry.

'Yeah…' Eva hesitated.

'I sense a but coming.'

'It's just…there's something about him…'

Beth frowned, puzzled by her comment. 'What?'

'Do you think he looks familiar?'

Beth considered the question for a moment. 'No. Why, should he?'

'I can't help thinking I've seen him before, you know, that déjà vu feeling?'

'Then why don't you just ask him?'

'I can't… I think there's more to it.' She didn't divulge the conversation she'd overheard between him and Alex, it seemed inappropriate and disloyal.

Beth studied Eva's troubled expression, then spoke quietly. 'Eva, you've been through a lot. Please don't look for problems which aren't there.' She nudged her playfully. 'Just relax and enjoy getting to know him.'

Eva chewed her lip, then turned to her.

'Am I overthinking this?' She searched her best friend's face for an answer, longing for some sign of reassurance.

'Maybe?' Beth suggested. 'Honestly, Fitz came across as a down to earth guy.' She crossed her arms over her chest. 'I swear, I got nothing but good vibes from him.' Eva smiled in relief. 'I suspect you're gonna get a whole lot more from him though,' Beth added in a low voice, making them both double over in laughter.

Chapter 18

Fletcher eased himself into his favourite armchair. He was tired, having done quite a lot lately. That party at Wolven Hall he'd thoroughly enjoyed, sat next to Lilly on the 'oldies' table, along with other guests his age. It was getting a habit, this; socialising more and more with Lilly, so they were almost seen as a couple in the village, such was their long and lasting friendship, dating back since childhood.

Not for the first time, Fletcher contemplated what might have been. Deep down he'd always known of Lilly's feelings towards him. Ever since she'd been a small lass, she'd worshipped the ground he walked on. There had been times in his life when he had thought of reciprocating those feelings, of course there had, but something always — or rather *someone* — had prevented him. Alice, Jasper's mother, his sister-in-law, his undeserving brother's wife. Only one good thing had come from that obsession and that was undoubtedly Jasper.

So, for Fletcher, it was hard to say he had regrets, as there would be no Jasper if the turn of events hadn't unfolded. But that didn't deter Fletcher from imagining what he may have missed out on for all these years; he'd never had that close partnership he envied Jasper and Adira having and, what made it worse, was knowing he *could* have had something like that with Lilly. Instead, he'd made do with having Lilly about The Laurels as his housekeeper-cum-companion for all these years. Had he been fair to her, knowing how her affections had been ignored?

No, not ignored, thought Fletcher, that was a tad harsh and actually untrue, more… not fully acknowledged, in the way he knew she had always wanted. Still, she seemed happy enough to keep turning up at The Laurels, day after day, week after week, doing his laundry and cleaning and keeping him company. Yes, Lilly deserved to be treated to river cruises and parties.

Then his thoughts spun back to the last night of the cruise. The weather had taken a turn for the worse and a storm cloud had gathered. Well into midnight, flashes of lightning sparked the black night sky and rumbles of thunder echoed through the river, sending the boat to rock. It had awakened Fletcher and instantly he'd thought of Lilly. She hated thunder and lightning, always had, it absolutely terrified her. He heard her in the cabin next door, banging about, obviously up and fretting. Fletcher flung back the covers and went to tap on her door.

'Lilly, it's all right, lass, let me in,' he said calmly.

An anxious face appeared round the door.

'Oh Fletcher, it's awful!' She was trembling as she let him pass into her room. Just then another crack of thunder roared, followed by a bright flicker of lightning.

'Aaaargh!' jumped Lilly in horror.

'Oh Lilly, come here.' He wrapped his arms around her and rocked her softly. 'Shush,' he soothed. Lilly sank into his strong embrace. 'It's all stuff and nonsense, it'll die down soon,' he whispered. Another clap of thunder contradicted him though, and Lilly screamed in fright.

Knowing sleep would be impossible, he offered to stay the night with her.

'Please,' she squealed, 'don't leave me.'

'I'm not going anywhere lass, now come on, let's huddle together.'

He pulled back the bed sheets and gently guided her in, then snuck in beside her. Lilly clung to him in terror as the commotion outside rolled on. At last, it finally subsided. Fletcher looked down at Lilly; she'd fallen into an exhausted slumber. Holding her warm body and watching her gently breathing, his heart cracked. What had he missed out on?

'You bloody stupid man,' he cursed himself.

Chapter 19

Eva had had a busy time throwing clay down on the potter's wheel and mauling the wet lumps of earth into long, elegant vases. Seeing them lined up on the shelf, waiting to be glazed, reminded her of a set of vases that had been packed up and stored in the attic at her parents' home. She made a mental note to collect them. It didn't make any sense to have stock tucked away in boxes when they could be on her shelves selling. Looking at the clock told her it was break time. Eva fancied a decent cappuccino from the cafe, and she would stop by the Crafty Carpentry to see if Fitz wanted a coffee too. Having Beth stay had been good not only to catch up with her, but she'd also really helped put her mind at rest regarding Fitz. Deciding to take her advice and just relax getting to know him, Eva tapped on Fitz's door.

'Hi, it's me!' she called over the loud noise.

Fitz was blasting wood with his sander when she came in. He switched the machine off and removed his face mask.

'Hi,' he smiled, pleased to see her.

'Fancy a coffee?' She tipped her head towards the cafe.

'Yeah, why not.' He joined her and locked the work-shop behind him.

It was warm and sunny, so they picked a table outside on the cafe's decking.

'Let's have an early lunch, on me,' Eva said.

'Why's that?' he frowned.

'For sanding my floor.'

'I've told you, that was nothing,' he brushed off casually.

'It was a great help, Fitz, don't underestimate your generosity,' Eva replied looking straight at him. He stared back, hoping she'd always have such a good opinion of him. He decided to take the initiative.

'OK, you buy lunch, if you let me cook dinner tonight.'

'Deal,' she smiled. Then, on impulse she leant forward and kissed him on the lips, taking him by surprise. 'I'll get the menus.' Eva suddenly darted off, not quite believing she'd just done that.

–

Later that evening, Eva was at pains to take great care of her appearance. In the end, she opted for a pale green linen dress and ballerina pumps, all the better for walking through the woods to get to Fitz's cottage.

Carrying a bottle of wine as she strolled through the leafy trees, Eva wondered what meal Fitz would have cooked. She assumed he'd be a good cook, being so practical in other ways. The sun was shimmering between the branches as they waved slightly in the evening breeze and the faint scent of wild garlic filled the warm air, as well as the distant call of bird song. Eva's spirits rose, especially at seeing Fitz on the balcony stood over a barbeque.

'Thought we'd eat outside again,' he called upon seeing her approach. He looked totally in control as he turned the meat over.

'Hmm, smells good.' Eva's mouth watered at the juicy steaks sizzling away. There was a salad and pasta bowl too on the patio table, plus a bottle of wine chilling in a bucket. 'Thanks for this. It all looks delicious.' So did he, she thought, once again taking in his muscular, brown arms and broad shoulders. Her eyes followed the dark hair visible above his open necked shirt. Something inside began to stir, and a hot sensation filled her.

'How do you like it?' he asked.

'Pardon?' Hell, had he been reading her mind?

'Your steak,' he replied with a grin, causing her to blush slightly.

'Oh, sorry, medium please.' His lips twitched, then he nodded and turned back to the barbeque.

Soon they were sat at the patio table sipping cool white wine. Eva had relished her meal. As predicted, Fitz was indeed a fantastic cook. She took in his side profile as he cleared away the plates. Never before had she been so attracted to a man with facial hair, usually falling for the clean-cut type.

–

Back in the kitchen, Fitz too was fighting his self-control, but it was hard seeing Eva looking so beautiful. She had a natural glow about her, which was proving impossible to resist. Then he frowned at his own thoughts. Why *should* he resist? He'd clocked the way she had looked at him. It was pretty obvious the pull was mutual.

He returned to find her swinging in the hammock.

'This is so soothing, isn't it?' Fitz glanced at her long, slim legs stretched out before him and a switch flicked inside him. He moved to stand over her.

'Mind if I join you?' he asked huskily. Eva moved to give him space. Carefully he eased himself next to her, their bodies touching as they rolled together. Fitz's arm went around her shoulders as she rested her head on his chest. There was something so intimate about her hearing his heartbeat. Eva lifted her head up to look at his face. He stared intensely into her eyes. Then, like a magnetic force, their lips met, and they kissed gently at first, then more urgently. Fitz ran his tongue across her soft lips making her jolt with pleasure. Her hands brushed through his hair, enjoying the silky, smooth feel. He pulled her on top of him, slowly stroking her back as his mouth now reached her neck, then moved to her shoulders, loving the touch and taste of her golden skin.

'Eva,' he moaned roughly. She unbuttoned his shirt, desperate to see more of him and gasped at the solid torso before her. Fitz wanted the same, pulling the straps of her dress downwards to reveal more cleavage. His head moved towards the swell of her breasts, again his lips and tongue ran over the tantalising flesh as she shivered in response. Her dress had rived up, exposing her thighs. Then he felt Eva tense. With superhuman effort, Fitz slowed down. His chest was heaving, and his pulse was racing, but he managed to cradle Eva in his arms, who by now was teary eyed. 'Hey, come here,' he comforted, tightening his hold protectively.

'I'm sorry…'

He nudged her to look at him. 'There's nothing to be sorry for.'

'It's just… you know… the first time since the mis—'

'Eva, please, it's fine, really,' he softly interrupted, then kissed her again, softly.

For a few moments they just laid there, gently swaying in the hammock. It was therapeutic to be cuddled together, listening to the sounds of the night forest. And knowing they wouldn't be spending the night together didn't detract from the calming moment. It was a comforting understanding between them.

Fitz's mind started to kick into action. Was now the time to tell her about his past? He looked downwards to her face resting on his chest. Her eyes were closed. She looked so peaceful, so serene, he didn't want to break the spell. He then cast his eyes upwards over the night sky. A crescent moon shone down, surrounded by bright stars piercing the darkness. If only they could stay like this forever, in this tranquil cocoon, without any outside inter-ruptions; without the realities which would inevitably hit them.

Chapter 20

Fitz hadn't slept well. He'd woken with a splitting head-ache and decided not to go to the workshop. Instead, he made himself a cooked breakfast, a large mug of tea and took two painkillers. After an hour he began to feel marginally better. His thoughts turned to last night and a comforting glow warmed him from the inside. He'd walked Eva home on cloud nine, but the happier Eva made him, the more sinister the warning bells rang in his mind. If she hadn't brought their passion to a close, he was damn sure he wouldn't have. He had to come clean and tell her everything, too much was hinging on the relationship now.

He heard the post being delivered and went to the front door. One envelope lay on his mat. As he bent to pick it up, his heart skipped a beat. He recognised the handwriting immediately. It was his father's. His hand was shaking as he opened it up.

> Dear Theo,
> Please don't be alarmed by me contacting you. You will soon realise I really had no choice.
> For two years now I have sat back, whilst respecting your wish to have the time alone you need. Every day your mother and I have prayed that you contact us, that you would reconnect with

the family that so misses and loves you. We wanted
you to make the first move, when you were ready,
but matters have been taken out of our hands now
and we desperately need you. Your brother needs
you.

Lucas has been diagnosed with multiple
myeloma, otherwise known as bone marrow cancer.
In short, he needs a donor with a close genetic
match. That's you, Theo. I know this will all come
as a complete shock to you. But I can't sum it up
any other way.

It will also shock you to learn that we have
always known of your whereabouts. But Theo, it
really shouldn't. You're our son, and we love you
so much. Did you really think I'd let you disappear
from our lives without a trace? Not a chance. I'm
proud of what you have achieved and the life you've
made, but Theo, it's time to come home.

Dad

Fitz read the letter over and over again with tears pouring
down his face. Lucas, his little brother, had cancer. Oh my
God. His body shook with emotion. And all this time, his
parents had known where he was, waiting patiently for
him to come home. Now he was crying loudly, with great
wracking sobs. Eventually, forcing himself to take deep
breaths, he tried to sit still and process the shock. Home,
he had to get back to Cheshire. He had to be there for
Lucas and be his donor.

His mind was in overdrive as he packed a suitcase. He'd
ring Alex and let him know everything, ask him to keep an
eye on the cottage and studio for him. He mentally made

a list of the clients he was currently working for to send them an email, explaining he had urgent family business to attend to. Then his thoughts turned to Eva. How would all this affect the beginnings of their relationship? Then he cursed himself. *His brother had cancer, for Christ's sake!*

There was no time to start assessing his love life. At breakneck speed, he had packed and locked up Woodsman Cottage, before throwing his suitcase into the Range Rover and setting off to Cheshire.

Chapter 21

'Say hello from me!' called Fletcher as Adira and Jasper were about to leave. They had a hospital appointment. It was the baby's five-month scan.

'Yes, we'll wave and say you send your best,' Adira laughed. Jasper turned around to face Fletcher.

'We shouldn't be that long, a couple of hours tops.'

'Never mind me, concentrate on the little one,' Fletcher pointed to Adira's bump. 'Off you go,' he shooed them out, 'you don't want to be late.'

Travelling to the hospital they were filled with a mixture of excitement and trepidation. Whilst eager to see their precious baby, they were each secretly concerned that all was well and the baby was growing just as it should be, which was perfectly natural, but still worrying.

'Will they be able to tell us if it's a boy or girl?' asked Jasper as he searched for a car parking space once they'd arrived.

'I don't want to know,' replied Adira in surprise. 'Why, do you?'

'Not if you don't.' He smiled and patted her lap.

Once parked, they entered the hospital and followed the signs for the maternity ward. After registering and waiting a short while, they were shown into a room for the ultrasound scan. Adira's heart started to thud in anticipation as a cold gel was smeared over her abdomen. Jasper held her hand and waited with bated breath for the image of the baby to appear on the screen. And then, there it was! Jasper and Adira's eyes homed in, soaking up every detail of its head, spine, arms, and legs.

'I'll just look and take a few checks, make sure everything's fine,' said the nurse cheerfully as she looked back and forth from the screen to a clipboard.

After a few minutes, Jasper couldn't stand it anymore.

'Is everything all right?' he asked urgently. The nurse gave a nod.

'Yes, baby seems happy and content.'

His shoulders immediately relaxed, and Adira squeezed his hand. They both exchanged smiles of relief.

'Everything is developing as it should,' continued the nurse. 'Baby's head, heart and spine are all forming nicely.'

Adira felt a flutter inside, as though the baby was responding to the nurse.

'It just moved,' she said excitedly. Jasper quickly looked at the screen. Sure enough a tiny pair of arms and legs wiggled. They all chuckled.

'The baby is developing muscle and exercising,' the nurse told them.

Adira laughed. 'It feels like butterflies are inside.'

'The movement's called a quickening,' she replied, smiling. 'Baby's hair is also growing on its head now.'

'Really?' said Jasper in awe. Then he swallowed. It was so emotional; he could hardly speak.

Adira's eyes filled; never had she been so overcome with such feeling.

'How long is it?' she asked, trying to gauge its length from the screen.

'About sixteen centimetres,' answered the nurse.

'It's amazing,' Jasper's voice cracked.

'Yes, it certainly is.' The nurse could spot the first-time parents a mile off and never tired of seeing their reaction.

—

A comfortable silence settled in the air on the journey back home. Both Jasper and Adira were still in wonder from what they had just experienced, trying to absorb the momentous occasion they had been through. Finally, Jasper spoke.

'Can you imagine how excited Fletcher is going to be once it's born?'

'Fever pitch,' replied Adira with a grin.

Jasper shook his head wryly. 'He's already bought a nursery full of toys.'

'I know,' laughed Adira, 'it's going to be the most indulged child going.'

Jasper's mind flashed back to his own childhood and how special Fletcher had made it for him. He couldn't have asked for a better role model. Happiness filled his whole being, knowing his child would have the same.

—

'It's amazing,' admired Julia Partridge, 'you must be *so* pleased.' The *Lancashire Lifestyle* reporter was back with Rory and Cassie to capture the finished smallholding. She was genuinely impressed with all their hard work, recalling the dilapidated pile of stone that had been their home a few short months ago. The progress they'd made was remarkable, to say the least. 'We are,' they said in unison, turning to each other and laughing.

'And rightly so,' nodded the reporter.

After a tour of the outside and livestock, Julia had been ready to take her leave, especially when Belinda the goat had promptly urinated, splashing her suede boots. Kevin the cockerel hadn't taken too kindly to her either, shrieking an ear-splitting cockerel call, making Julia jump out of her skin.

A few weeks later, Rory and Cassie were able to see the finished article. Sat at the kitchen table, the *Lancashire Lifestyle* magazine spread out before them, their article had made it to the centre pages, with a charming update on their smallholding and eco-way of life, complete with photos of the couple inside their barn renovation and stunning scenes of the local landscape.

'We'll make an eco-warrior of you yet,' said Rory, smiling at the picture of Cassie feeding the hens, dressed in work overalls, beaming into the camera. Her pixie cut hair was ruffled by the breeze and her cheeks had a rosy glow. He'd never seen her looking so natural and pretty.

'Hey, I told you I was a farmer's daughter,' Cassie chided and nudged him playfully. She too was taking in how handsome Rory appeared in the photos, with his dark curls hanging over those bright blue eyes of his, as he leant against a spade.

They epitomised the idyllic country couple, living a healthy, organic life. The complete antithesis to how they used to exist, with Rory working all hours in the city and Cassie as a hotel manager. Never had either of them looked back. It might have been a hard slog to get where they were and they both knew more hard work was to come, but it was a standard of living they believed in and were equally committed to.

The book deal they had signed required them to keep a diary. The book was to be entitled, *Life at The Harvest*

Barn and it was to depict the early stages of setting up the smallholding and the growth of their business, plus the progress on the restoration of the barn. They had had several Zoom calls with the top publisher's senior editor, who had wanted to arrange to meet them. Initially they had assumed this would involve a trip to London, but to their surprise, the editor had wanted to travel up north to see them.

'It would be good to come to Lilacwell and see you on site,' he'd told them.

So, all in all, they were busy and thriving – tired, but happy. They enjoyed the simple luxuries, like hot, deep bubble baths after a day's manual grafting; cooking wholesome dinners on the AGA; sipping wine by the cosy wood burner and tumbling into their comfy, king size brass bed, to wake up the next morning and start all over again.

Chapter 22

Eva's mood initially had been buoyant after her evening with Fitz. Butterflies fluttered inside every time her mind replayed them together in the hammock. What pleased her most, though, was Fitz's total acceptance of her sudden resistance. It was too soon – and he clearly understood it.

Eva's miscarriage and subsequent break up had scarred her. She knew it wouldn't always be like this – after all she was attracted to Fitz and had loved being touched by him – but her body simply wasn't ready in the full sense. She had appreciated Fitz's patience and felt safe with him, which had put her mind at rest regarding her previous reservations. Evidently there was something in his past, something he was concealing, but whatever it was, Eva knew fundamentally Fitz was a good man. It was blatantly obvious judging by the way he acted. He was a good friend, a loving Godfather and… son? He never discussed his family.

Eva was resigned to accepting that Fitz would hopefully open up fully to her when he was ready. When the time was right. In the meantime, she intended to enjoy being with him and get to know him better.

Over the next couple of days, however, Eva hadn't seen or heard from Fitz. It was starting to worry her a little. He hadn't been next door to his workshop. It had remained locked up, empty. She had called his mobile a few times but been put through to voicemail. She'd even visited his cottage, but unusually that had been locked too – the place was silent. What had happened?

Eva asked Max after him when she saw him at the cafe.

'No, I've not heard from him recently either.' He frowned. 'It's not like Fitz to disappear.' Eva stared at him briefly. Wasn't it? A churning sensation gripped her stomach. What if he had just taken off? Because from what she had gathered, he'd done this before. That conversation she'd heard between him and Alex came back to haunt her. *Have you ever thought of going back? Home, I mean, or at least contacting your family? They must be worried sick.* Then Fitz's reply, *I can't face them.* Anxiety swamped her, tightening her chest. What if he was in trouble?

'You Ok, Eva?' Max was looking at her with concern.

'I… I'm worried about him…' Her chin wobbled.

'Hey, come on.' Max put his hand on her shoulder. 'I'm sure there's a logical explanation.'

'But where is he, Max?' she implored, wide-eyed.

'I'll ring Kit and Pru, see if they know anything.'

'Thank you.' She looked over her shoulder at the Crafty Carpentry unit. There it was, standing vacant and still. A sense of foreboding spread through her.

'It'll be right,' Max gently told her, perhaps startled by how fretful she appeared.

'Let me know, won't you? As soon as you hear anything?'

'Of course,' he nodded and watched her walk back to her studio.

Eva had tried to keep busy, occupying her mind. She'd started to get a few orders in from her website, so concentrated on those. One of them was a vase, which reminded her of the box she wanted from her parents' attic. Later that afternoon, after finishing the ceramics and putting them in the kiln, she rang them, finding it immediately reassuring to hear her mum and dad's voices and to catch up on their goings-on. They were due to go on holiday in a few days but promised to send Eva her box of vases in the post.

'Is it just that one box?' her mum asked.

'Yes, it's been up there for ages. I'd forgotten all about it.'

'OK, I'll make sure it's packed safely and send it on.'

After hanging up, Eva stared at her phone. Should she try Fitz again? She didn't want to appear like some kind of stalker, but then again, what would *he* think if she'd suddenly gone off the radar? With force, she pressed his contact button. It rang, and rang... then the voicemail kicked in. It wasn't even his voice, just some automated, bland instruction telling her to leave a message. A touch of annoyance pierced her. Well, yes, she *would* leave a message after the bleep.

'Fitz, it's me, Eva. Is everything OK? Ring me, will you?'

—

It had been eight days since Fitz had sped back to Cheshire, and already it felt like weeks, so much had happened in such a short space of time. Travelling down the leafy lane where his parents' house was situated, he swallowed tightly at the sight of the rather modest looking bungalow – a far cry from Hazelgrove, his childhood's large country home. As soon as he pulled into the drive, Miles had come bounding out, arms outstretched, tears pouring down his cheeks. Fitz stood still, overcome with emotion.

'Theo, Theo,' his dad cried, hugging him so hard it took his breath away. Then he pulled back to take a good look at his son. His eyes searched his face. For a moment they were motionless, staring at each other, no words necessary. Finally, Fitz broke the silence.

'Where's Lucas?' he choked, barely able to speak.

'He's here, with us. Come this way.' He put an arm round his son's shoulders and gently guided him safely inside.

Dimitra was just coming down the stairs.

'Theo,' she gasped and rushed to hug him. Fitz breathed in that familiar jasmine scent of hers and at once he felt comforted. Tears threatened to spill.

'How's Lucas?' he managed to ask. 'Can I see him?'

'He's asleep. Let him rest for now,' she replied in hushed tones.

'He'll be delighted to see you,' said Miles, as he ushered them into the sitting room.

Time passed so quickly as the three of them talked and talked. Miles had explained how friends of friends knew the Tomkin-Jones' and the connection they'd had to his life in Lilacwell. Fitz had sat and listened in shock at just how much his parents had actually known all along about his new life.

'Tell me, Theo,' his mother softly asked, 'would you ever have come home, if it wasn't for Lucas?'

'Yes, of course. But I can't say when.' He looked at them both and gulped. 'It's hard having to face what I've put you through.'

At this, both his parents interrupted.

'Theo, we never blamed you,' his dad instantly replied.

'You're our son, we love you so much. We never held you responsible and we certainly never wanted you to just leave us...' His mother started to cry.

'I'm sorry... I'm so, so sorry.' The three of them wrapped together in a tight hug.

Later that afternoon, when Lucas was awake and sat up in bed, the two boys reunited. It was hard seeing his little brother so pale and weak. Although tired, Lucas was still able to talk, and the sight of Theo gave him such a lift. He constantly thanked his brother for hopefully becoming his donor, all being well.

'Don't thank me, Lucas, it's the least I can do,' Fitz told him.

'No, Theo, it's the most. You're giving me my life back.' Lucas looked him in the eye. Fitz couldn't hold out anymore. All the emotion of the day had built up and came gushing out. Lucas too was crying, but it was tears of happiness that stung his face at seeing his brother back home.

In the evening Fitz's dad took him to one side and explained the imminent procedure he was about to undergo as a donor.

'Cells will be collected from both your hip bones through a needle, under anaesthetic. These will be harvested a day or two before the transplant.'

'How will it work?' asked Fitz.

'Lucas will be regularly monitored. Your cells will travel to Lucas' bone marrow, where they produce new blood cells and promote growth of new marrow. You'll have a blood test first, to make sure your stem cells match Lucas'.' Fitz's head shot up.

'But I thought I'd be a perfect match? Being his brother?'

Miles nodded, 'Yes, highly likely, but there's still a chance you might not be. You're going to be the best chance Lucas has, though.'

'Good.'

'There may be side effects,' his dad gently warned.

'Don't care.'

'From a drop in blood pressure, headaches, nausea or pain, to more serious—'

'I don't care,' cut in Fitz firmly.

'—to damage to vital organs, bleeding in the lungs, brain, or other parts of the body,' continued Miles, knowing he had to tell his son every aspect he might endure.

'I'm doing this for Lucas,' Fitz said with force. His dad's hand reached out and covered his.

'You're doing this for all of us and we can't thank you enough.'

Somewhere, way down in the heart of Fitz's soul, a small chink of light broke through. Could this be the ultimate act of recompense?

Blood tests revealed Fitz to be a perfect match to Lucas, as predicted. The subsequent donor procedure had all gone to plan and had been carried out safely. Fitz was feeling a touch sore and tired, but the utter feeling of fulfilment far outweighed any discomfort he had.

The next few days would tell if the donation had been successful. The results were looking positive. The first sign in Lucas was the rise in his white blood cell count, which showed that the transplant was starting to make new blood cells. So far so good.

Now, knowing he had done all he possibly could, Fitz was recuperating at his parents' house. It felt strange being back in the spare bedroom which housed all his old clothes and belongings, packed up from Hazelgrove. It was past midnight, and he couldn't sleep. All the events over the past few days had stopped and the waiting game had begun. His head was packed with worry and hope, his mind was fully focused on helping his brother, so he hadn't had time to think about anything else. It was as if he lived in some kind of parallel world, switching from his life in Lilacwell to that of Cheshire. Would the two ever meet? Common sense told him that of course they would; he couldn't keep them apart forever. For in Lilacwell, he had set up a new business through which he thrived and met someone who he very much wanted to be part of his future.

Eva. He sighed and rolled over on his side. His mobile was there, sat silently on the bedside table. Fitz had turned it off when setting off to Cheshire, as if doing so was distancing his life in Lilacwell and hadn't looked at it until now. His hand reached out and took the device. As soon as he'd switched it on, it bleeped and flashed to life. He'd had numerous missed calls, four of them from Eva. Seeing a notification for a voicemail, he pressed to hear the last voice message he'd received, again from Eva.

'Fitz it's me, Eva. Is everything OK? Ring me, will you?'

He closed his eyes in anguish. Poor Eva. What must she be thinking? He wanted to reply to let her know everything, but where to start? A text message couldn't possibly suffice. She deserved a long conversation, and it was far too late to ring now. Besides, it didn't seem right not telling her face to face. He badly needed to see her but wasn't up to the drive back to Lilacwell just yet. His head ached with all the pent-up stress and his eyes grew heavy. Within a few minutes his breathing became deep and steady, and he fell asleep.

–

Max's mind was full of a pressing matter – Fitz. Where the hell was he? He remembered thinking how quiet and withdrawn he had appeared over the past few weeks and concern edged further in. It unsettled him to see how anxious Eva was too. It was blatantly clear how the two had connected, so for her not to know of his whereabouts disturbed him even more.

With purpose, he strode over to Wolven Hall, hoping Kit and Pru would be able to shed some light on the matter. As before, Max felt slightly intimidated by the grandeur of the place whilst pulling the cast iron door-bell. He was soon shown inside by the housekeeper and directed to Kit and Pru's quarters.

'How the other half live,' he muttered to himself, climbing the huge sweeping staircase. He could hear Pru's voice down the corridor and followed it until he got to their drawing room where the door was open.

'Hi Max,' Pru called from where she was standing by the fireplace, looking pleasantly surprised at seeing him in the doorway. Kit leant forward from where he was sat on the sofa to see him.

'Come in, Maxy boy. What brings you here?' He sensed something was afoot, judging by the serious expression on Max's face.

'Hi,' he said entering the room, 'sorry to turn up unexpected.' Then moved to sit next to Kit.

'Is there something the matter?' asked Pru, picking up on the vibes.

'We're worried about Fitz, me and Eva that is. We haven't seen him for days. His workshop's locked up, he's not answering his phone and his cottage is empty and locked, too.' A short silence followed. Pru and Kit exchanged cautious looks. 'Do you know where he could be?' asked Max, turning from one to the other.

'Sorry, no mate,' Kit shook his head frowning.

'I could ask about?' replied Pru. Max knew what she was implying. Pru was offering to use her family's contacts, which most aristocratic families had.

'Would you?' implored Max. Then, turning to Kit said, 'What if something's happened to him?'

'It's unlikely,' he comforted. 'Sounds like his going away was planned if he's locked up his studio and home. Normally Woodsman Cottage is left open.' He himself had often wandered in when calling to visit Fitz. It was basically a free for all.

'Yeah, that's true,' Max replied, nodding his head thoughtfully.

'Don't worry, Max. I'll see what I can do.' Pru tried to sound reassuring but did concede it was out of character for Fitz to disappear like this. Then, on reflection, she realised that they'd only actually known Fitz for two years. And come to think of it, *why* had he even come to Lilacwell? All anyone had gleaned from him was that he was from Cheshire. That was about it. There was no mistaking he was a respectable chap, even Mummy and Daddy could see that and liked him – and they were *very* picky.

She stole a side glance at her husband, who never had quite made the mark with them. Yes, they had recognised that Fitz had had a similar upbringing to her. He was well spoken, 'polished' was how her mother would describe him. Again, her eyes cast over Kit and saw how he must appear to them. Slightly scruffy, with his bohemian sense of style, floppy fringe covering his eyes and fingernails caked with dried paint. At least he *was* painting again, she quickly thought with relief. She wondered if her parents had secretly wished Fitz had stumbled into Lilacwell a whole lot earlier than he had. They certainly had been at pains to help him set up his business and gain permission from the local council to build his cottage in the woodland. The more she considered this, the more inquisitive she became. At the time she'd just been pleased with their assistance to help her friend, but now, contemplating the matter, she was left questioning their behaviour.

'You OK?' asked Kit. He saw her chewing her lip, forehead creased in thought, and he knew her mind was ticking over.

'Hmm?' she jolted, then gave a tight smile. 'Yes, yes of course.'

'Do you think he's had an accident?' urged Max, his eyes widening.

'No mate. I don't. We'd have heard from the police by now if he'd been involved in an accident.' Kit patted his shoulder. 'He's probably had urgent business to attend to. Something that couldn't wait.'

'Like what?' shot back Max.

Kit sighed and shrugged his shoulders. 'I dunno Max. But I don't think we should jump to conclusions.'

–

Later that evening, a very pensive Pru tapped on her father's study door.

'Enter,' he called, then smiled at seeing his daughter. 'Prudence, darling.'

'Daddy, there's something I need your help with.'

'Certainly, what is it sweetheart?' he asked.

'Fitz. He's gone missing.' His smile faded. She was surprised to see that a part of him half expected this to happen. He put down his pen, folded his arms and looked her in the eye.

'Take a seat, Prudence,' he replied in a low, quiet voice.

Chapter 23

Fletcher was marvelling at the baby scan photograph on the fabric notice board in the kitchen. He gazed in wonder at the details of the tiny creature, *his grandchild*. His eyes filled every time he contemplated the future years and how they would pan out. He envisaged days filled with fun and laughter in the nursery and cosy bedtime stories. His mind then fast-forwarded a few years and he pictured a toddler, learning to walk, his or her first words, then further on, learning to ride a horse, being led through the estate on their first pony... all the things he'd done with Jasper.

Lilly was in the kitchen too. She'd just finished the ironing and was putting the kettle on. She smiled to herself at seeing Fletcher staring at the photo.

'You can't wait, can you?' she said warmly.

He turned and grinned. 'No. I can't,' he agreed, then paused before adding, 'I've waited a long time for this.'

-

Lilly nodded sagely, fully understanding what he was implying. She, more than anyone, knew what Fletcher had been denied for years. The true acknowledgment of Jasper's parentage.

It was Lilly who had witnessed Fletcher and Alice's chemistry the night of the summer ball all those years ago, having spotted them coming down the stairs looking somewhat dishevelled – and guilty. Lilly had instantly realised what had gone on in the privacy of Fletcher's bedroom, whilst the rest of the party was in full swing. She'd seen first-hand how they had danced in each other's arms on the lawn, which the rest of the guests had apparently been oblivious to. Why? Because she'd quietly watched Fletcher like a hawk her whole life, wishing she was the one being held in his arms.

Nine months later, when Jasper was born, Lilly had had no doubts as to who the father was. Jasper was Fletcher's. For years Lilly had kept it to herself, until a few months ago, when she had confronted Fletcher with what she had known all along – his secret.

–

He had been staggered to learn that Lilly had known his family secret. He'd been even more staggered at her silence for all this time. Once more he was reminded of the loyalty Lilly had shown. She hadn't pried, or made things difficult or awkward, just conveniently kept it to herself. Lilly was and always had been, a true friend.

Fletcher sat down at the kitchen table and glanced at Lilly, busy making the tea. She was a trooper. He didn't know what he'd do without her. Lilly was part and parcel of The Laurels, bobbing away in the background, a constant companion, and he suddenly realised how empty his life would have been, had she not been there, especially before Jasper and Adira had moved in. He remembered the long days that she had filled, chatting over memories past. They went back a long way.

The 'what if' game started to play on his mind once more.

Lilly turned, placing a cup of tea in front of him, along with a slice of cake.

'Coffee and walnut, your favourite,' she smiled.

'Oh lovely, thanks Lilly,' he rubbed his hands together, then looked into her pale blue eyes. Was it too late? Could he rectify what should have been? He continued to gaze into that kind, familiar face.

'Fletcher, are you all right?' Lilly frowned.

'Aye lass, never better,' he quietly sighed.

Chapter 24

Eva had just finished serving a customer when the courier arrived with the box her mum had sent. Placing the wooden crate down carefully, he passed her a piece of paper to sign.

She was looking forward to opening all its contents, meticulously wrapped in newspaper. The vases had proved to be a good seller and having so many ready-made would be a big help. Already her shelves were looking a little bare, which was encouraging, she told herself, but she hadn't anticipated just how quickly she needed to replenish stock. At least the business had kept her occupied, in between agonising about Fitz, who still hadn't made contact. She'd contemplated approaching Alex, to see if he knew anything. Out of all the people in Lilacwell, he would be the most likely to know where Fitz was. But how would it appear? Could she be misconstrued as being plain nosey? Would she be putting Alex in an uncomfortable predicament, especially if he had been confided in with confidence? It was all so maddening.

One thing this did reveal though, was how strong her feelings for Fitz were. And this in turn told her she was moving on; no longer did her mind rewind to those dark days filled with loss, not just of her baby, but all that having a baby would have entailed. She didn't even think about Simon much now. On the odd occasion when he did filter into her mind, he was always happy, living his free, independent life in her mind's eye. Never could she picture him sad, regretting what might have been. In fact, the more she considered Simon and their relationship, the more she realised just how selfish he was. Looking back, it was incredible how she hadn't seen it before.

Moving to Lilacwell had been the best thing she could have done, giving herself distance from him, not to mention a new lease of life. The Potter's Bolthole had been a blessing. She loved working in her cosy, little studio, and getting to know the locals. Eva was at her happiest when shaping cold, wet clay into beautiful pieces of ceramic. The hours whizzed by when she was fully absorbed in her craft. Eva imagined Fitz feeling the same way about his carpentry; it was a gift.

By late afternoon Eva closed the studio and decided to get some fresh air. A walk along the river would clear her head.

Strolling along the lush, green grass, she marvelled at the scenery before her. Clear water glistened and bubbled along the rocks into the stream, while tall fir trees stood proud, providing a canopy of shade against the sunrays. She took a deep breath and inhaled the fresh air. It was refreshing to feel the gentle breeze against the heat of the sun. Wood pigeons faintly called in the distance as they flew out into the forest. Lilacwell really was a special place. It was her haven.

In the early evening, Eva was thoroughly revitalised from her walk and ready to tackle emptying the box of ceramics. Carefully she took out the top layer of objects wrapped in newspaper. One by one, she unfolded each vase, discarding the newspaper into a pile. After placing all the vases on the shelves in her studio, she collected the crumpled pages of the newspaper. Then, the writing of one headline instantly drew her attention, but more significantly did the photograph underneath it. Taking a sharp breath, Eva knelt at the coffee table and spread the creased page flat on top of it, flattening it down with her palms. The whole time her chest pounded, knowing the enormity of what she had stumbled across. There before her, in black and white, was the missing piece. The answer to all the nagging doubts she had had about Fitz. There he was, staring up at her with those clear blue eyes she'd recognise anywhere. The rest of his face was completely different, no beard, but a clean cut, fresh face. His hair was short too, cut into a sharp, snappy style. His usual checked shirt had been replaced for a collar and tie. A total contrast to the Fitz she knew, though reading the headline told her even his name wasn't the same. *Golden Boy Theo loses his touch.* Eva gasped, reading on,

> *Theo Fitzgerald gambled his entire family's fortune and lost everything. His father, Major Miles Fitzgerald and mother Dimitra, have been forced to sell their spectacular country home Hazelgrove, thanks to their eldest son's risky investment in Aerospace Plus, the company whose stocks and shares plummeted as drastically as their latest plane had plunged into the Indian Ocean…*

On she read, not quite believing her eyes. She vaguely remembered reading this article the first time, obviously the photograph of Fitz had stuck in her head, lodged there innocently until meeting him in the flesh and triggering her mind. Eva *knew* she'd seen him somewhere before, back in the past. Now it all made sense; his reluctance to talk about his family or his previous life before coming to Lilacwell. His words to Alex about 'not being able to face his parents,' even his name being 'just Fitz' when she had first enquired. Theo. His name was Theo Fitzgerald. She looked again at his photograph. How suave and sophisticated he appeared, exuding an air of confidence, self-belief. Very polished. So not Fitz.

Eva could only imagine the kind of money he had been used to dealing with. He hadn't been dubbed the Golden Boy for nothing. Now look at him, living the most modest, simple life, working with his hands, and practically hiding in a cottage tucked away in the woods. It beggared belief that the Fitz Lilacwell knew was the polar opposite to the city stockbroker, Theo Fitzgerald. Eva understood his need to disappear from a world where money reigned. She envisaged the cut-throat dealings and back-stabbing it inevitably must create. How shallow it all would seem compared to the close-knit community within Lilacwell. Here, Fitz was one of them. He had friends, good friends, that genuinely cared for him. A lump formed in Eva's throat. Had he gone back home for good? Had he tired of his simple life here in Lilacwell and craved the buzz of the city again? Deep down in her gut she refused to believe this… Yet still, he hadn't contacted her. Should she try one last time to ring him?

No. It was his move now. All she could do was wait in the hope he'd return her message. Eva neatly folded the page and put it safely in a drawer. Something inside stopped her from throwing it away with the rest of the newspaper.

-

Fitz was returning from the hospital after visiting Lucas. Thankfully, Lucas was making excellent progress and was looking more and more like the brother he knew and loved. Initially, it had been agony to see how thin and pale Lucas was, lying weak in his bed. Now, he had more colour in his cheeks and the dark shadows under his eyes had vanished. The white blood cell count was still rising, which indicated that the new blood cells were successfully producing – all positive signs. This in turn had given Fitz a boost too, knowing he had made this happen. It was as if a huge weight had been eased off his shoulders and in his own way he felt as though he had made amends. He had helped Lucas regain his life. His actions had made the family whole and happy once more.

With all this, Fitz's mood had lifted, he no longer felt tired and, more than anything, he didn't have that constant anxiety looming over him, or the incessant fear of his past life exposing him. In short, he had forgiven himself, and this alone made all the difference. Fitz had seen first-hand the impact of Lucas's recovery on his parents. Now, they too looked years younger – all the worry lines had faded, and their eyes danced with joy.

It was too emotional at times. The enormity of it all hit Fitz in waves, and in those instances, he had to just be alone, away from all the activity. In those quiet moments, he missed his life in Lilacwell terribly. It felt like months since he'd been there, rather than weeks, so much had happened in such a short spell, but after seeing Lucas steadily recuperating, Fitz was ready to return. He had a business to run, clients to see and an empty home waiting for him. Would Eva be waiting too? A stillness filled him. Would she have given up on him? He thought of those unreturned calls and the message she left on his phone.

He hadn't contacted her. He hadn't contacted anyone in Lilacwell. What kind of reception was he about to receive?

For once, that all too familiar torment didn't take root, knowing he could finally face them all with his head held high. Whilst being away from his friends in Lilacwell, he had achieved the pinnacle achievement of his life. The punishing, pitiless, monumental foul-up of his bad investment no longer played centre stage. He was Theo Fitzgerald, who had saved his little brother's life. Getting ready to pack, he opened his wardrobe. There before him were rows of suits hanging meticulously. All dark, pressed, and clean, waiting to be worn. Not by him, he thought, that was for sure. Life had taught him a lesson the hard way – money was not the be all and end all.

Chapter 25

Jasper was busy painting what was going to be the baby's nursery. Not knowing the sex meant they had opted for neutral colours and, after studying various colour charts, they had gone for pale lemon walls and a pure white ceiling.

Jasper was happy that it was his old bedroom, tucked into the eaves, which was to be his child's nursery. Clearing the room out had been so nostalgic for him. Fletcher had left his wooden train set on the cast iron fire mantelpiece and even his bookcase was untouched, packed with his very early Beatrix Potter books and his Enid Blyton's *Famous Five* series. It all took him back to his childhood days at The Laurels, having Fletcher make every summer holiday an adventure.

Adira entered the room. Under strict instructions not to even lift a paint brush, her maternity denim dungarees ironically made her look the part of a painter and decorator.

'Hi,' she said, making Jasper turn around on his step ladder.

'Hi, what do you think?' He had painted all four walls and was onto the ceiling now, stretching high from the top step of the ladder.

'It looks great,' she replied, then gently rubbed her bump. 'Cassie's just delivered the fruit and veg box and she's invited us over for a meal.'

'Oh, when?' asked Jasper.

'Next Saturday. It's a celebratory do for friends and family.'

'Celebrating finishing the barn?'

'That and getting married,' replied Adira, still admiring the couple for having the guts to elope. 'I think it's a bit of a peace offering, for not throwing a traditional family wedding.'

'Ah, I see,' said Jasper as he rolled the white paint, trying his best not to splash.

'Do you think you should have done the ceiling first? Then the walls?' Adira questioned, reading his mind.

'Probably,' Jasper dully agreed. 'Still, it's going to look great, isn't it?' He grinned, hardly able to contain his excitement. It was infectious, and Adira beamed up at him.

'It certainly is,' she replied, looking round the room. 'Where should we put the cot?'

'By the window?'

'Hmm, maybe.' Adira walked towards it and looked out at the lawns spread before her. Colourful flower beds blossomed with roses, cornflowers, sweet peas, and peonies.

'Right, that's it,' said Jasper, climbing down from the stepladders. He squinted up at the ceiling to assess his work. 'I don't think it'll need another coat.' He moved to hug Adira from behind and kissed her head. 'How are you feeling?' The morning sickness had long since abated, only to be replaced with fatigue.

'I'm fine, really.' She patted his hand. Then she suddenly remembered something that Cassie had just told her. 'Hey, have you heard about Fitz?'

'What about him?' asked Jasper.

'He's gone, left The Cobbled Courtyard and nobody knows where he is. Cassie's just delivered there, and Max told her.' Jasper frowned.

'Perhaps he's decided to take a few days break, a holiday?'

'And not tell anyone?'

Jasper shrugged. 'Maybe he doesn't feel he needs to?'

'Seems a bit odd though,' Adira remarked.

'Says you, who took herself off in a camper van,' he laughed, 'and never returned home.'

'That was different, at least my family knew where I was!'

'Well, his might, too,' reasoned Jasper.

Chapter 26

Eva was on edge. She'd seen Fitz's Range Rover pull into The Cobbled Courtyard that morning. She had also witnessed Max practically run to the Crafty Carpentry studio moments later. He was still there, obviously catching up with his friend, and Eva had been touched at Max's response. As for her, she needed a little time to adjust – not really knowing how to react. Inside, she was a cocktail of emotions; hurt, questioning, concerned, mixed with a trace of anger at the way he had ignored her efforts to contact him. Ultimately, she was left feeling unsure. Had she totally misread Fitz? She pictured them the last time they'd been together, snuggled up on the hammock and how attentive he'd been. Surely, she hadn't got him so wrong? But then again, she never would have pegged Fitz as a stockbroker, gambling with his parents' money. Every negative thought and scenario spun round in her head, along with all the words printed about him. Confusion swamped her and a part of her wanted to barge into his shop and demand an explanation.

Instead, she kept quietly busy. As if to remind herself – which she really didn't need to – Eva took out the newspaper article from the drawer and re-read it. It was still hard to comprehend, yet there it was, in black and white. There *he* was, those blue eyes looking into her. She jumped at hearing a knock at the door, her head turning sharply towards it and suddenly he was there, in the flesh, standing before her.

'Hi,' he said quietly, scanning her face. Was he trying to read her? Gauge her mood? Eva stared blankly at him, refusing to give anything away. She discreetly moved the article out of view, behind a pot of paint brushes on the workbench where she was leaning on.

'Hello,' she replied coolly, still staring impassively at him. He looked just the same. Nothing had changed, except something *was* different. It was hard to put her finger on it, but somehow an air of confidence exuded from him. Not in an arrogant way, but more self-assured. Was he really the same person she'd just read about?

–

Fitz gave a deep sigh. So, this was how she was going to play it, cold and aloof, judging by her demeanour. He took in the rigid stance and detached expression. Did those sea-green eyes look a little wounded? He moved closer, wanting to spill everything he'd been through, wanting her to be warm and welcoming, not freeze him out.

'Eva, I need to talk to you,' he said gently. He tried to reach out and touch her hand resting on the workbench, but she instantly snatched it from him.

'You've had weeks to speak to me,' she answered in a small voice, not trusting herself to speak further. She watched him avert his gaze and swallow.

He tried once more. 'Eva, please, I can explain everything.'

The sound of his voice stilled her; it was sincere and almost pleading. She searched his face for a hint of what could be going on inside his mind.

'Why… why didn't you contact me?' she choked.

'I couldn't. Believe me.' Sighing again, he moved to stand beside her, desperate to touch her, hold her, but knowing that's not what she wanted right now. As he moved closer to the workbench, he caught sight of the newspaper article and froze. His eyes flew to hers. His jaw tightened and a condemning glare blazed from him. 'So, you've read all about me,' he said in a low, accusing tone.

She wanted to run, away from his stare and away from the pent-up emotional turmoil.

'I… I…' she stammered, whilst her heart hammered. He tilted his head slightly and narrowed his eyes to slits.

'Been researching me, have you?'

'No! I…' Eva started to go a little dizzy, a whooshing noise pounded in her ears.

'How long have you known, Eva?' he asked in a quiet voice.

'I didn't—'

'Oh, I think you did,' he cut in, 'from the moment you first met me. I saw the flicker of recognition in your face.' The fury rising in him was evident. Eva looked frantically for a way to escape. She hated the way he was looking at her, full of revulsion, so different from just moments before. Tears stung her eyes. Above all, she felt disloyal, fickle, when at the same time not sure why. He'd been the one hiding a secret, not her. 'Did I interest you, Eva? Were you just plain curious?'

'Stop it!' Eva's hands covered her ears, and she snapped her eyes shut in an attempt to block him out. Silence, followed by a loud bang. He'd left, slamming the door behind him.

—

A burning rage rumbled inside Fitz as he marched his way through the woods. It boiled and bubbled with each stride he made until reaching Woodsman Cottage and pushing the door open. He needed a drink. Grabbing his bottle of whisky and not bothering to pour it into a glass, he knocked the drink back then wiped his mouth. The strong liquid stung the back of his throat and made his eyes water. They were already heavy with the tears he refused to spill.

How could she? How worried he'd been about her, longing to talk and confide in her, when all along she'd been bloody well reading up on him! He thought she was different, had felt a real connection, but he'd been so wrong. Eva was just like all the others. Prying, judgmental gossips, who gave him condemnatory looks and accusing stares, *'the poor Fitzgeralds,'* they'd whispered, *'they didn't deserve that,' 'how could he do that to his own parents?'* they'd hiss slyly. He'd been subject to all the malicious, hushed insults, and the outspoken ones, where people would openly point the finger and on one occasion, actually hurled, *'Robbing bastard!'* from their car window. It had been relentless, unavoidable, and in the end, Fitz felt like he'd had very little option but to run away, escape for good. And he had, for a while. At least now it was different. Now he had made amends. He had saved his brother, and in turn, saved his family. In his own world, an atonement had been reached. Fitz was finally ready to move on, and he'd wanted to do so with Eva.

He took another swig of whisky, wanting to dampen the pain mounting in his heart. He dully realised he'd invested too much in Eva. He'd been foolish. Then he turned, hearing the door slowly open. He rubbed his eyes and made out two blurry figures.

'Fitz?' It was Kit's voice. Shaking his head, his vision became clearer. Pru was with him, frowning.

'Fitz, are you all right?'

'Fine,' he replied, then hiccupped. He walked to the sink and quickly poured himself a tall glass of water then necked it back. Kit and Pru exchanged a concerned look. 'So, I take it you've been filled in?' Fitz asked in a flat tone, edged with derision. He was done with what people thought. Why should he give a damn? For all he knew these two probably knew all along who he was. He stared confrontationally.

'Fitz, my father only just told me,' replied Pru in a quiet voice. Then added, 'How is your brother?'

At this Fitz stopped still and swallowed, his throat suddenly dry, ashamed that his main concern had been himself, instead of his little brother.

'He's… he's getting there, making good progress.'

'Good, good,' gushed Pru. Then she walked over and gently wrapped her arms round him. He sought solace in the comfort of her warm body and sunk his head into her shoulder. Finally, the tears came pouring out, fast and furious. Kit came to join them, and he too put his arms round them in a group hug.

'Welcome home, mate,' he soothed, 'welcome home.'

–

Half an hour later, once they'd all absorbed the high emotions, Fitz sat down with them over a strong pot of coffee. He relayed all the details of the past few weeks. It proved cathartic being able to offload it all and it was also good to be home, in the sanctuary of his little cottage.

'You should be so proud of yourself,' Pru said, huge eyes staring into him.

'Absolutely,' agreed Kit, 'you're a lifesaver, Fitz.'

'And what about the rest?' Fitz looked down to his clenched hands.

'The rest?' Pru asked.

'The money I lost my family.'

'You had every good intention of making a decent profit for your parents. What happened with that airline company was a genuine disaster,' Pru said almost indignantly.

'Yeah, how could anyone have foreseen that?' cut in Kit.

Fitz looked away. 'Not everyone shares your views,' he answered in a quiet voice.

'Well, we support you,' Pru instantly responded with passion. 'In fact, we were *all* worried about you.'

'All?'

'Of course! Us, Max, and Eva in particular, apparently.'

Fitz's head turned sharply towards Pru at those words. 'Eva?'

'Yes, Max said she was frantic after you took off. Sent him round to Wolven Hall to see if we knew where you were.' Fitz blinked. Pru leant forward. 'Incidentally, since Daddy told me of his connection to your parents, it's remained confidential.'

'I know. Max has been around this morning. I've told him everything, the past and being a donor to Lucas.'

'Right,' Kit nodded his head, 'so does Eva know too, why you urgently went back home?' He eyed his friend thoughtfully, suspecting she was the reason for Fitz's early drinking. A short silence followed.

'No. But she knows who I am,' Fitz replied in a stilted voice. Kit stared at him pensively. Another pregnant pause filled the air. A raw nerve had been struck.

'She was anxious at the way you suddenly disappeared,' Kit softly spoke. Fitz swallowed the flicker of emotion. 'Ask Max, she was distraught.' Kit was twisting the knife now it seemed. Pru coughed and broke the silence.

'Fitz, come back with us to Wolven Hall. Stay for dinner, don't be on your own,' she urged.

Fitz shook his head. 'No really, that's very kind of you Pru, but I need some space right now.'

'Of course,' she replied tight-lipped.

'We'll be off now mate.' Kit slapped Fitz on the back and signalled to his wife for them to leave.

'Thanks for… everything,' Fitz said, somewhat still in a daze. Thoughts were tumbling over and over in his head. Somehow, life in Lilacwell was never going to be the same again.

Fitz spent the rest of the day chopping and stacking wood. He badly needed to get rid of the surplus energy jolting in his blood. He wanted a decent night's sleep and in order to do so, knew he had to physically exhaust himself. After four solid hours of throwing his axe and packing the logs up into the stack, he collapsed into a hot bath. Closing his eyes, he let the warm bubbles soak into his skin, relaxing him muscle by muscle. But try as he might, Eva still remained stubbornly in the forefront of his mind. She'd been worried about him. Distraught, they'd said. But then he knew that from the voice messages she'd left him. *The ones you ignored*: a voice inside chided him.

But where had she got hold of that newspaper article? It would be years old now. *Maybe you ought to have let her explain*, continued the same voice. Maybe he should, thought Fitz bleakly. He looked through the open bathroom window to the night sky; the same beautiful indigo, pin pricked with diamonds, just like the one he and Eva had gently swayed in the hammock under. He gulped, remembering how he hadn't wanted that evening to end. How much he had craved them to be together, cocooned safely from the outside world. Little had he known then just how much things would change.

Chapter 27

In the drawing room late that night, Fletcher was sat drinking whisky by the open fire. It was quite late, and the sun had long set, leaving a cool, dusk evening.

He watched the amber flames flicker, quietly contemplating. For some reason, the past was playing on his mind – again. Whereas once his memories would have been intermingled with regret concerning Jasper's mother, Alice, his reflections now tended to steer more towards Lilly.

His thoughts were also tinted with a shade of guilt. Ironic really, when perhaps culpability ought to have played a major role involving his feelings for Alice – she was his brother's wife after all – but Fletcher never had felt a tinge of blame for loving his sister-in-law, because he knew Alice hadn't been loved properly by her husband. Rufus had neglected her.

With Lilly it was different. She had shown nothing but care and devotion to him, asking very little in return. And Fletcher, rightly or wrongly, had allowed it to happen. He'd let Lilly carry on working at The Laurels as his housekeeper, knowing full well where her affections lay, and he'd been quite happy for her to wait on him, albeit she'd been paid, very well in fact, but not in the way Lilly had wanted.

In short, Fletcher had let his futile obsession with Alice take over his life. Had he seen sense all those years ago, he could have had a contented married life, maybe had more children, one big happy family packed to the rafters at The Laurels, instead of rattling around the place a lonely, old man.

He supposed all this gloomy pondering was evoked from seeing how happy Jasper and Adira were. Not that he resented them – far from it, he more than anyone wanted to see the couple content, but Fletcher couldn't help thinking, *Why not me?* Was he to live out the rest of his days full of regret and *what might have beens*? *Do something about it, man!* a voice inside told him firmly.

'OK Fletcher? You're up late.' Jasper stuck his head round the door. Fletcher turned to face him.

'Aye, I'll not be long up. Has Adira gone to bed?'

'Yeah, she went hours ago,' said Jasper. Sensing something was amiss, he went to sit opposite him. 'Come on, what's up? You look…' he paused, not sure of the right word.

'Melancholy?' offered Fletcher with a wry grin.

'Yes,' agreed Jasper, frowning.

There was a short silence as Fletcher stared back into the fire, he swallowed before speaking.

'Have you ever regretted something so badly it… it… eats you up?'

Jasper blinked; concern started to edge in. After considering the question he gave an honest reply.

'No, I don't think I have.' Then added as an afterthought, 'But I would have severely regretted not leaving Dubai to return here.'

Fletcher gave another rueful smile.

'Ah, but you *did* leave Dubai,' he said, now looking into Jasper's eyes. 'You made exactly the right decision, and it paid off.'

Jasper tilted his head, puzzled.

'What's all this about, Fletcher?' he asked softly, hating to see him so sad.

'It's about... missed opportunities... not doing the right thing.'

Jasper frowned again. 'Well, is there an opportunity to do the right thing now?' he asked. It seemed the most logical suggestion, even though he didn't really know what Fletcher was talking about. He'd noticed an empty whisky tumbler and guessed that might have had something to do with it.

Fletcher narrowed his eyes in consideration.

'Yes, there just might be.'

'Right, now we've sorted that out, come on, it's time for bed,' Jasper smiled.

'Aye,' agreed Fletcher and slowly rose from his chair.

Chapter 28

Max was in good spirits. Having Fitz safely back at The Cobbled Courtyard, he was genuinely pleased, not to mention relieved, to see his friend. He'd been equally shocked, too, upon hearing the reason for his absence. Max had stared, open mouthed, listening to Fitz explain how he had had to return home urgently to be a donor for his brother. He'd learnt how Fitz, or Theo, as he now knew was his real name, had lost a vast amount of money on the stockmarket – his parents' money, to be exact. Max had sat in silence, stunned by what his mate was revealing, almost like he was confessing. After a few moments, when he'd absorbed everything, Max had nodded, at a loss what to say. Only when he noticed how troubled Fitz looked did he speak.

'You made a mistake, Fitz. You're human, like the rest of us.' Then he added, turning to look at him fully, 'You'll always be my mate, no matter what.'

'Thanks,' Fitz croaked, on the verge of tears.

'Come here, man.' Max got up and hugged him hard. He was surprising himself at how sensitive he was becoming, learning to listen, then say the right thing. Perhaps his reputation as a Jack the Lad was slowly transforming.

Feeling pleased with himself, he decided upon a course of action. He'd arrange a small gathering, just his close-knit circle of friends. It would do them all the world of good, call it… bonding. Yes, they all needed a get-together. Plus, he rather warmed to the idea of inviting and seeing Janey; his thoughts often flashed back to her at Kit's birthday party and how sexy she'd looked. Buoyed by the idea, he thought he'd call on Eva, not having seen her for a few days, and run the idea past her.

On hearing the doorbell, Eva's head turned sharply. She'd been on edge since Fitz had slammed out of The Potter's Bolthole, half anticipating another visit from him, demanding explanations. The other half of her was disappointed to see Max standing at her doorstep with a cheerful smile, which promptly dropped at seeing her face. She looked terrible, pale, and drawn, with dark circles shadowing her eyes.

'Eva? Are you all right?' he asked, frowning.

'Hmm,' she managed to reply, refusing him eye contact. She pretended to be busy tidying her workbench.

'Ri–ght.' He moved closer to speak and saw her shoulders shake. To his horror, she then openly started crying. 'Eva! Whatever's the matter?'

'It's… it's Fitz. He's furious with me,' she spoke in a strangled voice, hating the way she was breaking down in public. What was wrong with her?

'But why?' Max asked incredulously.

Reaching out for the incriminating newspaper, which was still on her workbench, she unfolded it for him to see.

'Because he caught me reading this,' she said, pointing to the page. Max took in the headshot of Fitz and squinted to read the headline.

'Ah, I see.'

'Did you know?' she asked abruptly.

'No, of course not. But he's since explained everything to me. And what he's done for his family is admirable.'

'What?' Eva's brow puckered, perplexed by Max's reaction.

'Saving his brother's life like that,' he replied. Then he paused. 'You do know, don't you?' Seeing her puzzled face streaked with tears told him that no, she most definitely did not. 'Eva, sit down. I need to fill you in.'

My God, he was getting good at this, talking and reasoning with all and sundry. Maybe he should join the Samaritans.

After telling Eva all that had happened, she just sat staring in silence. Suddenly it all made sense; the pressure Fitz had been under, no wonder he hadn't had the headspace to communicate. And when he had been in a good place to talk, she'd rejected him. A tight knot formed in her stomach and began to grip hard. She fought the urge to vomit.

'Listen, I think you need to lie down,' Max gently told her.

'Oh Max, what have I done?' she whimpered. 'He tried to tell me, but... I... wouldn't let him...'

'Shush,' he soothed, patting her back. 'It'll be OK.'

'Will it?' she asked wide eyed. 'He looked so ...*angry*.'

'Where did you get that article?' he asked softly, curious to know.

'Purely by chance. I was just unwrapping some ceramics sent from home, then suddenly there he was, I couldn't believe it.'

'Blimey, the chances of that,' he remarked. Then he remembered, 'Oh, but you're from the same area, aren't you?'

'Almost. I must have stored his photo in the back of my memory. I was so sure I'd seen him before when we'd first met but couldn't place him.'

'I see,' Max nodded. 'I'm sure it'll all work out once you've talked.' He tried to reassure her. Maybe now wasn't the best time to organise a get-together at The Inn after all.

–

In turmoil, Eva's first instinct was to ring Beth; she'd know what to say, but it was midday and she'd be busy working on set. Although gutted by her last conversation with Fitz, still a small part of her was hungry to discover more about him. She knew his real name now – Theo Fitzgerald. Theo, what a lovely name. It suited him; he looked more like a Theo than just plain 'Fitz'.

Opening her laptop, Eva typed his full name into it and immediately a long list of results came up. Quickly checking out the shop window in case there were any potential browsers about to come in, she clicked the first on the list. The last thing she wanted was to be caught red-handed again by Fitz, so she positioned the screen at an angle where no incoming customers, or visitors, could see. Her eyes scanned the first article, which had the same picture of him as the newspaper, with similar information on how he had plundered his parents' money. She went down the list and found they were all pretty much the same. One or two articles had pictures of him frantically trying to avoid the news reporters. He had visibly been hounded, and Eva gave a shaky sigh. Poor Fitz. Another site gave a more detailed background of him, and Eva learned he came from a wealthy, middle-class family. His father had been a Major and his mother was Greek, which must be where the name Theo had derived from. That and his dark, good looks.

Further down the page showed a photograph of the family home with a caption underneath: *Hazelgrove – the grand country house which had been gambled away.* How heartbreaking it must have been, Eva reflected. Above all, she felt incredibly sad reading it all. That knot in her stomach was still there, refusing to disappear. Eva hadn't been sleeping well. Her mind was constantly bombarded with her last encounter with Fitz. Eventually she closed her laptop, having exhausted all the search results. What a shame there weren't any articles depicting how he had saved his brother's life, she mused. Typical how bad news always travelled fast, when Fitz deserved to be applauded for his good deed. But no, there was no accolade, except from his friends and family in private, without the press to acknowledge it. *So* unfair. Which was why she needed to go and face him, to make her peace.

Eva planned in her head what to say – she would calmly explain exactly how she'd come into possession of that wretched newspaper article, then she would apologise for not letting him speak, but try to explain how hurt she'd felt. He had, after all, not returned her calls and disappeared without a word for weeks. Surely, he'd understand? Well, if he didn't, he simply wasn't the man she thought he was. She could almost hear Beth's voice telling her this.

So, now she had a plan, it was just a case of implementing it. Seizing the moment, Eva turned the shop sign to 'Closed' and made her way next door to Crafty Carpentry. It was shut, with no sign of movement when she peered through the window. Should she try calling at Woodsman Cottage?

'Hi Eva.' She jumped. Max stood behind her.

'Oh, Max,' she laughed. 'Sorry, you startled me. I was trying to find Fitz.'

'Good,' he smiled. 'Eva, I was thinking of arranging a get together, just a few drinks at The Inn. Maybe it'll do us all good meeting up?'

'Definitely,' she nodded in agreement. That sounded exactly what she needed, a bit of fun amidst all this drama in her life.

'Great. Well, I'll invite Fitz, obviously, Kit, Pru and… err…Janey?'

'Yeah, sounds good.' Eva gave a thumbs up.

'Right. What about this Saturday night? Or is it too short notice?'

'No, not too short at all,' Eva answered immediately. A night out couldn't come quick enough for her, the sooner the better.

'OK, I'll contact everyone,' he said.

Finally, something for Eva to smile about. She'd focus on Saturday night, when everyone was there. Hopefully, the atmosphere would be upbeat.

That evening, Eva called Beth and they chatted for over an hour with Beth listening intently.

'I told you he was a good guy,' she said, glad that all of Eva's doubts had at last been quashed.

'But Beth, what if he doesn't want to speak to me?' urged Eva, desperate to hear reassurance.

'Of course, he will,' she instantly replied, her confidence easing Eva's fears. Then she added, 'And if he doesn't, he's simply not the man I think he is,' which made Eva grin wryly to herself.

Chapter 29

'How does it look?' Cassie turned to Rory as he entered the kitchen. Today they were hosting the party they'd promised friends and family. They'd both been up first thing in the morning, as ever, tending to the animals and smallholding before Cassie had hastily changed from her overalls into leggings and a hoodie to prepare everything inside while Rory set up deck chairs and patio furniture outside.

Bunting swooped from the kitchen ceiling beams, all the champagne flutes sparkled on silver trays, while the bubbly chilled in ice buckets. Cassie had made huge dishes of pasta, chilli, and salads, along with cheeses, olives, and rustic bread. The desserts she'd cheated on and shop bought, but the pavlovas and gateaux still looked the part. Nobody would know and who cared anyway, Rory had told her.

'It looks amazing, Cass.' Rory put his arms round her and kissed the top of her head. 'Now go and get ready before they start arriving.'

Cassie gave one last glance round the kitchen and shot upstairs to shower and dress.

Rory was looking smart in his black jeans and check shirt. He'd just washed his hair, leaving the dark curls to dry naturally. He wandered around the farmhouse table, picking bits of bread and cheese to nibble.

'And no nicking the food!' shouted Cassie from the top of the stairs.

'I won't!' he shouted back between mouthfuls. He chuckled to himself, looking out of the window, and catching Belinda staring in. She obviously sensed something was happening. Even Kevin the cockerel wasn't crowing quite as much, choosing to keep a beady eye on them instead. The hens were oblivious, clucking away as usual, their main concern picking up bits of grain still remaining on the ground.

Rory stood still and took stock. It wasn't often he actually had time to find a quiet moment and do this. Usually there weren't enough hours in the day, always rushing about doing one job or another. It certainly kept him fit working the land; no need to join an expensive gym, like he had when living in London – then hardly finding the time to go. Life was certainly different nowadays. Running a smallholding might be backbreaking, but he loved it, all that fresh air and exercise; and what they were contributing to the local area was commendable. The Harvest Barn was growing from strength to strength, and he was fast beginning to realise that it was going to need more than just him and Cassie to work it. They'd need help, a few staff to assist in sowing and reaping the crops and packing up the wooden crates for delivery. More and more customers were getting in contact, wanting their services. All good, but still time consuming nonetheless. Plus, they had to find the time to dedicate to their other projects, like the up-and-coming book, it all required attention.

–

In the shower, Cassie was contemplating more immediate matters, like had she prepared enough food? What would everyone think of their new home? Would the animals behave with a large number of visitors? Her lips twitched remembering how Belinda had practically peed on Julia Partridge's suede boots. Most of all she was anxious as to how Rory's family was going to react to them eloping. Were they going to take it in good cheer and wish them well, or would it create a tinge of resentment?

Her parents, she knew, had been quietly disappointed, but had tried to hide it. As their daughter, Cassie knew they had been put out, despite their cheery faces. How were Rory's parents going to be? She dreaded any form of confrontation, especially from his brothers, who were like Rory, and not scared of speaking their minds.

Still, face everyone they had to. It had been their decision to run away and get married, now they had to stand by their convictions. Cassie had made a small wedding album from the few pictures taken of the wedding ceremony by the anvil in the Blacksmith's Shop, as well as the honeymoon, and had put it on a side table for people to look at if they wanted.

After showering and slipping on a simple summer maxi dress, Cassie blow dried her short hair and was applying a touch of make-up when she heard the music Rory had just put on. Instantly she began to relax on hearing 'their' song. It was the Stereophonics, 'Maybe tomorrow, I'll find my way home...' She smiled, remembering the first time Rory had played it in his car, whilst they travelled to Lancaster, his home city.

'Mum and dad have arrived!' Rory called.

Quickly Cassie finished with a brush of lipstick and fled down the stairs to greet her guests.

Rory had met his parents outside and was pointing out various spots of the smallholding when Cassie joined them.

'Well, congratulations Mrs Molloy,' smirked his dad, making Cassie grin up at him.

'Yes, congratulations to you both,' smiled Rory's mum, looking from one to the other. She added wryly, 'Although we're not at all surprised you ran off in secret. Typical of you.' With a wink, she poked her son's chest in good humour.

Then Rory's brothers arrived shortly after, followed by Cassie's parents. The brothers pelted out of their cars to slap Rory's back, with mutterings of 'sly dog' and 'robbed us of a good knees-up,' could be heard; all which Rory accepted in good spirit. Cassie's parents just nodded politely, feeling slightly uncomfortable amidst all the boisterous cheer. When Adira and Jasper arrived minutes later, it came as a relief to Cassie, knowing her mum and dad would be preoccupied by them. She could see how they were a tad intimidated by the whole of Rory's jaunty family.

As the music played and the bubbles flowed, everyone seemed to blend together effortlessly. Even Belinda remained placid once she grew accustomed to so many people on her territory. Kevin only crowed once, making Cassie's mum jump and spill her champagne, much to Rory's dad's amusement who pointed and laughed, making her blush slightly.

'Here love, never mind,' whispered Cassie's dad, passing her a napkin. Jasper, who had witnessed the incident, tactfully interjected.

'What do you think of the barn, Mrs Wright?' he asked politely.

'Oh, I think they've done a marvellous job!' she gushed, quickly blotting her skirt of the drink stain.

'Yes,' agreed Cassie's dad, 'and the work they've done on the land is remarkable, given the time they've had.'

'I know!' said Adira, sipping her orange juice.

'Not too long to go now,' Cassie's mum tipped her head towards Adira's bump.

'I can't wait to be honest,' replied Jasper with a huge beam, putting an arm round his wife.

'Neither can Fletcher,' said Adira dryly, making them all chuckle. They were then interrupted by Rory's eldest brother, who stood on a chair clinking his glass with a spoon.

'Ladies and gentlemen, if I may have your attention, please!'

Rory rolled his eyes, clearly this was an impromptu speech which he had had no idea about, though it didn't exactly come as a shock either.

'As our darling brother has robbed me of being best man at his wedding—'

'He would have chosen me,' interrupted the younger brother wittily, to everyone's laughter.

'Yeah, right! *Anyway*, as I was saying,' he continued, 'just because Rory and Cassie eloped, doesn't mean they're not getting a best man's speech.'

Cassie's eyes darted to Rory, who appeared relaxed, leaning on a patio table with his arms folded and legs crossed out in front of him.

'There's never been any dispute that our Rory is the brains in the family—'

'And the looks,' called Rory to a peel of laughter.

'Whatever,' came the quick response with an eye roll, 'but I will say this: although Rory used his nowse to get a top-class job as a barrister, it never went to his head. He never forgot his roots, or his principles, and we're proud of him, especially the way he stuck his career on the line and represented the climate activists.'

'He is one!' shouted Cassie.

'Absolutely and it's good to know he's chosen a feisty wife, to match his own personality,' winked back the brother. 'So, can we all raise our glasses: to Rory and Cassie!'

'Rory and Cassie!' They all cheered.

As the early evening dusk set in, the lanterns dotted around the garden glowed warmly and a gentle breeze filled the air, along with the sound of chat and laughter.

'It's been a success,' sighed Cassie in Rory's ear, 'thank goodness.'

'Never doubted it,' replied Rory with a grin and kissed her lovingly on the lips.

Chapter 30

Saturday had finally come around, and more than anything else, Eva was looking forward to an evening spent at The Inn with friends. Eva had been busy in The Potter's Bolthole all day and she still hadn't managed to see Fitz, but knowing he'd be at the pub tonight helped ease her mind. Perhaps it would be better if there were others present initially, it might help break the ice.

After a hectic last rush hour, she gladly turned the door sign to 'Closed' and gave a sigh of relief. She was tired from being on her feet all day and was desperate to eat, shower, put on her glad rags and go for that well-earned drink. Noticing the shelves were virtually empty again, she quickly pulled out the box with the rest of the vases from under the workbench and decided to replenish at least the top one before locking up the shop. Gingerly climbing the stepladders, with two vases in her hands, she reached out to put them securely at the back.

Mid-reach, she lost balance. The ladder wobbled and with a scream, Eva tumbled down onto the floor with a thud.

–

Fitz, too, was contemplating the evening ahead. Taking extra care of his appearance, he had made the decision to call at Eva's first, before facing her in the pub in front of an audience. He wanted to clear the air between them in private, not public. So, with a sense of resolve he strode through the woods and made his way to The Cobbled Courtyard. As he approached The Potter's Bolthole, he was surprised to see the shop light still on. Surely it wasn't still open? He knocked on the door and was even more surprised to find it unlocked.

'Eva?' he called, entering the studio.

'Help!' came a voice from the floor. He turned sharply to see her lying in a heap by the stepladder.

'Eva!' He bent down to her in panic.

'I fell off the ladder,' she winced in pain. 'I've done something to my ankle,' she managed to say in between gasps of agony.

'We need to get you up.' Fitz took hold of her and gently eased her onto a stool. 'Let me see,' he squinted at the swollen ankle from underneath her jeans. 'Can you move your toes?' She did so, letting out another yelp. 'I don't think you've broken it,' he said. 'It's very bruised though.'

'Thank God you came,' replied Eva. 'I'd have struggled to move.' Their eyes met, both had much to say, but obviously now was not the moment. A short silence followed. Then Fitz interrupted it.

'Have you got any painkillers?'

'Yeah, first aid box in there.' She tipped her head toward the tea point in the corner of the studio. He quickly returned with a glass of water and a small packet. 'Thanks.' She gulped back the water and urgently swallowed two tablets.

'Well, I don't think you'll be going out tonight,' he joked, trying to comfort her. Eva gave a shaky smile.

'Come on, let's try and get you upstairs.' Together they just about manoeuvred her up the stairs and onto the settee. Fitz plumped up the cushions behind her and very carefully placed one under her ankle to support it. Once settled Eva looked directly into him.

'Listen, Fitz, I'm so sorry—'

He cut in instantly, shaking his head, 'No, I'm sorry Eva. I shouldn't have judged you like that, and I certainly shouldn't have flown at you that way. I wasn't thinking straight, my head's been all over the place, what with Lucas being so ill, going home for the first time and facing my family... it's all...' his eyes began to fill, 'got on top of me.' He gave a shuddering sigh, 'I'm afraid you bore the brunt Eva and I'm so, so sorry.' He swallowed. 'I honestly did want to contact you... but I just couldn't. I wanted to tell you everything face to face.'

'The article, it was—'

'Purely chance, yes, I know. Max told me.' He looked into those mesmerising sea-green eyes of hers and his heart skipped a beat. How he'd missed gazing into them. How he'd missed *her*. He leant down, his face inches away from hers. He breathed in that intoxicating floral scent of her and was unable to stop himself from moving his lips to cover hers. His tongue tasted her, and she was sweet like nectar.

–

Eva's pain had dulled, and all she could focus on was the way her body responded to him. Her fingers instinctively ran through his dark, silky hair, relishing the touch of him. The kiss deepened and her heart hammered inside her chest, all she wanted was him closer. He pulled her further into him, rubbing his hands up and down her back, all the time his lips probed hers, wanting more. They became frenzied, desperate to feel each other, when her legs moved, and a searing ache jolted through her. Jerking backwards she cried out in agony.

'Sorry!' Fitz looked horrified. 'Eva, I'm sorry...' He moved away to give her space.

'It's OK... ah!' It clearly wasn't.

'I'll be OK in a minute, once the painkillers kick in.' Eva was touched at just how concerned he was.

'Tea?'

She shook her head. 'No way. I deserve that drink I've been promising myself all day.' He gave a wary look. 'I'll be fine, go on, there's a bottle of wine in the fridge.'

'Sure?' he still looked apprehensive.

'Yes, yes,' she waved him away laughing.

Within half an hour the soreness had indeed subsided, and Eva was enjoying her cool, refreshing wine. It was good to have him nearby, chatting and relaxing together. Fitz told her about the donor procedure he'd undergone and all about his family. Eva sat transfixed, totally absorbed with every word he spoke. Talking about it proved therapeutic to him, as he poured out the remaining pent-up emotion and all that the past had brought him. She could almost see him visibly unwind and couldn't help but think at last the real, *whole* Fitz − or Theo − was eventually emerging.

'So now you know it all,' he shrugged and threw the last of his wine back.

'Oh Fitz,' it was all she could say. A huge lump in her throat had formed.

'I was so frightened of how you'd react,' he explained, then looked away self-consciously.

'It wasn't your fault,' she softly replied. 'You only acted with the best of intention.' It killed her to see him look so tortured. 'Come here.' He moved from the chair to kneel by her side. She wrapped her arms round him protectively, like a mother would her child. 'It's over now. Don't dwell on the past Fitz. Just think of how you've saved Lucas' life.' He nodded, then looked straight at her.

'Thank you.' This time his kiss remained gentle, but every bit as heartfelt.

–

Meanwhile, Max and Janey were at The Inn waiting for the rest to arrive. Both sat relaxed, shoulder-to-shoulder, sharing a bottle of red wine. It was as though both of them were seeing each other in a new light. Secretly, Max had always suspected Janey's affections lay with Fitz, noticing how she had often gravitated towards him. But now, was she a little more tactile with *him*? The way her hand touched his arm when talking and how close they sat together? He certainly felt a pull towards Janey, almost surprising himself that he hadn't previously noticed just how attractive she was. He waved up at seeing Kit and Pru enter, hand in hand. Together they all chatted, mainly about Fitz and his return to Lilacwell.

'I wonder where Fitz and Eva are?' Max looked at his watch. It was over an hour since they were due to arrive.

'I hope nothing's wrong,' said Pru with a look of concern.

'I'll give him a ring.' Kit reached for his mobile out of his jeans pocket. They all sat in silence, trying to listen to the conversation. 'Eva's fallen? Oh no, how is she?' Kit asked. The three of them leant forward a little, straining to hear more. 'Right, yeah. No, that's fine, Fitz. Send our best. Bye mate.' He hung up and faced them. 'Eva fell off a stepladder and badly sprained her ankle.'

'Oh no!' Pru exclaimed.

'He found her on the floor in her studio,' he explained.

'Good job he called there first,' remarked Janey.

'Yeah, it is. Good old Fitz,' said Max, glad his friend had finally caught up with Eva.

Chapter 31

Eva's swollen ankle began to calm down over the next few days. Having closed The Potter's Bolthole and under strict instructions from Fitz to rest it, she'd had plenty of time on her hands. Fitz had been a huge support, constantly calling on her and attending to her every need. He'd made a crutch for her to use, which had proved a blessing. That first night of her fall he'd stayed over on the sofa, after carefully assisting her into bed and making breakfast in the morning. Eva had been touched by the care and attention Fitz was showing and was quite getting used to having him around. It was a comfort to know he was never too far away, working next door.

Sat in her armchair, leg resting on a footstool with her laptop open, her thoughts flashed back to the evening when Fitz had stopped by and the conversation they'd had. A huge part of her still felt so sorry for the trauma he'd endured. To think he'd been practically living a double life in Lilacwell beggared belief. The guilt he'd carried obviously still had a big impact on him. Fitz had told her about the idyllic childhood he'd had in the beautiful country home, Hazelgrove. Eva pictured a long, gravel driveway with large, cast-iron gates opening up to a magnificent sandstone building with stained glass windows, and acres of lush, green lawns manicured to perfection. It sounded splendid, but now, apparently, it belonged to a young couple who had transformed it into a boutique hotel. Eva hated seeing the pain in Fitz's face when he'd revealed the sad end to his story.

It was at this point she'd gently reminded him that Hazelgrove was just bricks and mortar, as opposed to the life he'd saved. Eva sighed; would he ever truly forgive himself? Yes, he did seem much more relaxed, but there was still that degree of regret about him. It was plainly obvious his family had moved on, not that they had ever blamed him in the first place, but deep inside, would he? He needed to say a final goodbye to his past; he needed closure of some sort.

That's when the idea came to her. Eva typed *Hazelgrove, boutique hotel, Cheshire* into the search bar and gasped at the image appearing on the screen. Her imaginings of the splendid country house weren't far off the mark. It truly was a grand building, full of character with stone Georgian pillars and sash windows. The owners had kept the name, using Hazelgrove written in gold lettering as the title of the website. Eva clicked on the gallery page and various photographs of the house flowed across the screen; the oak panelled dining room, a residents' lounge with a wide, marble fireplace, a curved staircase in the hall boasting a huge stained-glass window, immaculately kept gardens and the bedrooms looked amazing. Eva clicked on each one. They all had four poster beds, with rolled top baths in the rooms, clearly decorated to a high spec with tasteful patterns and textiles. Eva whistled softly to herself; the place looked awesome. Just then she heard Fitz call and make his way up the stairs. She decided to leave the laptop open.

'Hey, you,' he lent down to give her a kiss. 'How are you feeling?'

'I think it's going down now, look,' she pointed to her ankle on the footstool. Fitz examined it.

'Yeah, it has.' Then he saw what was on the screen. He paused and peered at Eva, waiting for an explanation.

'Fitz, I think we should go,' she spoke quietly.

'To Hazelgrove?' he asked sharply. 'To see my family home that's been turned into some B&B?'

'It's a classy, boutique hotel, Fitz. It's still beautiful… just… no longer your home,' she gently replied. 'I think you should visit it and finally let go.' Her eyes explored his face, hoping he could see the logic in her suggestion. 'Say goodbye and move on,' she added softly.

'I… I don't think I can,' he spoke in a choked voice.

'Yes, you can. I'll be there. We'll do this together.'

Could he deny her anything? 'OK, let's go then,' he said in surrender.

To lighten the mood, Eva suggested opening another bottle of wine.

'There's chilli in the freezer, if you fancy making dinner?' she added with a cheeky grin. She was keen to keep Fitz as relaxed as possible before committing and actually booking a room.

'Sure,' he smiled.

Whilst Fitz was busy in the kitchen, Eva took the opportunity to go back to the Hazelgrove page.

Hazelgrove provides exceptional accommodation, the finest cuisine, and a genuinely warm welcome.

Eva had already chosen which bedroom she wanted. A family room with a double and single bed, a balcony overlooking the lawns at the rear of the house, decorated in pale green and gold décor and a tasteful chandelier, the room was classy yet not overdone and had the rather grand name, The Grosvenor.

After eating, Eva showed it to Fitz, clicking through each photo of the room.

'What do you think?' she tentatively asked.

His eyes swept from the laptop screen to rest on hers.

'That was my bedroom,' he stated flatly.

'Oh… right—'

'Book it,' he told her firmly. Eva was right. He badly needed closure.

Eva was now able to move without the support of the crutch Fitz had made her. Although she was glad to be moving painlessly, without assistance, a part of her was a tad disappointed to lose the excuse of having him around most of the time. The more time she'd spent with him, the more she liked him – more than like, if being completely honest.

Eva had had plenty of opportunity to sit and contemplate whilst being immobilised. The vast majority of her thoughts had turned to Fitz, or Theo, as she now preferred to think of him. Theo suited him so much better. He *looked* like a Theo, a handsome, dark Greek figure of a man. She wondered how he'd react if she called him by his real name, instead of Fitz as he was known to all. Well, everyone in Lilacwell, she reflected soberly. This then gave her something else to ponder about. Would Fitz's life change here in Lilacwell, now his cover had been blown? Would he be regarded in the same light as before, or would people's perceptions change? Did it matter?

Eva had been cooped up inside since Fitz's return to Lilacwell, so hadn't really witnessed how everyone had interacted with him. She knew his close friends, Max, and Kit, wouldn't be any different with him, and as for Alex, he already knew the real Fitz. It saddened her to think that he'd been worried about *her* reaction. Now though, after they'd spent so much time together with her ankle injury, they had grown closer; Fitz had elaborated about his past, and everything was in the open. He'd given her details about his childhood, his upbringing, and his family. He had even told her about his career in the city as a stockbroker.

At first, she'd been almost incredulous to imagine him as the Golden Boy, handling vast amounts of money. The idea of Fitz wearing a suit, commuting with the rest of London, to work on the stockmarket floor, was a hard one to picture. She simply couldn't comprehend it. It just didn't make any sense, especially seeing how he was now, with long hair, a beard, always dressed in jeans and working with his hands. Whilst obviously highly intelligent, he clearly had a creative talent too.

The evening Eva booked the overnight stay at Hazelgrove had encouraged Fitz to really open up and expose all. Eva had been mesmerised when he'd directed her to the website of the stock exchange. She took in the glass walls and the huge screens all around the room depicting various amounts of figures and information.

'What are world indices?' she'd asked, squinting at the screen.

'They're a yardstick to evaluate strength or weakness in the overall market,' Fitz had explained.

'Ri-ght… and risers?' Eva had asked, still a little confused.

'They're the sudden uptrend, causing a rise in price,' he'd simply replied, like it was just everyday chat to him, which at one time it would have been.

'…and the FTSE 100 index?' she'd frowned, trying to comprehend all the information before her.

'The global benchmark of the largest premium listed companies,' Fitz grinned, knowing all this was complete double Dutch to her. He shut the laptop and kissed her lips. 'It doesn't matter anymore.'

'Really?' asked Eva, looking closely at him. 'Don't you miss it?'

He gave a harsh laugh.

'No. It was another life.'

So now, all the pieces fit together. She knew *all* of Fitz, and any doubts Eva had had previously were now well and truly quashed. But what about him? Exactly what was going through his mind? Judging by the attentive way he had cared for her; she could only assume he had real feelings for her. In a way, Eva felt privileged to be privy to so many of the details of his life, especially after he'd gone to such great lengths to conceal it, realising that she was the only person to know so much about him. Not even his family would know what she did. That then led her to another question to ponder: Would his family come to Lilacwell and meet everyone? Or, even more significantly, would he follow them back to Cheshire?

A dull realisation filled Eva. The thought of Fitz leaving Lilacwell was unbearable. Surely, he wouldn't give up his carpentry business and sweet, little cottage? What about his friends? Could he leave them too? *Look how he had scampered home to Cheshire, without a backwards glance,* a voice inside her head goaded. Those unanswered phone calls and voice messages crawled into her mind, casting doubts. Oh, this was impossible! She couldn't keep mulling things over and over.

In an effort to do something positive, she opened her wardrobe. Yes, she needed to decide what to pack for their imminent weekend away. Keep herself busy.

–

Meanwhile, Fitz's mind was also in a quandary, but not about his future – about his past. He too was thinking about the weekend with Eva. In many ways he was glad of the break and a chance to get away with her. However, the one huge obstacle which threatened him relentlessly was Hazelgrove, his family home until it had been desecrated and transformed into a boutique hotel. He couldn't decide if it was a good or a bad idea to stay there. One minute he agreed with Eva, in that it would provide closure, but the next he feared it would open up old wounds.

At one point he'd even considered counselling. Maybe he ought to talk to someone? There was no denying that saving Lucas' life had helped him enormously and it had provided a gateway back to his family. But it was the memories that haunted him, not the here and now. He just couldn't get those precious childhood recollections out of his system. When he'd mentioned this to his parents during a heart to heart with them, they had said it was *good* to have happy memories; but they didn't get it. Fitz was wracked with guilt that *future* memories could no longer be made at Hazelgrove. He'd wanted his and Lucas' children, his parent's grandchildren, to enjoy the same joyous experiences there. He'd pictured family get togethers at Hazelgrove – toddlers playing on the lawn, whilst grown-ups looked on with smiles, chatting over drinks; his dad, always master of the barbeque, cooking up a treat; mum fussing round her brood on the terrace, ensuring nobody wanted for anything. Then he imagined family Christmases and how magical they'd been when he was little. The whole house would be decked with holly, mistletoe and berries from the garden and the open fires would crackle as they roasted chestnuts. Once, when he and Lucas were very small, his dad had made a Santa's grotto in the small wood at the back and dressed up as Father Christmas. Even growing up, Hazelgrove had provided a sound base for him and his teenage friends. Having so much room meant that all his mates were able to stay over together. The parties they'd had in the summer house were legendary.

Yes, his parents had made the most of their spectacular house and really created a loving, family home for them. And now it was gone.

Fitz wondered how he'd feel when stepping back inside Hazelgrove. Would he be impressed with the renovations of its new owners? Or would he resent the changes? Then he considered Eva's choice of room, his old bedroom. Was it fate? Or, had she chosen it because it had more than one bed? He remembered how she had backed off that time in the hammock when things had become heated between them, which naturally led to another question: Was their relationship ready for the next level? Would they be sharing the same bed?

Fitz gave a heavy sigh. There was certainly a lot hinging on this mini-break.

Chapter 32

Fletcher made good use of having The Laurels to himself while Jasper and Adira were dining out. He had decided to cook a meal for himself and Lilly. Only this wasn't just any old meal, no, this was going to be a romantic candlelit dinner for two. Well, as romantic as he could muster.

It hadn't helped burning the garlic mushrooms, but who needed a starter anyway? He cursed, shovelling them into the bin and promptly turned on the extractor fan in an effort to get rid of the smell and smoke. It was probably a blessing if the evening went the way he planned… Then he popped the plastic coverings on the ready meals he bought and shoved them in the oven. Once ready, he'd just pour the beef stew in a casserole dish and pass it off as his own. The baked potatoes he couldn't go wrong with – even he could stab spuds with a fork and bung them in the microwave. The vegetables would go in the microwave too, once snipping the corner of the plastic bag. As for dessert, that was easy. Adira had made an apple crumble yesterday and there was plenty left over. So, hey presto, a meal was made!

All he needed to do now was chill the prosecco. Personally, he'd like a deep, fruity red wine, but knew Lilly didn't care for it and much preferred a lighter drink with fizz, so prosecco it was.

He only hoped and prayed his efforts were not in vain – because tonight was The Night. Tonight, Fletcher was going to propose to Lilly. He was, after fifty-odd years, finally going to right the wrongs in his life and ask Lilly the question he should have asked her years ago. This fact alone made Fletcher sweat. How was she going to react? Would she say, 'Too little too late, Fletcher' or, just a simple, all out, 'No.'? Fletcher gulped. Was he doing the right thing? *Of course you are, man!* said that voice in his head. Then, on a calmer, more rational note he reasoned and asked himself, *what have you got to lose?*

Lilly tapped the kitchen door and entered, taking him unawares.

'Hello, Fletcher, oh, what's that awful smell?' she said sniffing the air.

'Oh, Lilly. I've burnt the... never mind, here, let me take your jacket lass.' He helped her out of her coat and went to hang it in the hallway. On returning to the kitchen, he found her opening the oven. 'No, no, don't do anything, tonight's all about you,' he said, ushering her away.

'But I always cook,' replied Lilly, frowning.

'Not tonight. Go into the dining room, I'll fetch you a drink.'

'The dining room? Aren't we eating in here?' Lilly questioned, clearly confused with formal dining.

'No. Dining room tonight, Lilly,' said Fletcher firmly. 'Now go, I'll bring everything through.'

'Are you sure?' Lilly's eyebrows rose.

'Yes lass, go on.'

Once settled nicely in the dining room and Fletcher had managed to serve up the meal, he poured them another glass of prosecco before clearing his throat.

'Lilly, I've been a fool…'

Lilly put down her fork in alarm. 'Fletcher?'

'No, hear me out, please. I want to… will you… err,' his hand trembled and he gulped back his drink, then caught her gaze, holding it fiercely. 'Lilly, will you marry me?'

Silence. Fletcher swallowed dryly.

'Don't ask me to go down on one knee Lilly, I might never get up,' he attempted humour.

But still there remained a stunned quietness.

'How does the saying go, Fletcher?' she finally replied, with a slight curve to her lips.

Fletcher's shoulders sagged.

'There's no fool, like an old fool?' he weakly replied.

'No, I was thinking…' she paused, making him raise his head sharply. 'It's better late than never.'

'What? You mean—'

'Yes, Fletcher, I'll marry you.'

Was that a tear in her eye?

'Oh lass, come here!' He jumped up and hugged her hard, never wanting to let go.

–

Jasper blinked in quick succession, standing rigid on the spot.

'You're getting married?' he asked incredulously.

'Aye, I am that,' came Fletcher's fixed reply.

Jasper came to sit opposite him by the fire in the drawing room, just like he had that night when Fletcher seemed troubled. Little had he known then how the conversation they'd had would pan out. The penny dropped. Jasper vaguely recalled the words they had exchanged regarding 'missed opportunities' and 'doing the right thing,' but he'd assumed it had been more due to Fletcher's empty whisky tumbler. How wrong he'd been.

'Fletcher,' Jasper said calmly, looking him in the eye. 'Are you sure about this?' His face was etched with concern, the news he'd just been given coming as a total shock.

'Of course I am!' retorted Fletcher impatiently. 'I should have asked her years ago.'

With that Jasper couldn't argue. He had often pondered why Fletcher and Lilly had never got together after all this time. He'd completely understood the circumstances way back when he was born and to some degree even after, but as Lilly had always shown such loyalty and devotion to Fletcher, he had wondered why they'd still remained single all these years. It was obvious the two complemented each other, with Fletchers' gregarious spirit and Lilly's peaceful stability, not to mention the long history they shared. Their genuine affection for each other was blatant. But why now? That's what Jasper couldn't comprehend.

Fletcher eyed him carefully, knowing full well what was going through Jasper's head. Hadn't he been toying with the same question himself? Sighing, he leant forward and patted him reassuringly.

'I know what I'm doing. It'll not change anything between us you know.'

'I know that,' Jasper half laughed. 'It's not me I'm thinking of. Why didn't you ask Lilly years ago?'

Fletcher gave another sigh.

'To be honest, I think I let the past govern me.' He looked at Jasper sorrowfully. 'Do you understand?'

'You were waiting for my mother, weren't you?' came the quiet reply. Finally, the words were being spoken, out in the open.

'Aye, I was Jasper,' Fletcher nodded, then added in a small voice. 'But she never came.'

Jasper's own eyes filled. It was such a heartbreaking, hopeless situation. He didn't know how to feel, apart from incredibly sad.

'And then, as the years went on,' continued Fletcher, 'you were enough for me, it's that simple. Though I now know I did take advantage of Lilly's good nature,' he conceded.

'Well, did you? Lilly was happy to be housekeeper here at The Laurels and you paid her very well,' argued Jasper.

'But I let things drift on, really knowing how she felt about me. Maybe I prevented her from meeting someone else. Selfishly I let her carry on, looking after me.'

'Oh Fletcher, I wouldn't say that,' Jasper tried to reassure him. 'You both love each other's company and Lilly's always had her sister Ruby, too. She's never been lonely, has she?'

This seemed to appease Fletcher.

'Aye,' he agreed, 'I suppose.'

'So, now you're tying the knot,' Jasper couldn't help but chuckle. 'Good for you.'

Fletcher smiled up and winked.

'Life in the old dog yet.'

–

When Adira was told the news that night as the four of them shared supper, she was equally surprised and delighted.

'Oh, how lovely!' Her eyes too were filled with emotion. 'When's the big day?'

Lilly gave a coy smile.

'It won't be a big day as such, Adira. Just a registry office.'

Adira glanced at Fletcher for confirmation. He gave a noncommittal shrug.

'It's what Lilly wants. No big song and dance, just a quiet do.'

'Oh… I see,' replied Adira looking at Jasper. It really didn't seem Fletcher's style, but she obviously wasn't going to voice her concern.

'You could always have a church blessing?' suggested Jasper. 'Afterwards, in the chapel, just immediate family?'

Fletcher looked at Lilly for her response. A glimmer of a smile hovered over her lips.

'What do you think, Lilly?' Fletcher asked hopefully. Truth be told he did want more of an occasion than just a registry office service. He was, after all, a bit of a showman.

'That would be nice,' she said, nodding in approval.

'It'll be splendid Lilly,' enthused Adira, 'and afterwards we can have a small wedding breakfast here, in the orangery. I'll arrange—' then suddenly stopped after seeing Lilly's face fall. Jasper discreetly put his hand on her lap. Clearly Adira was excited and wanted to give her input, but they had to stand back and let Fletcher and Lilly decide what *they* wanted.

Fletcher coughed. 'We've agreed to have a celebratory meal at The Inn, for close family afterwards,' he explained, looking a touch uncomfortable, not wanting to cause any offence.

'Ah, right,' said Adira cheerfully.

'We don't want a fuss you see,' said Lilly, who didn't want another replica wedding of Adira and Jasper's. They had had a spectacular Christmas wedding at The Laurels but the last thing Lilly wished for was that kind of affair; it was for the young ones, not her.

'Well, I'm here if you need a hand with anything,' Adira smiled, taking the hint.

'Thank you dear,' said Lilly. 'That's exactly what Ruby said.'

Jasper smothered his laugh at seeing Fletcher roll his eyes.

'Yes, I'm sure that sister of yours is ready to lend a helping hand,' he remarked wryly.

Chapter 33

The day had come. Fitz was to face his demons and step foot once more into Hazelgrove, this time as a paying guest. Seeing Eva ready outside her pottery studio, with her small wheelie suitcase, gave him comfort though, especially when he noticed how excited she looked.

'Ready?' he smiled, coming around his Range Rover to open the passenger door and help with her bag.

'Yes,' she kissed his cheek, then looked him in the eye. 'You can do this, Theo.'

He flinched slightly at hearing his name. It sounded odd coming from Eva, but another part of him liked it, because it spoke volumes. Being called by his real name meant that Eva knew him; all of him. And still here she was, about to enjoy a weekend away with him.

Of course, it was more than just a mini-break. It was a whole load more. Visiting Hazelgrove was closure, a chance to accept what had happened and what it now was – a boutique hotel, not his family home. It was a chance to confront his mistake that had cost his family so dearly and move on. *Fully* move on.

Fitz had finally realised that in order to move on, he needed to unite both his worlds. His present life in Lilacwell had to meet his past life in Cheshire. The first step towards this was to introduce Eva to his parents and brother, which he intended to do, but not this weekend.

This weekend was all about them. He dearly hoped Eva was comfortable enough to share a bed with him, though he would respectfully wait for her signal and assume he'd be in the single bed. He wanted the closeness, not just the physical proximity, but the emotional bond. Only recently was he beginning to realise how much he had distanced himself from people in order to keep his cover. Now he craved an intimate relationship, without any complications. In short, he had denied himself love for too long.

–

Meanwhile Eva was determined to be as positive and supportive as possible. She refused to allow herself any negative thoughts, whether it be Fitz's future, or anything else remotely unconstructive. She'd taken Beth's advice, who had told her not to maudle.

'Fitz is hardly likely to up sticks and go,' she'd said reassuringly, 'he's established his business and built a home in Lilacwell.'

'I know, but only because he was made to leave Cheshire,' Eva had countered. 'What if he decides to return, now that he's reunited with his family?'

'Cheshire's not a million miles away!' exclaimed Beth in exasperation, then quickly added, 'Why not just talk to him? See what's on his mind?'

So, that's what Eva intended to do. Talk.

In just under two hours, they'd reached Cheshire. Fitz knew the area well as he drove through all the streets lined with large, impressive houses. When Eva noticed his hands tightly grip the steering wheel, showing white knuckles, she knew they had reached Hazelgrove.

'This is it,' he stated, as they entered through the huge iron gates. Eva gasped. Although she had seen it on the hotel's website, it still hadn't prepared her for the grandeur of the place.

'It's amazing,' she whispered in awe, taking in the big Georgian house with extensive grounds. Ivy grew up its stone pillars and hanging baskets bursting with colourful blooms hung either side of a solid oak door.

'It certainly is,' replied Fitz quietly. Automatically he drove to the left, round the back of the house to park, barely noticing the car parking signs. Then he switched off the car engine and sat back for a moment to survey the sight before him. Quite a bit had changed. A rear entrance had been made, with the back door being replaced with double glass doors and a ramp leading up to them. A fire escape, too, had been installed, with metal steps and railings running across the building. The garden was exactly the same, though, with its immaculately cut lawns, vibrant flower beds and stone terrace leading into the house. This was a relief; he'd have hated to see them undo his parents' hard work. By 'them' he was of course referring to the new owners. The couple on the website hadn't looked all that old, probably not much older than him, Fitz had dully thought, and look at what they'd achieved with their life. Unreasonably, Fitz had already decided he didn't like them. He resented everything that the young couple stood for – success, at his cost. Deep down, he knew how irrational he was being, after all, they were strangers to him. And it was his fault they lost the house, not theirs for buying it. They would be totally unaware of the fact that he knew every single nook and cranny of the place.

'OK?' Eva gently asked, seeing how his eyes were scanning every detail.

'Yes.' He gave a tight smile. 'Come on, let's do this.'

Together they wheeled their suitcases to the front door. Fitz hesitated for a moment, prompting Eva to take the initiative and open it. As they entered the hall, Fitz walked steadily to the reception desk at the far end, where his mother's console table used to stand, usually holding a vase full of fresh picked flora from the garden.

'Theo Fitzgerald,' he said to the receptionist, 'we're here for two nights.' He couldn't help but notice a flicker of recognition across the woman's face. Then he realised this was the owner. The name Fitzgerald would resonate with her, especially his after buying the place from his parents. Embarrassment flared up inside him.

'Ah yes,' she said whilst looking at a screen in front of her. 'If I could just ask you to fill in this form?' She then slid a pen and paper in front of him. Fitz quickly completed it and was handed a key. 'The Grosvenor is at the end of the corridor,' she smiled politely. Fitz resisted the urge to say, 'I know, I slept in it for twenty-nine years.' The irony of being given a key to his own bedroom wasn't lost on him.

Eva quietly observed, knowing how much this was costing Fitz. For a moment she worried if this was such a good idea after all. Too late now, she thought, they were here. In silence they climbed the stairs, taking in the newly painted apple white walls and tasteful artwork. The floor to ceiling stained glass window from the hall reached up past them, shining multi-coloured rays across the ceiling. They walked down the corridor, passing the bedroom doors, each with its name neatly inscribed, until they reached The Grosvenor. Fitz stifled a laugh, *The Grosvenor*, how fucking pretentious was that? He remembered the very same door plastered with his Stone Roses poster!

Smirking to himself, he unlocked it; maybe he'd be able to see the funny side of things after all.

Eva seemed struck by the opulence of her surroundings; she dumped her case on the double bed and went straight to open the glass doors which led out to the balcony overlooking the gardens. Fitz watched her and wondered if it meant she'd staked her claim on sleeping in the double. If so, where should he put his? On there with hers, or on the single bed? He opted to just leave it standing in the middle of the room and went to join her on the balcony. Turning, Eva smiled and reached out for him. They wrapped their arms around each other in comfort.

'It sounded strange hearing you say your real name,' she said, staring ahead, admiring the beautiful lawns and terrace below. Then she turned to face him. 'Fitz, I hope I've not bullied you into coming here.'

'No. I needed to confront things head-on. It's no good being in denial, or hiding away,' he replied and took a moment to reflect on what he'd just said. Yes, his days of hiding were well gone now.

Chapter 34

Cassie was on tenterhooks. She was expecting Rory to arrive any minute, along with the editor from the publishing house they had signed with. He had caught the train from Euston to Lancaster, where Rory was meeting him, to then drive back to Lilacwell.

She had prepared them lunch, all with their own fresh produce, naturally; a broccoli, basil and spinach quiche with new potatoes and a rocket, radish, tomato and beetroot salad. Then strawberries, blueberries, and blackcurrants with ice cream. So hopefully the editor, Craig, would be impressed.

As promised, Craig wanted to sample for himself a taste of the good life which Rory and Cassie had created. He was keen to visit and see first-hand their achievements both with The Harvest Barn smallholding and the barn conversion.

'Renovating old buildings into new life is what people love,' he'd told them. Craig had been equally enthusiastic about Rory's back story. 'A barrister in London jacking it all in to work the land is a real rags-to-riches story in reverse – but in a good way,' he stressed. 'And as for the Climate Warrior the media dubbed you, well you couldn't have asked for better marketing!'

However true this was, Rory still felt a touch uncomfortable with all the attention the Climate Warrior brought him. He point-blank refused the title originally suggested for their book. *The Climate Warrior's Diary* had made him balk. Still, as Craig stated, it most definitely had provided endless promotional openings and for this he was grateful.

Cassie only hoped Rory and Craig were hitting it off in person, having only met the editor over Zoom calls until now.

As instructed, they had kept a journal, along with photographs depicting their story so far. It had been something they would most likely have done in any event, marking their journey to date. They only hoped it would be edited sympathetically, keeping their informal style. Would the publishers appreciate the humour Rory and Cassie had injected into their diary? Being up to your eyes in mud, misbehaving animals and living in a shepherd's hut had certainly brought them a few giggles along the way.

Cassie spotted Rory driving the Range Rover down the field. He appeared to be laughing, whilst Craig at the passenger's side talked animatedly next to him; a good sign, she thought. As they pulled up next to the barn, Cassie went out to greet them. She heard Rory telling Craig about the party they had just hosted, and Craig replying with mirth.

'Must have saved a fortune eloping. Wish I'd done it.' Then he turned at seeing Cassie join them and reached out his hand. 'Hi, so pleased to be here.'

'You're welcome,' she replied with a handshake. 'Come inside, I've made some lunch.'

Lunch was a casual affair with Craig doing a lot of the talking. He was easy company and both Rory and Cassie were a little surprised at how relaxed they all were together. They had been slightly wary of the meeting

– Rory in particular – feeling almost as if the editor had come to size them up. But Craig seemed straightforward and neither of them felt intimidated in any way.

Craig noticed the wedding album still on the side table from the party.

'May I?' he tipped his head towards it, wanting to take a look.

Cassie's head turned to Rory, taken unawares. She'd meant to put that album away.

'Sure,' replied Rory.

'These are amazing,' he said looking up at them, as he turned the pages. 'Can we include a few in the book?' Again, Cassie's eyes flew to Rory. 'They'd make a brilliant feature,' Craig pressed. Then another idea hit him. 'In fact, could we have photographs of when you were a barrister, in wig and gown? And Cassie, maybe you as a hotel manager in uniform? We need your back stories, you know, what you did beforehand.'

Rory met Cassie's gaze. He raised an eyebrow in question.

'What do you think, Cass?' he asked.

'If it'll help sell the book…'

'Too right it will,' replied Craig with gusto. Then added passionately, 'Also, what about photos of your childhood to early teens?'

Rory snorted imagining the photographs of him as a student, spearheading demos, and various rallies, appearing in the book. When he voiced this, Craig's face lit up in delight.

'That's *exactly* what I'm after!' he exclaimed.

All in all, the meeting went well. After taking a tour of the barn and smallholding, Craig seemed more than happy with his findings.

'Well, thanks for a fantastic visit,' he turned to Cassie with a huge beam. 'I'll be in touch.'

Rory drove him back to the train station, and Cassie wished the book, once published, would be everything they hoped for; not just about them as a couple, but also what they were doing and more importantly, what they stood for.

Chapter 35

Fitz and Eva were exhausted, but a happy exhausted. After checking into Hazelgrove and unpacking, they had ordered tea and sat on the balcony overlooking the garden terrace below. This had given Fitz time to adjust to his environment. Slowly, he was beginning to unwind, chatting to Eva about various points of interest surrounding them.

'See that grotto over there?' He pointed in the distance to the very far end of the lawn giving way to a small wood. Eva blocked out the sun with her hand and strained to see piles of stone built into a banking, forming an arch shape hollow.

'Yes, just about,' she said.

'That was where Father Christmas left our presents.' He gave a grin, his eyes sparkling with a joy that had long been missing.

'Oh, how sweet!' exclaimed Eva. 'This must have been a magical place to grow up in.' She carefully looked at him, hoping he took the comment in the way it was intended and not a dig at what had been lost. The smile and shrug he gave told her he had.

'It was. But it's only bricks and mortar at the end of the day,' he said, sitting back. Eva nodded but remained silent. 'It's family that matters. Come on, I'll show you the local area,' Fitz said, quickly changing the mood.

Together they strolled through the high streets, shops, parks, and cafes. Fitz had given Eva a potted history of his upbringing, showing her his primary school, rugby club and his local pub. Eva was more than happy to learn of his past, relishing every detail.

'Where do your parents live now?' she asked, curious to know.

'Not too far away, in a bungalow on a new estate.' There was a slight pause. 'I will introduce you to them, but not now. You do understand?' He reached for her hand and held it tightly, searching her face hoping she would.

'Of course,' she replied immediately, eager to make him feel as comfortable as possible. She completely understood that Fitz was still adjusting to his new lease of life, and the tentative relationship he was rebuilding with his family, and the last thing she wanted was any extra pressure for him.

Later they had travelled into Manchester and taken in the vibrant city. Eva suddenly realised how much she had missed this and thoroughly enjoyed being amongst the hustle and bustle of city life.

–

Fitz relaxed and let it all unfold around him. It had been a long time since he had felt so free, especially on this territory. No longer was he half expecting a flash of recognition from a passer-by, or insults hurled in his direction. He was just an ordinary bloke with his girlfriend, enjoying an afternoon out.

By early evening they made their way back to Hazelgrove. Deciding to eat supper there meant neither of them had to worry about driving back, so they could both relax and have a drink.

It was now eight o'clock and both had showered and dressed for dinner. Eva looked elegant in a close-fitted black dress, sitting slightly off shoulder. It reminded Fitz of the first time he'd seen her through the pottery studio window. She'd worn a similar style top on that day, show-casing her slender neckline and shoulders, tanned and lightly dusted with freckles.

She caught the lustful expression on his face and felt a jolt of anticipation. He cut a fine figure in black trousers and a crisp, white shirt. Together they made a handsome couple as they walked down the stairs into the dining room.

Eva glanced over at him as Fitz gave the name of their room before being shown to a table. He seemed to be in his comfort zone, pulling a chair out for her and sitting opposite with ease. She saw him discreetly look around, his eyes darting to each corner of the room.

'Has it changed?' she asked quietly.

'Apart from there being more tables?' he gently teased.

'Well, yes,' she softly laughed.

'Not really, the wallpaper and the curtains are the same,' he acknowledged, then added dryly, 'but then, my mother had just had it redecorated.'

'Well, she has very good taste,' approved Eva, looking at the pale lemon walls and the heavy tapestry fabric. It all resonated with class.

Soon they were sipping wine and browsing the menu. Fitz, though he hated to admit it, was impressed with the choice on offer, as was Eva. He suddenly wondered if his parents had ever visited here? He doubted it.

Eva noticed a flicker of emotion in his face as his eyebrows briefly furrowed, and she reached out to touch his hand. His eyes shot to meet her gaze and a quiet understanding passed between them. The evening was pleasant and easy-going, despite Eva's reservations. Together they talked and laughed, basking in each other's company. It was good to enjoy just being alone, albeit in Fitz's former home.

By the time Eva checked the grandfather clock by the door, it was almost ten thirty and the evening had flown by. Then, there was a frisson of excitement as a few of the diners all looked towards a table tucked into the far recess behind the bay window, with big smiles and eager faces. Eva turned around to see what the commotion was. A man was knelt on one knee, obviously about to propose to the young woman sat at his table. Hushed oohs and aahs filled the room. Eva couldn't help but grin at the romantic gesture. The girl sobbed her acceptance through obvious tears of joy, and everybody clapped and cheered when her now-fiancé placed a ring on her finger. Then he turned to acknowledge the applause and Eva's heart dropped like lead.

It was Simon. Her ex.

His eyes, roaming around the jubilant crowd of diners, eventually found hers and widened with astonishment at seeing her. His expression visibly turned from elation, to shock, to horror. He sat back down quietly. His fiancée hadn't noticed any awkwardness, still wrapped up in the moment, admiring the sapphire on her finger.

Fitz had, though, quickly putting two and two together. Eva had turned a pale white. He drew up and quietly went around to move her chair back, helping her up from the table.

'Let's go,' he gently whispered, and they retreated back up the stairs to their room.

A cocktail of emotions flooded through Eva's blood. A mixture of surprise, disbelief, confusion, and anger. Simon, wanting to *marry* someone. Who? And how long had he known her? She rushed to the bathroom and threw up the dinner she had just eaten.

Fitz sat on the bed in silence, not quite knowing what to do. Clearly seeing Simon had an impact on Eva, which naturally made him question her feelings for him.

Eventually he heard the retching stop and the toilet flush. Then the splash of water. Eva rinsed her face before opening the ensuite door. She still looked a little shaken, but managed a small, embarrassed smile.

'Sorry about that,' she spoke quietly and sat on the double bed next to him.

'That was Simon, wasn't it?' Fitz softly asked, putting a protective arm around her waist.

'Yes.' Then she turned to him and stared into his eyes. 'It was such a shock. I can't believe he's here, *proposing* to someone.' She sucked in a shaky breath. 'I was pregnant… and he never—' then she stopped abruptly.

'Proposed to you?' he said. Eva nodded, a sudden calmness falling over her.

'But, do you know,' she reflected, almost as if realising it for the first time, 'it's a good job, because I might just have said yes, and it would have been a huge mistake.' Fitz felt like punching the air in celebration but refrained with a small smile instead. 'Theo?' she said, making him gently chuckle.

'One minute I'm Fitz, the next Theo.'

'Which do you prefer?' she asked, head tilted to one side, assessing him. He gazed pensively into the distance in consideration.

'I've grown accustomed to Fitz, I suppose. That's who I was when you first met me.'

'And thank God I did.'

He turned to face her.

'And I you.' There was a moment's pause. 'What were you going to ask me?' he said.

'I was going to ask you to share my bed.' Eva gave a coy smile, suddenly feeling a tad self-conscious.

'Sure?' he touched the side of her cheek. At least she had regained a bit more colour now.

'Very sure,' she replied, craving to be held by those strong, shielding arms.

Chapter 36

Well, what a weekend, thought Fitz as he drove out of The Cobbled Courtyard. He'd just dropped Eva off and was making his way back to Woodsman Cottage. They'd shared a long, lingering kiss goodbye before Eva had got out of the car and waved him off. Fitz had seen Max and Janey from his top window, who had blatantly been watching them. Max knew no shame as he gave him the thumbs up and a wink, having witnessed their intimacy. Fitz shook his head and laughed to himself. He was pleased that Max seemed to be happy with Janey, obviously things were progressing nicely between them, too.

Although he'd loved being in Eva's company, Fitz was glad to be home in his own cottage. He needed space and time to think, to consider and digest all that the past few days had thrown at him. In many ways he'd changed as a person. Having to deal with such a catastrophic financial loss, together with the humiliation of it all; running away to create a new life in Lilacwell; becoming a donor to his brother and saving his life; trusting to form a new relationship with Eva. It was a lot to absorb.

Having parked up at his cottage, he opened the front door and collected the post lying on the mat. Then he promptly poured himself a whisky and sank into the armchair. Closing his eyes and taking a deep breath he replayed the weekend with Eva. It had gone well, very well in fact. Better than he had been expecting, truth be told. Visiting Hazelgrove had slotted things into place in a way, making him realise that it was just in fact bricks and mortar, nothing else. Yes, it had made a spectacular childhood home, but he was a grown man. And that's when it struck him – the enormity of what he had actually done. He had *saved* his little brother's life. Lucas was a grown man too and thanks to him, he'd continue to be. Lucas was not going to wither and die. Fitz gulped at the mere thought of losing him. It was inconceivable. How would his parents ever have come to terms with it? They would *never* have recovered from the loss, and had they not known where he was all this time, it might have been too late. And then it really would have been his fault. He took a swig of whisky. That alone put everything into perspective.

Then there was Eva. Just the thought of her made him smile. Ironically, the episode with her ex-boyfriend in the restaurant had distracted them both from the weekend's mission and, instead of their stay giving him closure over Hazelgrove and all that it encompassed, it had ended up giving Eva a form of conclusion also.

Seeing Simon with someone else had clearly made her realise what a close escape she'd had. Of course, Eva had been shocked initially, especially as Simon was proposing to the girl sitting opposite him, but after getting over the surprise, Eva had become rather philosophical about it.

They had given each other support and comfort. They were a good team, thought Fitz. Then flashbacks of just how good they were together made him shiver inside. Blood started to pump through his veins at the memory of her. Sleeping next to her warm body and waking up beside her had been heaven. The close intimacy of another human being had been sadly lacking in his life for so long.

Fitz finished his whisky and contemplated further. Life was a sequence of events, all waiting to unfold. Had he not lost a fortune on the stock exchange, he wouldn't have fled to Lilacwell, which meant he wouldn't have met Eva. He never expected to see a silver lining from the past, but… well, there it was. Life events had brought him to Eva.

–

Eva too, was taking stock. *What was the chance of bumping into Simon?* Then, thinking about it, she wasn't too surprised that he would choose such a flash place to pop the question. She smirked, a part of her was glad she'd ruined it for him. Not that she was jealous, she really wasn't, probably more offended than anything. Even though Eva knew she and Simon were not right for each other, it still stung to see that he had moved on so quickly. But then, hadn't she? The voice of reason sounded inside her head. The answer was yes, she had most definitely moved on. Eva had willingly given herself to Fitz, knowing she was in safe hands, in every sense.

The last thing she had wanted the following morning was to face Simon again. Thankfully, he wasn't to be seen in the breakfast room, much to her relief. She envisaged him checking out as soon as possible, not wishing to confront her either. It could have been comical, had it not been so unexpected. Wait till she told Beth!

Still, a nagging doubt persisted. It had been exacerbated by the fact that Fitz had chosen not to introduce her to his family. Although she had understood why, it gave her insecurities. Fitz clearly wanted to keep his life in Lilacwell totally separate from his roots in Cheshire. It troubled her, made her feel vulnerable; it was as though she was a secret, someone to be kept hidden in the distance. And thinking about it logically, *why* did she have to be concealed? Surely his parents would have expected him to form relationships? Their son was a handsome young man, they wouldn't be expecting him to remain single forever. Had they even asked if he had a girlfriend? Had he denied her existence?

She stopped herself, knowing that once again she was working herself up into a frenzy. Fitz had said he *would* introduce her, just not on that occasion. All in good time, she told herself. For now, she would savour the moments and enjoy every precious memory that spending time with him had brought. Eva had never felt so secure than in his strong arms.

Her phone bleeped with a text message from Beth.

> How did the dirty weekend go?

It was followed with a winking, smiling face emoji. Typical Beth laughed Eva.

Wonderful, she replied simply and copied the same face back.

> Tell me all about it. I'll ring you tonight.

Beth was obviously keen to hear all the details. Eva chuckled again, anticipating how her friend would react to all she had to say.

Chapter 37

The summer days rolled on bringing glorious sunshine to Lilacwell. Adira was also blooming as she entered the final two months of her pregnancy. It was the first week in August and the day of Fletcher and Lilly's wedding.

Whereas The Laurels had been a hive of activity for Jasper and Adira's Christmas wedding, today a quiet calmness surrounded the place. Fletcher stood in front of the full-length mirror and examined his reflection. Not bad, he concluded, taking in the navy suit, crisp white shirt, and paisley tie, complete with matching pocket square.

Jasper wore a navy suit too, while Adira had sought the most flattering maternity dress she could as befitted a wedding. Together they waited in the hall for Fletcher, ready to drive them all to the registry office in Clitheroe. Lilly was making her own way there with Ruby and Ruby's gentleman friend, Alfred.

Adira caught sight of Fletcher at the top of the stairs.

'Oh Fletcher, how dashing you look!' cheered Adira, looking up at him.

'Thanks, lass.' He made his way down.

Jasper grinned at him. 'Ready to go?'

'Aye, ready as I'll ever be,' replied Fletcher, appearing a tad nervous to their surprise. For once, he wasn't the loud and ebullient showman.

When they arrived at the registry office, Ruby and Alfred were waiting for them inside the foyer. As arranged, Lilly wanted to make an entrance alone.

They were all gathered into a room and seated. Fletcher anxiously fidgeted in his chair, until he noticed Lilly hesitating by the door. His face creased into a huge smile as she serenely walked down the centre of the room, wearing a cream silk dress, mid-length, with full sleeves and a drop waist. She carried a small bouquet of white roses. Jasper and Adira turned tearfully to each other as she joined Fletcher who stood up to meet her.

'You look beautiful, Lilly.' Fletcher's voice broke with emotion.

The ceremony was short and sweet but touching nonetheless. When Fletcher placed a wedding ring on Lilly's shaking finger a tear ran down his face. Jasper gulped back the lump in his throat.

'I now pronounce you husband and wife,' announced the registrar to a small applause.

'About bloody time,' muttered Ruby under her breath. As Lilly's twin sister, she'd always resented Fletcher not making his move years ago. Thankfully, nobody heard her comment.

After congratulatory hugs and kisses and a few photos, they left the registry office, where a silver Rolls Royce decorated with cream ribbon awaited the newlyweds.

'Is that for us?' asked Lilly in awe.

'Aye, it is,' said Fletcher. 'Thought we'd do it in style.' He held his arm out for her to take as they walked down the registry office steps. The chauffeur opened the door and Lilly climbed inside, followed by Fletcher. 'Well, Lilly, how does it feel to be Mrs Hendricks?'

'Just fine,' she laughed, snuggling into him.

As the Rolls Royce pulled into The Inn at Lilacwell, a small party had gathered to clap the bride and groom in. Although Lilly had wanted a quiet do, a few locals couldn't help but show support, thanks to Ruby who had rallied them up.

The conservatory overlooking the river and terrace had been decorated with lilies, as per Adira's instruction, and a white linen table shone with silver candles, cut-glass and white porcelain, surrounded by seats with white sashes, waiting for the wedding guests.

There were no speeches, just the sound of chatter and laughter. Every so often, Fletcher's eyes would fill, so overwhelmed by the fact he was actually married to Lilly, and, oh, what a fine-looking bride she made.

–

Lilly, with a quiet composure, took everything in her stride. It was the day she had dreamed of, ever since she was a little girl, truth be told. Now it had happened – she was Fletcher's wife at long last. She turned to view his profile as he sat leaning sideways talking to Jasper. He still had it. He was as handsome now as he had been all those years ago, when she'd pined away for him in vain. But not anymore. Today he had promised to love and look after her until their dying day. He'd always looked after her though, she knew that deep down.

'Well, you finally made it,' Ruby barged into her sentimental thoughts. There was never anyone quite like her twin sister to do that. She turned to face her.

'Yes Ruby, I made it and I've never been happier.' Lilly looked her in the eye, rather challengingly.

'Yes…of course,' blinked Ruby, unaccustomed to her sister's tone. They were interrupted by Alfred.

'Ruby, dear, would you like—'

'I'll have a whisky,' she ordered, making Lilly's lips twitch. It looked like poor Alfred was about to take her place in Ruby's pecking order. Still, he looked happy enough being bossed about by her twin.

'Maybe it'll be them next?' joked Fletcher in her ear softly. They both giggled like school children.

'Aw, look at them,' said Adira, observing Fletcher and Lilly as they laughed, leaning into each other.

'I know,' replied Jasper smiling. 'It's good to see them so happy together.'

'Do you think that'll be us, thirty or forty years down the road?' Adira held his hand on the table.

'Absolutely,' Jasper kissed her lips. Then, rising to his feet, he proposed a toast to the bride and groom.

Later in the early evening, as the sky turned a burnt orange and pink, all the guests bid their farewells and left the newlyweds to enjoy the beginning of their married life. Fletcher had booked the suite at the top of the hotel to stay overnight. Lilly had never known such luxury.

'It's palatial!' gasped Lilly on entering the bedroom.

'It's what you deserve,' countered Fletcher, enjoying her reaction. He himself couldn't help but be impressed with the huge four poster bed, antique furniture, plush carpet, and Juliet balcony with a view of the river and the Pennines beyond. The sun was beginning to set, casting magnificent hues over the countryside.

He'd never felt so complete, so content. It was a moment he'd cherish forever.

-

'The house is so quiet without Fletcher,' remarked Adira as she sat in the nursery, keeping Jasper company.

Fletcher and Lilly were on their honeymoon; having decided to spend a few days in Paris, Fletcher had surprised Lilly and whisked her away on Eurostar. However romantic the gesture was, Adira couldn't help but wonder if that was exactly Lilly's style. Then again, judging by how happy she'd looked waving them goodbye, maybe she was having the time of her life. One thing was for certain, Fletcher would be lapping up all the attention. Adira could just imagine him in the bistros ordering champagne and making a fuss of his new bride.

'It sure is,' replied Jasper, distracted as he tried to fathom the instructions before him. He was assembling a cot and was currently knelt on the floor surrounded by various bits of wood and small plastic bags of screws.

The nursery was complete, all it needed was for the baby's cot to be put up. They'd bought a few bits of furniture; a small wardrobe and baby changing unit, plus a comfortable chair for Adira to breastfeed in. She'd positioned it by the window for a good view of the gardens.

It felt strange thinking that in just a matter of weeks she'd be a mother. Her whole life was about to change. In her quieter moments, she recalled the photographs of herself as a baby, born two months prematurely. It was hard to believe that the tiny new-born, covered with wires, kicking in an incubator, had grown into the healthy, young woman she now was. The name Adira had been chosen by her parents as it meant 'strength' in Hebrew – and strength was exactly what Adira had needed in her early days.

Jasper had asked recently if any reason had been given for her premature birth. Adira knew he was secretly worried if history would repeat itself and *she* might also go into premature labour. But nobody could explain why Adira had been born so early and, so far, Adira was feeling fine. Her blood pressure was regularly checked and there wasn't anything to suggest she wouldn't go full term.

She rubbed her bump and smiled, wondering if there was a boy or girl inside there. She hadn't any inkling either way. To date, the only name they had agreed on was having Fletcher for a second name if it was a boy. Other than that, they couldn't wholeheartedly come up with anything particular either way.

'That's it,' said Jasper with satisfaction. He'd managed to attach both ends of the cot together with the frame. 'Now for the sides.'

'You're doing a great job,' laughed Adira, sat back in the chair relaxing. She put her feet up on the cardboard box the cot had arrived in.

'So are you,' said Jasper, smiling lovingly at her. My God, he'd never loved her more. She was positively glowing, with flawless skin, shiny blonde hair, and bright blue eyes. He too could hardly believe that in just a short while he would be a parent. The impending birth he was naturally wary of, but he tried to prepare himself as much as he could. He found it difficult to imagine his offspring. Would they have olive colouring like him, or a paler complexion with blonde hair like Adira? It was all so overwhelming and thrilling in equal amounts. Finally, he stepped back to look at the completed cot. 'There, what do you think?' he asked.

'Brilliant,' she nodded in approval.

Just then Jasper's mobile phone rang.

'Ah, it's the old boy himself,' he grinned, pleased to be hearing from him. 'Fletcher how are you?' he answered.

'Never better, never better!' shouted Fletcher down the phone. Adira could hear him clearly and smiled to herself. 'How are you both?'

'We're fine,' Jasper replied, then added, 'missing you.'

'Soon be back,' said Fletcher. 'Lilly's ready for home I think.'

'You've enjoyed yourselves though?' asked Jasper.

'Aye, it's been grand. Been up the Eiffel Tower today,' he announced.

'Really?' laughed Jasper, picturing Fletcher and Lilly taking in all the sites. Good for them. A pang of emotion hit him hard, he just wanted them home safely.

'You still there?' Fletcher called.

'Yes, yes still here.'

'Well, better get going. Just a quick call, Lilly's waiting to go down to dinner.'

'OK, say hi from us,' replied Jasper.

'Will do! Bye!' he boomed down the phone.

Jasper shook his head in amusement. 'He thinks he needs to shout because he's ringing from abroad.'

'I know, I heard every word,' chuckled Adira, then she suddenly stopped abruptly. A tightening gripped her abdomen and her hand rushed to her belly.

'What is it?' asked Jasper immediately, quickly kneeling at her side.

'Phew, Braxton Hicks, I think,' said Adira, taking deep breaths.

'What?' Jasper's eyes widened.

Adira laughed. 'It's OK. Perfectly natural, just the body preparing the cervix for birth.'

'But… you're not ready to give birth yet. It's too early.' The concern in his voice was evident.

'They're common around this time,' she reassured and put a hand on his shoulder. 'Don't worry, it's fine.'

Jasper wasn't convinced and an uneasy sensation began to rise up inside him. He wasn't going to let Adira out of his sight. He just wanted his family secure; Fletcher and Lilly home, Adira fighting fit, and the baby born safe and sound. Anxiety was etched in his face.

'Jasper,' Adira softly spoke, 'stop worrying.'

But it was easier said than done.

Chapter 38

Craig had sent Rory and Cassie his book edits. As the two of them read through the editor's comments, they were both pleased that he had overall kept to their manuscript. Craig had altered a few details and made helpful suggestions throughout, which in the main the two agreed with. The only thing which Rory objected to was the editor's proposal of naming the chambers he had worked for in London.

'Why, what's wrong with naming Goldgate Chambers?' asked Cassie, frowning.

'Because there's no way that creep, Nigel Kerfoot, is milking anything in my name,' retorted Rory.

He was of course referring to the Head of Chambers, who had been more than happy to have his chambers promoted, thanks to Rory's highly publicised win in court when defending the activists. Had Rory lost his court case battle, then he would have been disassociated with the chambers instantly and sacked on the spot, he had no doubt. As it was, Kerfoot actually offered Rory more prestigious, high-profile briefs, but only once he had struck victory in court. Rory had told him where to go.

'Hmm, I see,' said Cassie. 'But won't people already know which chambers you worked for anyway? You were filmed outside them.'

'Maybe, but I'm still not having them in our book, no way.'

'Fine by me,' shrugged Cassie.

There was one particular suggestion with which Cassie was delighted and took as a compliment – Craig had wanted a few recipes to be included in the book, due to the superb lunch which he had enjoyed on his visit. He thought that recipes which only included their produce would be a great addition, and both Cassie and Rory wholeheartedly agreed.

'That's a fantastic idea, and brilliant for our business too,' he shrewdly noted.

'You're right,' replied Cassie. Already she was picturing the images of her homemade cooking appearing in the pages of their book.

All this was good news, but it brought to mind Rory's thoughts on hiring some staff. There was no way just he and Cassie could cope with The Harvest Barn's inevitable expansion; already they were snowed under with customer's orders. He had thought of advertising locally, hoping that Lilacwell and the surrounding area would produce enough willing workers. After all, Adira and Jasper had managed to put together a good team at The Laurels glamping site without too much trouble. Cassie had agreed with Rory when they'd discussed it.

'I bet a few of the staff at The Inn would want extra work,' she'd told him, knowing that many of the cleaners and waiters would appreciate the money.

So, although living an extremely busy life at the moment, both Rory and Cassie were content in the knowledge that things would soon ease off. It was just a matter of time before helping hands would ease the burden. Rory was just plain relieved he no longer worked-for the likes of Nigel Kerfoot, while Cassie reflected on her days when she had been a student, picking fruit on The Laurels estate. Now look at her, running a business of their own and about to have a book published. Happy days.

Chapter 39

Fitz had been in his workshop all day and was ready to lock up and call on Eva at The Potter's Bolthole. It had become a ritual over the past few weeks since their weekend away in Cheshire. A comfortable routine had been established where either he would call at hers, or Eva would return with him to Woodsman Cottage at the end of the working day. He looked forward to sharing an evening meal together, they always had lots to talk about, especially knowing the rest of The Cobbled Courtyard residents and what they were up to. Max, it seemed, was seeing more and more of Janey. James was organising a trip to Barcelona. Tom and Tess were still busy at the cafe whilst parenting little Chloe. And when Kit and Pru had called in to see Fitz the other evening, he sensed that the Tomkin–Jones' were still half keeping an eye on him somehow, but in a caring, not prying, way.

Everything was ticking along nicely, but Fitz's intuition told him there was a touch of uncertainty about Eva. Every now and then he would catch her almost troubled expression and yet he was told, 'Nothing's wrong, I'm fine,' every time he enquired, followed with a false smile. Clearly something *was* bugging her. He had no doubt that her feelings for him were genuine, as were his, but there was definitely something upsetting her. Tonight, he intended to confront the issue and get to the bottom of it. He'd had enough of camouflaging, from now on he wanted transparency, all out in the open – full, honest exposure.

He tapped at The Potter's Bolthole door and entered. Eva was busy at the sink washing her hands after using the potter's wheel. A row of clay vases were lined up by the kiln, waiting to be fired.

'Hi,' he smiled.

'Hello, you. Is it that time already?' She'd been so engrossed in her work she hadn't noticed it was time to close. 'Yours or mine?'

'Mine,' Fitz replied assertively, making Eva glance up at him. 'I think it's time we talked, without any distractions.'

Often when they'd been at Eva's, she'd nip back down to the studio to check on something or other, or to answer her phone to take orders. Tonight, he wanted her undivided attention.

'Talk?' Eva tilted her head questioningly, a frisson of concern shooting through her. 'About what?'

'You tell me.' Fitz crossed his arms. 'There's something bothering you and I'd like to know what,' he said, challenging her.

Eva remained silent for a few moments, mulling over his words. He was right, of course he was. Try as she might, Eva couldn't hide her true feelings, her insecurity. A part of her was still waiting for that bombshell to drop, when Fitz would suddenly announce he was leaving Lilacwell, to return back to his family and life in Cheshire. She just could not get past it, that horrid dread of seeing Fitz pack up and go, as easily as he had appeared in Lilacwell, and as easily as he had disappeared so recently.

'Eva?' probed Fitz with a worried expression.

'You're right,' she eventually answered. 'We do need to talk.'

Later that evening after they had eaten and were snuggled up together by the wood burner, Fitz poured them each a generous glass of red wine before turning to Eva.

'Right, out with it,' he gently instructed, passing her glass.

Eva took a big gulp, then faced him head on. 'Fitz, what are your plans?'

'Sorry?' he frowned, honestly puzzled by her response.

'Your long-term plans.' She took another mouth full of wine. 'I mean, do you intend to go back to Cheshire, now that you've reunited with your family?' Her chest thumped uncontrollably.

'Eva, I'm not going anywhere.' He was still frowning. 'Why would I give up everything I've worked so hard for… the carpentry studio, this cottage, friends I've made and… you?'

The relief she felt was massive. Her whole being relaxed.

'But your life in Cheshire—'

'My life's here, in Lilacwell,' Fitz interrupted. 'Eva, is this it – what's been troubling you?' He pulled her closer to him. He suddenly realised how uncertain Eva actually was. Not only had he up and left her with no warning a few months ago, but from what she had told him, her ex-boyfriend had hardly been a picture of commitment and no doubt she still bore the scars from that past relationship. But nobody knew better than him how past events made you a product of the future. Hadn't his history dictated his emotions? He had to act, and fast. 'Listen, Eva, I'm now at that stage where my old life and current one are ready to meet.'

She looked up at him with searching eyes.

'I want you to meet my family,' he explained.

'Do they even know about me?' Eva asked in a small voice.

'Yes, of course they do, but they understand I needed time to introduce you.' Fitz's parents made sure they talked with their son every few days, having a lot to make up for and wanting regular chats. 'I had two years where I had no contact with my parents. We're all still adjusting, and Lucas is still recovering so it hasn't felt like the right time to bring you into our mess.'

'Yes, of course, sorry,' she replied, somewhat inadequately, digesting it all. She felt a tad foolish when considering what Fitz and his family had been through, and perhaps a little selfish, only thinking of herself.

'I understand how your ex must have made you feel,' he continued, 'but I very much want you in my life, for good.'

At this Eva reached up and kissed him. It was met with an urgent need as together they sought comfort, hugging each other tightly.

'Don't go, stay tonight,' whispered Fitz huskily.

Eva never wanted to leave this cosy, little cottage, hidden away in the woods, far away from the outside world, a secret sanctuary. She craved the warmth of Fitz's arms, the protectiveness he brought and the promise of a true, loving relationship.

Fitz felt a tremendous euphoria holding the woman who had changed his life for the better. She had taught him to forgive himself, to move on and more importantly, to love again. He knew Eva would be welcomed into his family and together he saw a bright, happy future before them.

Chapter 40

The nip of early autumn filled the air in Lilacwell, as the summer months hazily drifted into September. A sharper chill hovered in the morning and the dusky evenings were creeping in.

Jasper, as expected, had kept a close eye on Adira, even more so as her due date was fast approaching. An energised anticipation hung in The Laurels and Fletcher could hardly contain himself, despite Lilly's attempts to compose him. Adira had taken the doctor's advice and was being ultra-careful, especially in the past few weeks. Ever mindful of her own premature birth, she'd been at pains to be extra diligent by having as much bed rest as possible. Sleep had been difficult, and being so big meant getting comfortable was nigh impossible. Jasper had constantly been at her side, eager to assist in any way.

Then, the inevitable happened. Adira's waters had broken in the early hours of the morning, just as a golden-pink sunrise glowed through the village; a new day, a new dawn, and a new life.

Jasper, determined to remain calm, eased Adira into the car. He was grateful that his offspring had chosen to arrive at this hour, at least Fletcher and Lilly were still fast asleep. The last thing he needed now was an overexcited Fletcher hovering in the background. Once he carefully strapped Adira into the passenger's side, he slowly set off. He knew the best route to take to the hospital, having prepared for this very moment. His hands clenched the steering wheel.

'You OK, sweetheart?' He quickly turned to his wife, who was taking deep, steady breaths. She nodded whilst still concentrating on her breathing. His eyes remained steadfast on the road and his heart beat a solid, hard rhythm.

There was hardly any traffic on the road, another blessing, thought Jasper as he arrived at the hospital. Adira was by now panting heavily, clinging onto her husband as they shuffled into the hospital entrance. They were soon met by a nurse who ushered Adira into a wheelchair and together they all headed for the maternity ward. Adira let out a piercing cry, making Jasper wince.

'We'll soon be there,' soothed the nurse, alerting a doctor en route. The ward doors opened, and Adira was whisked into a delivery suite.

After being examined by the doctor, who told them Adira was fully dilated, it was all systems go. Adira's contractions started to come thick and fast.

'I want to push,' she gasped between gulps of air.

Jasper was then directed to stand at the top of the bed, where he clasped Adira's hand tightly. His eyes widened when the tip of the baby's head could be seen. It all happened so fast he couldn't take it in. Adira yelled out again and was told to push. After several more painful contractions, along with hard thrusts, she let out one last guttural groan and the rest of the baby's body gently eased out, followed by a high-pitched cry.

'A baby girl!' exclaimed the nurse gleefully, taking the babe and snipping its umbilical cord. She then wrapped her safely into a blanket and passed her to Adira's open arms.

'A girl.' Adira's eyes swam with tears, her skin was slick with sweat, hair plastered around her face, and she was still gasping for breath. But she'd never felt so serene in her life.

Jasper was openly weeping, tears running down his face. He leant down to put an arm round his wonderful, brave wife and look at his precious baby. They had a daughter.

'Well done, my darling,' he croaked, kissing Adira's cheek.

'Oh Jasper, look,' she choked. 'What shall we call her?'

'A miracle,' he gulped.

–

Meanwhile, back at The Laurels, Lilly was the first to rise. Pulling back the curtains in their bedroom, she admired the clear, blue sky. Birds flew in the distance and the gardens below glistened with morning dew.

'Wake up, Fletcher, it's a beautiful day!' she called over her shoulder. Fletcher was gently snoring, obviously still tired. Lilly had always been an early bird and she was used to quietly going about her business in the morning, careful not to disturb her sister, so she tip-toed out of the bedroom and down the stairs.

Entering the kitchen, she was surprised not to see Jasper or Adira. Usually at least one of them would be in there, propped up by the breakfast bar sipping coffee. Then, looking out of the kitchen window, she noticed Jasper's car wasn't parked up outside. All of a sudden, the penny dropped. Lilly scurried upstairs to check Jasper and Adira's bedroom. As she suspected, the bed was empty, unmade. Evidently, they'd left in a hurry. They must be at the hospital! Rushing to tell Fletcher, she burst into their bedroom.

'Fletcher! Fletcher, wake up!' She shoved his sleeping body.

'Err…' Fletcher slowly opened his eyes. 'What is it, Lilly?' he mumbled, yawning.

'Jasper and Adira aren't here,' hissed Lilly urgently.

'Egh? What do you mean?' Fletcher was only just coming to.

'They must be at the hospital!' trilled Lilly.

He became fully awake at hearing the word *hospital*. Fletcher shot up.

'Has the baby been born?'

'I don't know! We don't even know when they went,' exclaimed Lilly impatiently. The phone rang, and they froze.

'That'll be them!' cried Fletcher, bolting out of the bedroom, down the stairs and into the hall at breakneck speed. Flying to the phone, he grabbed the receiver.

'Jasper?' he gasped out of breath.

'Fletcher, I'm a… father,' Jasper could hardly speak, overflowing with emotion.

'Oh yes!' roared Fletcher at the top of his voice. Lilly had come to join him.

'You've a granddaughter,' Jasper said, then laughed at hearing Fletcher's loud cheer down the phone.

'We've a granddaughter, Lilly!' Fletcher exclaimed.

'How's Adira?' mouthed Lilly.

'Oh yes, how's Adira?' asked Fletcher.

'She's fine. Mother and daughter are both just fine.' In the hospital corridor, Jasper's eyes filled with tears again. All the pent-up anxiety was being released. He was so overwhelmed.

'Brilliant news, absolutely brilliant,' Fletcher boomed.

'What is she called?' Lilly mouthed again.

'What's she called?' Fletcher echoed.

'We haven't got a name yet,' replied Jasper.

'Well, plenty of time yet. The main thing is they're both safe and sound.'

'Yes, I know. Listen, I've got to go, but hopefully you'll be able to come at visiting time later today.'

'Try and stop me,' chuckled Fletcher. He'd waited a long, long time for this, he was going to savour every minute. Turning to Lilly, he grabbed her and kissed her hard. Lilly let him enjoy the moment, smiling with affection. 'I'm a granddad, Lilly,' his voice cracked.

'Come on then, let's get moving. We've a grand-daughter to meet,' she laughed, loving to see him so elated.

At visiting time there was no prouder grandparent than Fletcher, as he marched into the maternity ward, complete with a giant, pink teddy bear.

'He insisted on buying it,' whispered Lilly as they sat down next to Adira's bed. 'He's bought enough stuff to fill a crèche. We've been in every toy shop within a ten-mile radius since breakfast.'

Jasper and Adira laughed.

'Well, let's have a look at the little lass then.' Fletcher bent over the cot and gazed with adoration at the sleeping babe resting peacefully, totally oblivious to the commotion she'd caused. His face creased with emotion at the vision of his granddaughter, taking in her black, tufty hair and cupid bow pink lips. Tiny dark eyelashes suddenly flicked open, and a pair of blue eyes stared back at him. 'Hello poppet,' he whispered and gently touched her little, starfish hand. He was rewarded with the beginning of a smile, or so he thought. 'Look, she's smiling at me,' he chuckled.

Lilly was looking down into the cot too.

'Don't be silly. She's far too young to smile yet,' she softly chided.

'Probably wind. I've just fed her,' teased Adira.

'How are you dear?' asked Lilly.

'Tired, but OK.'

'She was incredible,' Jasper said. 'Absolutely magnificent.'

'Aye,' winked Fletcher. 'You've done a good job there, lass.'

Chapter 41

Rory was sifting through all the job applications received from the adverts he'd placed in the local newspaper. He was pleased with the response it had generated – over thirty emails had flooded his inbox. It was going to take some time to get through them all.

'Just look at the first twenty or so,' Cassie had advised. But Rory had disagreed.

'No, each one should be considered,' he'd insisted.

A whole range of people had applied to work at The Harvest Barn, whether male or female, young or old, each with varying experiences. The process of assessing them had proved entertaining and he had developed quite a skill at reading in between the lines of some of the applicants' claims.

Then something caught his eye. There wasn't anything flowery or false about this application, just a candid outline of his background, ending with a final sentence of, 'I really need this job. I need the money. I need a chance.' To Rory that smacked of a plea more than anything, and it had hit a nerve. Judging by the history this young lad had given, he hadn't had many breaks in life. Rory gave it his full attention. His name was Jake, he was seventeen and attending an agricultural college. Good start, thought Rory. Then he read on. Jake had stated that he'd had brushings with the police over a year ago but didn't divulge further. He also went on to say that he was from a single parent family and had two younger siblings.

Rory sat back, contemplating Jake's application. His eyes homed in on those words again, 'I need a chance.' Was this a cry for help? Jake's honesty was to be applauded. Not many teenagers would openly admit to having been in trouble with the police, especially on a job application form. Maybe he'd thought being directly truthful would save a wasted interview if it came out later?

Cassie came into the kitchen with a basket full of fruit and vegetables. Her overalls were soiled from digging potatoes, turnips and carrots and picking apples and black-berries.

'The sooner we get help the better,' she said, wiping her forehead and leaving a smear of dirt.

'Take a look at this one,' said Rory, moving the laptop on the farmhouse table to face her. She came and sat down in front of it. Squinting, she read Jake's application.

'Hmm, I wonder what the brush with police means,' she said, looking a touch wary.

'Might not be too sinister. At least he's declared it,' replied Rory. Then he realised why Jake's application had resonated with him. Hadn't he too had an altercation with a police officer at his age? He'd been on a rally when a burley officer had manhandled him, resulting in Rory lashing out. He had later received a caution, but still, technically he had had a 'brushing' with the police.

'Interview him then, see what you think when he's had chance to explain,' suggested Cassie.

'Yeah,' nodded Rory, 'I think I will.'

'What about all the others?'

'Not bad, by next week I'm sure we'll be able to put together a team.'

'That's a relief,' sighed Cassie. 'Don't forget, we're going to Adira and Jasper's this evening.'

Actually, Rory had indeed forgotten that they were due to visit The Laurels that night. He'd been so preoccupied with the job applications.

'Ah yeah, did you get them anything?' he asked.

'Of course, it's not every day your best mate has a baby.'

She got up and opened a drawer, then took out a small box. Opening it up to reveal the tiniest of silver bracelets.

'How sweet is this?' she said, showing Rory.

'It's so small,' he said incredulously. 'Is it engraved?' He narrowed his eyes to look for any markings.

'No. We don't know the baby's name yet. At the moment she's just Poppet, apparently,' laughed Cassie.

Later that evening as Rory and Cassie walked through the fields that joined The Laurels, they made their way to the back door and knocked gently. They didn't want to ring the bell at the front in case they woke up a possibly sleeping baby. Jasper was in the kitchen and opened the door.

'Hi,' he said, letting them in. Dark circles shadowed his eyes.

'Congratulations,' said Cassie, kissing either side of his cheeks. 'You look knackered by the way,' she smirked.

'Thanks Cassie,' Jasper replied dryly. Then shook Rory's outstretched hand.

'Congratulations mate,' said Rory. 'Sleepless nights?' he asked with a grin.

'You could say that, but you've come at a good time. Adira's just finished feeding her and she's in a good mood.'

'No name yet?' said Cassie, surprised.

'Still Poppet at the moment,' laughed Jasper. 'Come on, I'll introduce you.'

Adira and the baby were in the drawing room. A Moses basket was by the fire, but Adira was holding the tiny bundle in her arms.

'Hi,' she beamed, looking tired, but so happy.

'Oh, let me see.' Cassie rushed to sit next to her friend. There she was, the girl of the moment, looking angelic in her mother's arms. 'Adira, she's utterly gorgeous,' cooed Cassie, marvelling at the baby's minute, fragile fingers. 'Rory, come and look.'

'Hello gorgeous,' he whispered. He wasn't really a baby person but had to concede this one was a cutie.

'Want a hold?' asked Adira, thankfully in Cassie's direction, he thought.

'Too right,' answered Cassie, shuffling to get into position to receive her.

'There you go, hold her head, that's right.' Adira let go fully. Cassie was filled with a warm, heartening glow.

Rory's face dropped. Don't say she was getting broody, that's the last thing he needed right now.

'How's the smallholding, got any staff yet?' asked Jasper, to his relief. He was keen to remind Cassie how busy they were before she got any ideas of motherhood just yet.

'Manic,' replied Rory immediately. 'We're just looking at job applications at the moment. Aren't we, Cass?' But Cassie was too smitten with the baby to hear him. She and Adira were admiring her outfit; a petite pink dress with matching booties that Lilly had apparently knitted. Rory knew he had no chance of diverting her attention.

Jasper gave him a wry grin.

'Fancy a whisky?' he asked, raising an eyebrow.

'Yeah, just to wet the baby's head,' laughed Rory.

Not wanting to stay too long, Rory and Cassie left The Laurels after an hour. On the way home, Rory braced himself for the expected.

'Ro-ry…' began Cassie in a sweet talk voice.

'No. Not yet, Cass,' he cut in, wanting to nip the whole lets-start-a-family thing in the bud.

'But you don't know what I was going—'

'Yes, I do,' he chuckled, then stopped walking. 'Come here,' he pulled her into his arms.

'It's too early, isn't it?' she said.

'To have a baby, on top of running a smallholding and extending business, after having just finished converting the barn? Yes Cassie, it's way too early.'

'I guess so, even for us,' she agreed with laughter.

'Yes, even for us. But we can still keep practising,' he coaxed.

Chapter 42

Eva was mentally preparing for the big day. As promised, Fitz had arranged for his family to come to Lilacwell. A spark of anxiety simmered inside her at the thought of being introduced to his parents and brother, and yet, a huge part of her was also relieved that Fitz's former life was finally meeting his present one. It was good for him, she thought, helping to give final closure as both his worlds united. Hopefully today, when Fitz's family were introduced to his life in Lilacwell, it would draw a final line and a chapter would be well and truly closed.

Eva was also full of curiosity. She'd learnt from Fitz all about his parents' background – how his father, Miles, had been a Major in the army when meeting the beautiful, young Greek Dimitra and how they had married in the local village chapel in Patmos. It sounded so romantic! When Fitz had gone on to tell her about his childhood, she realised just how privileged it had been. It struck her how much love had been lavished on him and his brother, not just materially but with care and support. Miles and Dimitra blatantly loved their sons deeply. How much they must have suffered, first by Fitz's disappearance, followed by Lucas' diagnosis. It made Eva want to weep when listening to Fitz explain it all.

It also made her feel a tad guilty, after the way she had behaved when Fitz had returned from Cheshire. But, as he pointed out when she'd voiced this, she hadn't known the facts. He certainly didn't hold it against her, and if anything, it had made him realise how covert he'd been.

Together, they were resolute that communication was key. Too many doubts and uncertainties had caused needless torment and it was all so futile. They also believed that destiny had brought them together; that, by seeking refuge in Lilacwell for very different reasons, they had also sought support in a loving relationship. Gone was Eva's self-doubt, which had influenced a large part of her life. She had more confidence in herself, without having to have Beth bolster her up every time she felt down. Not that she didn't appreciate Beth, of course she did, but she had realised it was important to have conviction within yourself.

As for Fitz, he was also learning to value himself. Having Eva care for him the way she did made him understand that he wasn't this bad person that he – and the press – had dubbed him. He was a loving son, brother, and boyfriend. Yes, he'd made big mistakes, but he'd also made huge accomplishments – his cottage, his business, *saving Lucas' life*! Once again, he'd been forced to contemplate how catastrophic things could have turned out had he not been a donor to his little brother. In short, Fitz had forgiven himself and was ready to live his life as happily as he could. Life *was* for living, not hiding away, concealing himself from the rest of the world.

Today was symbolic for everyone, Eva, Fitz, and his family. It was the beginning of a new chapter.

–

For Miles and Dimitra, it was even more. The last few years had been a living hell for them. When Theo had bolted from their lives they had been devastated, putting the money they had lost into pale significance. Then, when Lucas had been diagnosed with bone marrow cancer, it had nearly finished them off. The only chink of light in that period of their lives had been the possibility of Theo returning to save Lucas. And he had. Their boy had done it for them. Theo had come back and saved them all. So today, having all the family together, and with Lucas making steady progress, they were going to celebrate like never before.

Miles also intended to call upon the Tomkin-Jones' at Wolven Hall. He owed them a great debt indeed. If it wasn't for Cyril and Patricia keeping him updated with Theo's life in Lilacwell, he didn't know how he would have survived; it had been them, together with their daughter, Pru – albeit inadvertently – who had kept his mind at rest, knowing his son was making something of himself. He was proud of Theo and what he had achieved, especially under the circumstances.

–

Autumn was putting in a full appearance with its russet and gold leafed trees majestically spread throughout the village. The whiff of wood smoke drifted in the cold air and cottage windows glowed with firelight. October was a cosy time of year, and there was nowhere more snug than Woodsman Cottage.

Fitz had lit the wood burner in good time to get the place as warm as possible. He and Eva had made a hearty winter casserole, to be followed by his mother's favourite dessert, bread, and butter pudding. That had made Eva giggle, expecting Dimitra to have somewhat more exotic tastes.

'She loves it, always has, since living in England,' Fitz had said, making Eva again inquisitive to meet her.

It was now one o'clock and his family was due any minute. As predicted, Miles had driven them there bang on time. Being a Major had made him strictly punctual, whatever the occasion. Fitz came out to meet them while Eva held back, giving the family a little space. She watched through the kitchen window discreetly, observing his parents' obvious delight at seeing their son. Big hugs and kisses were exchanged, and she saw Lucas high five his brother, followed by a tight embrace. Eva swallowed the lump in her throat and steadied herself. The last thing she wanted was for Fitz's family to meet her blubbering. Then, in they all came. Eva's hands gripped the edge of the kitchen top.

'And here's Eva,' announced Fitz with a big smile.

'Eva,' Dimitra sped over to her and enveloped her into a warm hug. Eva blinked, not expecting so demonstrative an introduction. Dimitra pulled back to take a good look at her. 'I'm so pleased to meet you. I can't thank you enough.'

'I… I'm pleased to meet you too,' stumbled Eva. Miles stood close by.

'I'm Miles.' He held out his hand. Eva smiled and shook it.

'And this is my little brother, Lucas,' said Fitz.

'Less of the little,' joked Lucas and turned to face Eva. 'Hi,' he gave an awkward wave.

'Hi Lucas,' replied Eva, taking in his appearance. Lucas' health was undoubtedly improving, judging from Fitz's previous description of him. Today he stood tall, he'd obviously put on weight, and his complexion was no longer a pale grey, but had pinpricks of colour.

They all gathered round the table and conversation flowed naturally. Dimitra was keen to know all about Eva's pottery business, information which Eva was happy to give, although suspected both she and Miles already knew a great chunk, thanks to the Tomkin-Jones.' Fitz had filled her in on their input over the past two years. Eva spoke of how her love of ceramics had evolved at college, which led her to renting The Potter's Bolthole at The Cobbled Courtyard.

'The Cobbled Courtyard,' laughed Lucas. 'It sounds so twee.'

'Quaint, I think is the word,' remarked Miles, not wanting any offence to be caused.

'Very quaint, or how you English say…quintessential?' said Dimitra.

'Hmm, I think so,' agreed Eva.

'And as for the name of the village, Lilacwell, how charming,' continued Dimitra.

'It's a charming village, mum, you'll love it,' said Fitz. This earned him a tender smile from her.

Miles nodded in agreement, approving of the future tense, indicating their expected involvement in Theo's home. It all looked promising. This was evidently the first of many visits. His mind fast forwarded to further get-togethers, hopefully including grandchildren… But that was way ahead. He was just going to enjoy today and the utter joy it brought.

Chapter 43

Adira gazed in adoration at her sleeping baby. She had just got Poppet nicely to sleep when Jasper entered the library carrying a huge bouquet of flowers. Turning hastily, Adira put a finger to her lips.

'Shush,' she whispered.

'Why are you in here?' he asked softly.

'It's the quietest place in the house.'

Fletcher was in the drawing room next door, with the TV on full blast watching the racing, and Lilly was in the kitchen with the radio on. The library was the only sanctuary in The Laurels.

Jasper had just returned from The Cobbled Courtyard. He had wanted to see all his tenants, not having been there for some time; being a new father was far more time consuming than he'd expected.

'Here, for you.' He handed Adira the flowers. 'A present from James.'

The tenant of the florist shop had made a beautiful bouquet of pink roses mixed with symbolic gypsophila – baby's breath.

'Oh, how kind, they're gorgeous.' Adira bent her head to smell their fragrance.

'Fitz was asking if we've decided upon a name yet. I suspect he's going to make something once he knows.'

'Yes, we're going to have to make up our minds,' replied Adira looking down at their daughter. 'Time's pressing on and everyone's asking.'

'I know,' agreed Jasper. 'The thing is, I've rather grown accustomed to Poppet.' He stood next to Adira, staring down at the Moses basket. 'She looks like a Poppet to me now,' he chuckled.

'Yes, she does,' laughed Adira. Then it came to her in a flash. 'What about Poppy? It sounds similar?'

Jasper tilted his head in consideration.

'Yeah, I like it. Poppy Hendricks.' He nodded approvingly.

'Poppy Grace,' replied Adira. Grace was a family name on her side that they had agreed on for a second name. When first arriving in Lilacwell, Adira had discovered the gravestone of her great-great-grandmother in the churchyard. Research had revealed that Grace Conway was in fact Edie's – her grandmother's – grandmother. Edie had managed to supply further evidence through a marriage certificate and other family documents which she'd had stored in the attic. It had all seemed so incredulous at the time, but Adira was convinced she was *meant* to find Lilacwell, and it was her destiny to be in the village where her family had come from. Edie also shared this belief and was delighted with the connection.

'That's it then, Poppy Grace Hendricks,' said Jasper assertively.

'At last,' sighed Adira. She was beginning to think they'd never reach a compromise.

Just then, Fletcher came into the room.

'Ah, there you—'

'Shush!' they both hissed immediately shutting him up.

'Oops, sorry,' he murmured, then walked to the Moses basket to admire his granddaughter. The baby shifted, then put a thumb in her mouth. 'Ah look,' he said, unable to take his eyes off her.

'By the way, we've got a name for her now,' said Adira.

Fletcher looked up. 'Oh yes, what?'

'Poppy Grace,' Jasper answered.

'Poppy, eh?' said Fletcher, then turned back to stare at the sleeping bundle. 'You'll always be Poppet to me,' he chortled, gently touching the side of her cheek.

Adira and Jasper exchanged a knowing smile.

In the evening, after bathing, feeding, and putting Poppy down in her cot, Jasper and Adira were enjoying a relaxing glass of wine alone in the drawing room. It was heaven just to be able to relax together in the peace and quiet. Snuggled together on the sofa, Jasper put his arm round Adira.

'The tenants were all asking about you today,' he told her.

'That's nice. I'll go and pay them a visit next week, take Poppy in her pram.'

'Good, they're dying to see her.' Then he smiled to himself. 'It seems strange calling her by a name now.'

Adira nodded in agreement, whilst wondering when she'd be able to see The Cobbled Courtyard crew. Then she suddenly remembered what Cassie had told her a few weeks ago. 'Did you ever find out where Fitz had been?'

'Yes. Apparently, he'd gone to Cheshire, where he's from, to be a donor for his brother.'

'Really?' Adira's eyes widened. 'I'd no idea he was from Cheshire.' Memories of the place came back to her when she'd stayed there overnight in her camper van, before stumbling across Lilacwell. It felt like an age ago now, so much having happened since.

'Neither did I,' replied Jasper.

'So, is his brother all right now?' asked Adira.

'Yes, he came with Fitz's parents to Lilacwell the other day, he was telling me.'

'Right...' Adira stared into the distance with a pensive expression.

'What are you thinking?' said Jasper, taking a sip of wine.

'Just that you never really know people, do you?'

'Sorry?' Frowned Jasper.

'Well, with Jessie, do you remember? It turned out she'd been a gangster's wife from way back and now Fitz... quietly disappearing to be a donor. Who'd have thought?'

Adira was referring to the previous tenant of The Potter's Bolthole, Jessie Carter. After moving out of her upstairs apartment, she had left a framed wedding photograph on a windowsill. It was easy to see who the bride was, as Jessie had had a birthmark on her cheek. It was Fletcher who had recognised the groom, with his pin-striped suit, pencil moustache and slicked back hair. Ronnie Taylor had been a notorious Midlands gangster in the sixties. They had all been gobsmacked to learn that Jessie had obviously started a new life as a potter in Lilacwell. There was clearly something about the village that attracted people on the run from their past.

'Yes, it just goes to show,' agreed Jasper. He raised an eyebrow playfully before adding, 'And I've more gossip.'

'What?' Adira was all ears.

'Eva and Fitz are an item.'

Adira gasped. 'They are?'

'Yep, apparently so. Max was telling me, they're practically inseparable these days.'

'Well, well.' Adira took a mouthful of wine, savouring the rich, fruity taste. She only allowed herself a very small glass, due to breastfeeding, so was really relishing it. 'And how is Max?'

'He's fine, dating the village doctor, more juicy gossip,' he laughed.

Adira moaned. 'I need to get out. I've missed loads.' She was looking forward to venturing out on long pram walks, feeling a touch cooped up inside of late. She understood how some mothers could feel isolated after having a baby. It was all so consuming, constantly being on call to such a tiny, vulnerable little being, and it was tiring, but rewarding. She thanked her lucky stars she had a good husband, and now father, in Jasper to help share the load. It beggared belief the way some single parents coped. How did they do it? Adira was full of admiration and respect for those who had to, and did, parent solo.

'Is there a mother and baby club you could join?' Jasper asked, not wanting his wife to feel secluded.

'No, I've looked and there's nothing, well not locally anyway.'

'Maybe set one up?' he suggested.

'Hmm,' Adira narrowed her eyes in thought. 'I just might.'

Chapter 44

Rory was at the kitchen table with his laptop and paper-work. Today, he was giving his last interview. Throughout the week he had seen several of the applicants who had responded to his advert and been pleased with the calibre of people it had attracted. Rory was confident that imminently they would be able to put together a decent team to work at The Harvest Barn.

The interviews had taken place in the small study which Rory and Cassie used as an office to run the business, but today was different. Rory had saved this particular interview to the very last, as it needed a little more time and thought, in his eyes at least. He was seeing Jake Mitchell, the young lad whose application had caught his attention.

Rory had deliberately chosen the kitchen to interview Jake, thinking it created a less formal atmosphere. He wanted Jake to be as comfortable as possible in a friendly environment, not in an office sat behind a desk. The radio was on very quietly in the background and two mugs sat on the table, ready to make Jake a drink; Rory was at pains to have Jake feel at home, to encourage him to open up and give a good impression. It dawned on Rory that he *wanted* Jake to impress him. Something inside Rory had already connected to this boy for some reason. Whether he had seen a younger version of himself in him, or even a cry for help, Jake's application had resonated.

Rory looked at the kitchen clock and checked the time. He was due to arrive in a quarter of an hour. Cassie was outside working in the polytunnels; she had wanted to meet Jake and so the plan was for her to show him round, after he had finished speaking to him.

Five minutes later there was a knock at the door. Good, at least he was punctual and not late, thought Rory. He opened up to see a slight-built teenager, wearing torn jeans, a puffer jacket and beanie hat, appearing slightly apprehensive.

'Hi, you must be Jake,' smiled Rory, welcoming him in.

'Hello,' he replied, stepping into the kitchen.

'Sit down.' Rory gestured towards a chair at the table. 'Would you like a brew?'

Jake blinked, taken by surprise, clearly this was not what he'd been expecting.

'Err... thanks.'

'Tea or coffee?'

'Tea would be good, thanks. No sugar.'

After making them both a drink, Rory took the seat opposite Jake and brought up his application on the laptop screen.

'So, you're at horticultural college?' started Rory. At this Jake's face lit up.

'I am. I love it,' he enthused.

'What do you love about it?' Rory was glad he'd set off on the right foot.

'Everything, being outside with nature, seeing the seedlings you've planted grow. It's a privilege watching nature flourish.'

Rory's jaw dropped. The joy in Jake's voice was evident. The answer he gave was a genuine one and clearly from the heart. There was no doubt even at this early stage, that he would be an asset, having such a passion. Jake went on to describe his course in more detail, without any prompting from Rory.

'At the moment I'm studying for a City and Guilds Level 1 Diploma in Practical Horticulture Skills,' he told Rory. 'I could be a groundsman, or greenkeeper.'

'What about the next level?' asked Rory, guessing those jobs weren't Jake's first choice.

This made Jake's face fall.

'Well… I've got to show commitment to English and maths to study Level 2,' he replied avoiding eye contact. 'And I'm no good with words or figures.'

Immediately Rory's brain kicked into overdrive.

'What would Level 2 mean to you?'

'Well, it would mean I could progress to become a landscape gardener, which is what I really want,' admitted Jake.

Rory hated to hear the regret in his voice now which had replaced the previous zeal. He decided to quickly move on.

'How long did it take to get here from where you live?'

'Not too long, it's about a twenty-minute walk. But I want to learn to drive, that's why I need the money. Amongst other things,' Jake quietly added.

Rory took in the pained expression.

'Can I ask, what other things?' he gently probed.

'To help Mum out, she's… skint,' he finished for want of another word.

Rory remembered Jake's application stating he was from a single parent family. As if reading his mind, Jake continued.

'Our dad checked out long ago when Caleb was born. Now it's just me, my mum and two brothers.'

'I see,' nodded Rory. Then, knowing he had to ask the question he was dreading, looked at Jake full on. 'I've got to ask, but what was the brush with the police about?'

Jake seemed prepared for this. Almost as if he was waiting for the question, he sat up and straightened his shoulders.

'I was defending a mate, a girl, who was being harassed.'

'What happened?' frowned Rory, sitting back, all ears.

'It was in town, on the high street outside a pub. I saw a girl I knew being shouted at by some bloke towering over her. I went across and by then he'd grabbed hold of her, she was screaming for help, so I went in and landed him one. Trouble was, the police saw me, and I was arrested.'

'But didn't you explain the circumstances? Or the girl, your friend, didn't she intervene?' asked Rory.

'She tried, but I think she was scared stiff of any repercussions from the bloke. He told the police it was an unprovoked attack.'

'But you just said the police saw the incident?' said Rory, the barrister in him surfacing.

'Yeah, but only the bit where I lashed out, not the stuff before.'

Rory sighed. His gut instinct told him to believe Jake. He had heard many a tale in court as a barrister and this one had the ring of truth about it. He wanted to help this youngster. In his opinion he deserved a break. OK, he was a tad scruffy, compared to the other smartly dressed interviewees, but so what? Smart dress or tailored trousers weren't much use to them on a smallholding. Jake obviously had good, solid grounding when it came to working the land and he had youth on his side, with plenty of vitality and gusto.

'Right, Jake, when can you start?'

Jake's face broke into a huge beam.

'You mean I've got the job?' he asked, amazed.

'Yes,' laughed Rory, 'I'm offering you a job.'

'Thanks!' gushed Jake. 'I'll start straight away if you want.'

'Well, let's show you round first,' grinned Rory. 'I'll introduce you to my wife, Cassie. She's outside in the polytunnels.'

'Cool.' Jake looked eager to get moving.

'Just one thing,' said Rory, making Jake's head turn sharply. 'I really think you should consider that Level 2 qualification.' He saw the beginnings of a refusal from Jake and hastily continued. 'Even if it means getting some tutoring in English and maths.'

Jake looked questioningly at him.

'But how? We can't afford a tutor.'

'I'll help you,' shrugged Rory. 'Free of charge, just as long as you don't let me down.' He eyed him carefully, desperately hoping he wasn't going to regret this.

'I won't. Promise,' Jake replied firmly.

Chapter 45

In his workshop, Fitz was busy concentrating on the matter at hand – he was making a doll's house for Jasper and Adira's baby. He had waited until knowing the name they had chosen before beginning the job. Now he knew their baby girl was called Poppy, he had made a start.

He rather liked the name Poppy as it had allowed him to be creative. The shape of a poppy flower had been carved into the side of the house and above the door he had chiselled the words, 'Poppy's House.' It was coming along nicely, he thought, standing back to admire his work. He'd made it in the identical Georgian style architecture as The Laurels, with sash windows, even giving it the same orangery.

This was the first time he'd made a doll's house, and Fitz was pleased with the result so far. He knew that uploading photographs of it onto his Crafty Carpentry website would create an influx of orders, but he wouldn't do that until he'd presented it to Jasper and Adira first. He wanted them to be the first to see it, not through his website with everyone else. The cute doorstops he'd made for their wedding had been a huge success, not just for the newlyweds, but for camper van lovers worldwide as Fitz had carved them in the shape of a small camper van with intricate details, including registration plates. This had proved immensely popular with his customers, who wanted the personalisation of their own number plate. Now he envisaged the same with the doll's houses. Every parent ordering one would want their child's name above the door.

Eva interrupted his work, coming through the studio holding two take away cups.

'Coffee break, I've been to the cafe and got us a couple of cappuccinos,' she said, passing one to him.

'Ah, thanks.' He took a sip while Eva gazed at the doll's house in front of him.

'Is this for Jasper's baby?' she asked, squinting to read the plaque above the door.

'Yeah, it's for Poppy.'

'It's amazing!' Eva gasped, taking in all the decorative detail.

'Hmm, I'm quite pleased with it,' he replied modestly.

'Fitz, it's brilliant.' Eva crouched down to peer inside. 'It's very generous of you. How long will it take to make?'

Fitz shrugged. 'Does it matter? Jasper's a good landlord. I'm happy to make it.'

'Well yeah, but how much would you charge for it?'

'I'll probably sell them for somewhere between six to seven hundred pounds.'

Once again Eva was reminded of how little money now meant to Fitz. He was just glad to make a present for his friend.

'You put me to shame,' she said. 'I'll have to think of something to make now.'

'I'm sure you'll think of something,' he grinned.

They both went to sit on a couple of stools in the corner of the workshop. Eva was dying for any feedback from Fitz's family visit. It was only natural that she would have been discussed amongst them and she was eager to know just what they had to say. She slid a sideways glance at him, waiting patiently for him to broach the subject.

Fitz sensed Eva was itching for something and guessed what she wanted. The corners of his mouth twitched. Eva gave him another look.

'What?' he laughed, unable to keep a straight face.

'Oh, come on, you know damn well what,' she shot back with frustration.

'Sorry, I'm not with you,' he feigned confusion, but still couldn't help chuckling.

'Yeah right. Come on, spill,' she ordered.

There was a moment's pause, then he relented.

'They loved you,' he grinned.

Eva's face broke into a wide smile. 'Really?'

'Yep. Really,' Fitz replied with a firm nod. 'In fact, Lucas wondered "how I'd bagged you." His words, not mine.'

Eva burst into happy giggles.

'Did he?'

'Oh yes. And Mum said you were extremely pretty.'

'Oh, how sweet,' Eva replied, loving the feedback.

'And Dad said you were a keeper.' At this Fitz turned to face her. Their eyes met, and time stood still. Eva gulped. She was so relieved, and a touch overwhelmed with all the kind words spoken about her.

'A keeper?' she faintly repeated.

'Yes, a keeper.' The two leant towards each other, bodies tilting as if drawn by magnets. Then the moment was lost when Max strode into the studio.

'Ah, there you are, hiding in the corner,' he called. He came over to them, oblivious to his bad timing. 'Up for a pint at The Inn tonight?' he asked looking at Fitz, then over to Eva. 'You too, Eva?'

'Sounds good to me, it's been a while.' He turned to Eva. 'You coming?'

Eva was looking forward to a quiet night in, desperate to ring Beth and relay all her news.

'No, you two go and enjoy a lad's night. I'm after a long, hot bath and an early night.'

'Sure?' asked Max.

'Yeah, thanks, go and enjoy.'

–

Fitz and Max didn't need any further encouragement. That evening they were propped up by the bar along with the locals having a whale of a time. Max was glad that Fitz had reverted back to his former self, as opposed to being subdued and withdrawn as he had been previously. Obviously understanding his circumstances, it was easy to see why Fitz seemed a lot more relaxed and content, but he was positive a lot of it was down to Eva. The two of them looked so good together and he was pleased for the pair of them.

'So, how are you and Janey getting along?' enquired Fitz, taking a gulp of his pint.

Max gave a wicked grin.

'Not bad.'

'And?'

'And what?' smirked Max.

Fitz was reminded of earlier that day when he had been teasing Eva. He appreciated her irritation in this moment, but he wasn't going to push Max for an answer. Instead, he just shrugged and took another drink of his beer.

–

Meanwhile Eva was busy on the phone to Beth. She had told her all about Fitz's family and how they had visited. More importantly, she had quoted every last word of praise they had given her.

'Oh Eva, sounds like you went down a storm!' trilled Beth, full of glee for her friend. It was high time Eva had such a confidence boost. She pictured her months ago, pale, insecure, and anxious. The damage from her previous relationship had taken its toll, but not anymore. Now she was positively buzzing with self-assurance.

Chapter 46

'There you go, all snuggled up.' Adira was gently tucking Poppy into her pram, about to venture out into the bright, cold morning.

Taking Jasper's suggestion, Adira had decided to set up a mother and baby group and had made flyers to put in the church hall and local businesses.

Poppy was enjoying the fresh air, her little eyes sparkling, darting back and forth, and she gurgled contently whilst Adira strolled along the hedgerows. Crossing over the humpbacked stone bridge, she made her way to the small high street. Here she called into the few shops to drop off the flyers, with her last stop the Puddleduck Cafe, intending to stop there for coffee and cake.

Entering the charming tea shop, she was pleased her favourite table by the window was free.

'Hi, Adira!' called the lady behind the counter, a familiar figure to all the locals.

'Hi, Ruth, can I have a decaf coffee please?' She peered into the glass cabinet at the tempting cakes displayed. 'And a piece of Victoria sponge please.'

'Coming up.'

Adira situated Poppy's pram next to her chair. The cafe was relatively empty, apart from two other tables which were taken; one by an elderly couple and the other a teenage girl, who kept stealing glances towards the pram.

Adira caught her eye, and they exchanged smiles. Then, typically, Adira needed to nip to the loo before her coffee and cake arrived. Not wanting to disturb Poppy, who was by now drifting off to sleep, she looked to see if Ruth was coming. She wanted to ask her to stay with Poppy, but the woman was busy behind the counter. The young girl could see Adira look at the toilet door and realised her dilemma.

'I'll keep an eye on her,' she offered in a friendly voice.
'Oh, would you? I'm getting desperate,' laughed Adira.
'Sure, no problem.'

–

The girl got up and sat next to the pram whilst Adira dashed off. She gazed at the sleeping baby before her and a chronic, crushing pain stabbed at her heart. She forced herself to breathe steadily, her eyes locking onto the stable, rhythmic movement of the baby's chest. Admiring her pale pink coat, the soft velvety blankets, the sweet cuddly teddy bear slipped in beside her, she could tell the little girl was obviously well cared for and well loved. Another sharp sting pierced through her. Unable to resist, she reached out to touch Poppy's tiny hand. To her delight, the baby's little fingers instinctively closed around her thumb. Oh, how cute! A tender sensation flooded through her. Then she ever so gently stroked Poppy's cheek. It felt soft and warm. She took in the baby's dark hair escaping from her bonnet, no doubt lovingly knitted. Hearing Adira's voice coming back from the bathroom, her head turned sharply, but the mother was talking to Ruth, so she still had a few more precious moments to admire this beautiful sleeping child.

'A mother and baby group? What a good idea,' Ruth was saying, which instantly caught the young girl's attention. She froze still, listening intently to the conversation.

'Yeah, I thought it would be good for any new mums in the area to get together and meet up with our babies. Give each other support and advice,' Adira said.

'Absolutely,' replied Ruth, reading the flyer in her hand. 'So, you'll all meet up at The Laurels?' she asked.

'Yes, there's plenty of room there, so why not?'

'Oh, it sounds lovely, Adira. I wish someone had done this in the village when I had my babies. I'll display it in the cafe window.'

'Thanks, Ruth.'

Adira was coming back to her table. The girl looked up with a pleasant smile, snatching her hand away from Poppy at the same time. She stood up to let Adira sit back down.

'Thanks for that,' Adira gave Poppy a quick check.

'She's been fine,' said the girl. Then, haltingly, asked, 'What's her name?'

Adira brushed a hand lovingly over her daughter's hat. 'Poppy.'

'What a pretty name.'

'Thank you,' Adira smiled. The girl was staring into the pram and in no hurry to leave. There was an awkward hiatus.

'Right... I'd better be going.' The girl turned to collect her coat and bag from her own table and made her way out of the cafe. Ruth came over with Adira's coffee and cake.

'There you go.'

'Thanks, Ruth, I'm ready for this.'

After finishing her coffee, Adira went to the church hall to drop off a flyer for the notice board. She wheeled the pram into the entrance and used the spare drawing pins to stick up her advert. Then she decided to call next door at the church. She and Jasper had been discussing a christening for Poppy. She hoped that Father Forbes would be in. He had been most helpful in the past, when Adira had requested to look at the church records in researching her great-great grandmother, Grace.

Entering the church, Adira was instantly surrounded by a peaceful presence. Poppy's eyes blinked open, immediately attracted to the colourful stained-glass windows high above.

'Aren't they beautiful?' Adira said, noticing how Poppy was drawn to them.

'They certainly are,' said a voice behind her she recognised.

Adira turned with a smile. 'Hello.'

'Hello there and what's this little cutie called?' asked Father Forbes over the pram.

'This is Poppy. I was actually coming to see you about her christening.'

'Ah, I see. Well, I'd be delighted to baptise her. If you email me with some dates, I'll check the church diary,' he replied.

'Will do.' Adira, realising she had caught him on his way somewhere, and didn't want to keep him. 'I'll let you get on,' she smiled.

'Yes, if you'll excuse me, I'm needed next door,' he grinned.

He made his way down the aisle and out of the church, leaving Adira in the tranquil ambience. With a glance down at Poppy, who was still captivated by the vibrant shafts of light shining from the windows, she sat on a nearby bench and absorbed the serene silence for a few minutes. A loud clatter as something hit the tiled floor made her jump and she turned abruptly to see what it was. In the distance by the porch, a large pillar candle had fallen from its stand. How had that happened? An uneasy feeling crept into her. She stood up.

'Hello? Anybody there?' she called.

A gust of wind fled down the aisle, followed by the sound of the door shutting.

Adira waited a few moments, then wheeled the pram back outside the church, all the time looking to see if anyone was about; but there was no one. Feeling a little unnerved, Adira decided to go home.

Chapter 47

As anticipated, Jake was the first to arrive on Saturday morning. He'd turned up bright and early, ready and willing to work at The Harvest Barn. Rory had set up a rota for the small number of staff, giving the older members hours during the week, as preferred, leaving the weekends for the younger ones, who were free from college. As Cassie had expected a few of the staff at The Inn at Lilacwell had wanted to work in between their shifts for some extra income.

Cassie was out delivering their crates of fruit and vegetables, while Rory worked in the field overseeing the planting. They had made over ten large, raised vegetable beds and had harvested pretty much most of them, giving space to sow afresh. Today Rory planned to plant lettuce, spinach, carrots, kale, turnips, and cauliflower. In the polytunnels, pot-grown fruit was also ready for planting. Blueberries, cherries, raspberries, and strawberries had grown in pots with acidic soil and been sheltered in a sunny spot and watered with rainwater, not tap water, as directed by Rory. Now they were ready to be transplanted.

Jake had loved digging up the rich earth and burying the seeds and bulbs, neatly covering them up, finishing with a sprinkling of water. It never failed to amaze him how nature would tend to the rest and in a matter of months, they would produce whole, fresh vegetables, ripe to eat. He saw it as a gift from mother earth. It *was* a gift.

Rory had given clear instructions to the small team and was keeping a close eye on them. They appeared to work well together, much to his relief. If anything, it had been the older members of staff who had caused him the most concern so far.

The manual duties on the smallholding had proved too strenuous for one or two. Not really appreciating the back-breaking work involved, they had been shocked at the sheer quantity and volume of the crops and the level of maintenance they took. A far cry from just the tomatoes grown in a greenhouse, as one lady who had been interviewed was used to. Rory had expected to lose a few along the way; it was all part of the process, separating the wheat from the chaff, he thought rather aptly.

With Jake though, he hadn't had such worries. Innately, he knew to expect the best from him. And so far, he hadn't let him down. Rory had observed the friendly assistance he'd given the others, offering to help when they struggled. Although slight in build, Jake was obviously strong, managing to wheel full, heavy wheelbarrows with ease and dig robustly. He outshone everyone, without meaning to, and Rory had clocked it all. So much so, he was considering upping his wages already. Another thought occurred to him, which he needed to run by Cassie first before making any decisions.

Rory made them all a drink mid-morning and the group were sat in one of the polytunnels on deck chairs.

'Well, what do you think so far?' he grinned, facing the three young workers before him.

'Hell, it's tiring,' laughed one teenage girl. Jake and the other boy exchanged a wry smile.

'You'll get used to it,' said Rory. 'Think of all the exercise, it'll be doing you good. What about you two?' He turned to Jake and the lad sitting next to him.

'It beats revising,' said the boy.

'And you, Jake?' asked Rory, knowing full well what the response would be.

'It's great. Can't wait to reap the harvest,' he beamed. *Is the right answer*, thought Rory.

In the evening, Rory told Cassie all about his day and how it went with the new team.

'Sounds promising,' said Cassie encouragingly.

'Yes, I think we'll soon have them whittled down to a decent few.'

'How was Jake?' Cassie asked.

'Very good. He knows his stuff and doesn't need prompting.' Then he paused in thought.

Cassie frowned. 'What?' She suspected something was on his mind.

'I was thinking, he'd make an excellent right-hand man, you know, like a permanent, full-time assistant.'

'But he's still at college?'

'Well, when he's finished.'

'If he's going to do that Level 2 you mentioned helping him with, won't he want to be a landscape gardener?'

'Maybe, but opportunities sometimes present themselves, don't they?'

He raised an eyebrow and gave her a pointed look. Cassie smiled knowingly.

'Like when you met me and thought, I'll pack it all in and live in Lilacwell?' she teased.

'Exactly. You never know who you'll meet and what life can throw at you.'

'Wise words, Mr Molloy.'

Cassie wrapped her arms round him and kissed his lips, ever thankful that life had thrown them together.

–

Eva, not to be outdone by Fitz, had made her own present for Jasper and Adira's baby. She had very cleverly sculptured a pair of child's praying hands. It would make a perfect christening present, she thought. When Fitz called in later that day, he'd been most impressed.

'What do you think?' Eva pointed to the worktop in the studio where the hands were drying out, waiting to be fired in the kiln.

'Hey, they're amazing,' he said, taking a closer look. The attention to detail was incredible, from the small fingers with tiny nails and lines in the palm of the hands. The sculpture was perfection and, from one craftsman to another, he appreciated her enormous talent.

'As good as your doll's house?' she kidded.

'Of course,' he laughed, as always finding her competitive nature amusing. 'I was going to call at The Laurels later this afternoon to give it to them. Fancy coming?'

Eva considered this. Truth be told, she'd been a touch in awe of The Laurels grand country house, looking so elegant with its Georgian architecture and vast estate. Often wondering what it was like inside, she'd quite like the opportunity to call and have a peek.

'Oh, I wouldn't mind,' she said. Greedy for more information, she added, 'What's it like?'

'Just a typical country house,' he replied with a slightly puzzled look.

Of course, observed Eva, Fitz would hardly be awestruck by such grandeur, having been brought up in comparable surroundings. She remembered him acting similarly at Wolven Hall, only then she hadn't a clue that Fitz's family home had been as fine as Hazelgrove.

Later that afternoon, they both shut their studios a tad earlier than normal and Fitz drove them to The Laurels. He didn't want to carry the doll's house all the way there, it was quite heavy and bulky.

Fletcher answered the front door, having spotted Fitz's Range Rover come up the gravel driveway.

'Well, well, what have we here?' he said, face lit up with eagerness.

'A doll's house for Poppy,' replied Fitz, as if stating the obvious, making Eva smile to herself.

As they entered the hall, Eva's eyes darted about the place, taking everything in. She knew Fitz had attended Jasper and Adira's wedding here and she could well imagine how special it would have been, especially at Christmas time.

Fitz placed the doll's house on a nearby console table, glad to put it down. Fletcher bent over it to take a closer look.

'Bloody hell, this is amazing,' he said, then shouted, making Eva jump. 'Lilly! Come and take a look at this!'

In she scurried.

'Oh, I say!' she exclaimed. She too joined Fletcher in crouching down to peer at Fitz's masterpiece.

'She's going to love this,' enthused Fletcher.

'Yes, all four weeks of her,' said Lilly *sotto voce*, which had Eva and Fitz exchanging wry looks.

'I've bought her a train set,' Fletcher said with a glance up at them.

'Along with everything else,' remarked Lilly drily.

They all laughed. Eva thought them a charming old couple. She'd learnt they had only recently got married, which touched her heart. In fact, everything about Lilacwell was affecting her. As each day passed, she simply couldn't imagine living anywhere else. This quaint, pretty village had totally enchanted her.

'They're upstairs bathing the little lass,' Fletcher told them.

'Ah, right, well I'll leave it for—' Fitz was interrupted by Jasper who appeared at the top of the bannister.

'Hi!' he called down the stairs.

They all looked up.

'Hi, Jasper, we've just come to give you this for Poppy.' Fitz tipped his head towards the doll's house on the table.

By now Adira had joined Jasper, holding a freshly bathed Poppy.

'Oh thanks, Fitz,' Adira said, coming down the stairs carefully, followed by Jasper.

They looked at Fitz's handy work, in awe of his talent.

'This is utterly brilliant,' gasped Adira, admiring the intricate features.

'It is, thanks, mate.' Jasper gave Fitz a handshake.

Eva moved to look at the baby who was lying comfortably in a cream baby grow in her mother's arms.

'Ah, she's gorgeous,' she cooed.

'Thanks,' smiled Adira.

'Oh, she certainly is,' agreed Fletcher, 'she'll be breaking a few hearts, will Poppet.'

Eva was struck by how close the Hendricks clearly were – happy in their own family bubble, with no apparent worries or cares. She thought how lucky baby Poppy was, to be loved and looked after by such adoring kith and kin. Little did she know the looming nightmare they would soon have to endure.

Chapter 48

A hive of activity filled The Laurels. Today was the first mother and baby group meeting. Having had a few emails and phone calls of interest, Adira was pretty optimistic about it. She had decided to hold the meetings in the orangery where there would be plenty of space and it was nice and light. It was a fairly bright morning, so the sun would be streaming through the windows, making it lovely and warm for them all.

Lilly had baked cakes for the occasion, while Adira had put down play mats and baby play gyms in the centre of the floor. Even Poppy seemed excited, sensing something was in the air as she kicked and gurgled in her Moses basket.

'Yes, all your baby friends will soon be here,' said Adira cheerfully, touching her cheek. This earned her a big smile, while Poppy's little arms moved furiously. Adira had dressed Poppy in her favourite pink dress, with matching tights.

'Won't you be the belle of the ball?' cooed Lilly over her basket.

Just then the front doorbell chimed.

'Here goes,' said Adira walking into the hall to open the door. She was greeted by three mothers, each holding their babies in a sling.

'Hello,' Adira beamed, 'come in.'

'Thanks,' said one of the mums. 'I'm Sally and this is Jo and Steph.'

The other two mums nodded their heads and said hello.

'We don't live far away, so thought we wouldn't bother with prams,' explained Sally.

'I see. It's good to know there are new mums so close by,' Adira replied. 'Come into the kitchen, I've just made coffee.'

After introducing Lilly and making them all a drink, there was another caller at the door. This time Lilly went. She came back with another mum, who Adira instantly recognised.

'Lisa! It's so good to see you.'

Lisa had sought Adira's advice before her pregnancy. She worked at The Inn at Lilacwell and had heard all the rumours surrounding Adira with her herbal remedies. As Adira's grandmother, Edie, was a naturopath, she had passed down all her knowledge, so Adira had a basic understanding of natural healing and had been sought out in the village by various residents for help. Lisa, who had had difficulty in conceiving, had contacted Adira. Obviously, Adira had explained she was no doctor, but had simply recommended a calming product to relax Lisa, to avoid any anxiety or stress. Within a few weeks Lisa was pregnant and as far as she was concerned, it was thanks to Adira, although Adira herself wasn't so sure; but still, she had been happy for Lisa. Now here she was with her baby girl, Jessica.

'Hi Adira, thanks for setting this up, it's a brilliant idea.' She held a bouncing baby, who was restless.

'How old is Jessica now?' asked Adira.

'She's eight months! Time flies, doesn't it?'

'Blimey, it certainly does.'

Adira showed them into the orangery. Wicker chairs had been placed around the play area, allowing all mothers to easily see the babies.

It made a pleasant change for the mums, to drink coffee and eat cake while still keeping an eye on their offspring. The ladies chatted, getting to know each other by sharing experiences and advice, as well as the inevitable humour to be found in caring for a baby. One or two of them knew of the latest sales and offers from companies selling baby products, while another came up with a good suggestion.

'Why don't we meet outside, weather permitting, for a "walk and talk"?'

'Excellent idea,' said Adira, rather liking the idea of them all strolling through Bluebell Woods or another beauty spot in Lilacwell.

All in all, the group meeting went very well. After a while, the mums picked up their sleepy babies and nestled them back onto their chests with the baby slings. Adira was left feeling like she'd created something constructive and worthwhile.

The sun was still shining, so she decided to make the most of it and put Poppy in her pram and wheeled her outside. Adira smiled to herself as she tucked a blanket around Poppy's sleeping body. Her gran's voice entered her head: *Fresh air, sunshine and sleep are what babies need,* she remembered her saying. She wouldn't argue with that, thought Adira, glancing up at the clear, blue sky.

Inside, the phone began ringing, and Adira dashed to answer it.

'How did it go?' Jasper was in the estate office. He'd had a meeting there with Colin, the estate manager.

'Really well, thanks. They've only just gone.'

'Ah right, I'll come back then if the coast is clear,' he chuckled, not really wanting to return to a house full of women and babies.

'OK, see you soon,' smiled Adira and put the phone down. Then Lilly called her from the kitchen.

'Do you want another cake dear, there's just one left?'

'No thanks, Lilly, let's leave it for Jasper, he'll be here in a minute.'

'Righty-ho.'

Her sudden activity had obviously kicked her bladder into gear, and Adira shot off into the cloakroom.

Meanwhile Jasper was back, chatting to Lilly in the kitchen and turned around when Adira entered.

'Hi, where is she then?' he asked, surprised not to see Poppy. He assumed she must be sleeping in the nursery.

'Outside in her pram,' frowned Adira. 'You must have passed her?'

Jasper stared at Adira, an ice-cold shaft of fear shooting down his spine. 'She's not outside.'

'What?' A bolt of panic punched Adira in the stomach. She fled through the hall and outside to where she'd left the pram.

It wasn't there.

'Oh my God, oh my God.' Bile rose up her throat and she spewed it out. Her chest hammered and everything became a blur… Lilly was holding her; Jasper was on his mobile ringing the police. Her head spun, where was Poppy? *Where was her baby?*

The next thing Adira knew she was being led back inside to sit down. Jasper's arms gripped her tightly.

'Adira, take deep breaths,' he was saying.

'Poppy… where is she?' cried Adira hysterically.

By now Fletcher had come in from the drawing room, concerned by the commotion. He'd gone white on hearing what had happened.

Jasper had rung the estate manager and instructed him to alert all the estate staff to search for Poppy.

'Whoever's taken her can't have got far,' Colin had tried to reassure him.

'I want every inch of land covered and fast,' ordered Jasper.

'My Poppet…' whimpered Fletcher. The doorbell rang and he rushed to answer the front door.

Two police officers entered the hall.

'We've got a team to search the village,' one told Jasper and Adira. 'If nobody's reported hearing any vehicle come up the drive, whoever took Poppy must be on foot.'

'Yes, that's right… I didn't hear a car or anything. Just the phone ringing… then—' Adira shook her head trying to recall.

Jasper immediately felt guilty. Had his call distracted her? Would she have left Poppy otherwise? He gulped, swallowing the overwhelming urge to vomit too. My God, where was his precious daughter who had only just blessed their lives?

Chapter 49

Jasper had not only rung the police and estate manager, but basically every contact on his phone who lived in Lilacwell, desperate for as many people as possible to be involved in the search for Poppy.

Cassie had frozen when told by a frantic Jasper of Poppy's disappearance. Her heart went out to him and Adira. She couldn't imagine what her friends must be going through right now. She pelted from the office into the kitchen where Rory was with Jake. As promised, he had been tutoring him with English and maths, going over previous exam papers that Jake's college had supplied him with.

Rory's head turned sharply when Cassie rushed in.

'What's up?' he asked, shocked at the state she was in.

'That was Jasper on the phone. Poppy's been taken,' she wheezed.

'Taken?' Rory's eyes widened in horror.

Jake sat silently, his head turning from Cassie to Rory.

'Yes, someone's taken Poppy. She was in her pram outside in the garden.' Cassie's voice rose frenziedly.

Rory got up. 'Come on, we'll have to search the village.'

Jake got up too.

'Poppy's pram is distinctive... it's pale grey with red poppy flowers on it...' sobbed Cassie, bursting into tears.

'Be strong, Cass, we've all got to look for her.' Rory held her by the shoulders, willing her to stay focused.

'Yes… yes,' she stammered, wiping her eyes.

Together they set off, all in different directions. Rory took the fields that joined his land to The Laurels estate, Cassie ran along the dirt track to the river, whilst Jake made his way down the footpath leading to the stone bridge into the village.

—

All the time Jake's eyes scanned through the trees and into the distant countryside, while he marched on steadily with purpose. He soon reached the village high street. Pausing at the top of the row of shops, he squinted for a clearer vision of all the people milling about before him. Nowhere could he see anyone pushing a pram of Poppy's description. He walked along one side of the pavement, going into each shop for a quick sweep of who was in, then repeated the same on the opposite side, but still, there was no sign of Poppy's pram.

Satisfied he had explored the high street, Jake walked further on. He passed the village green and approached the church hall. Going up to the entrance, he tried the door but found it locked. Then, seeing the church next door, decided he would check in there too.

It had been some time since Jake had been in a church, not since his little brother's christening. Walking quietly through the vestibule, he stopped dead in his tracks. There was Poppy's pram, in the middle of the aisle. His eyes slid over to the girl sitting in the pew next to it. He silently stepped to the side, hiding behind a pillar to take a better look without being discovered. The girl turned to the pram, and he inhaled sharply. He recognised her. It was Becky Stansfield. She had been a student at his college but had had to leave before finishing her course because she had fallen pregnant. Sadly, he'd heard from other college students that Becky had lost her baby.

He stayed where he was, rooted to the spot and feeling all manner of emotions – alarm, pity and above all a burning need to let Rory and Cassie know of the baby's whereabouts, ever mindful of the poor mother who must be suffering. A door shut, the sound echoing through the church. It was the priest, walking out of the presbytery, down the aisle. He stopped to talk to Becky. Good, at least she wasn't going anywhere. Jake hastily texted Rory.

Poppy in church. Give me 5 mins.

Hopefully, that should be enough time to approach Becky and the priest. Jake very cautiously crept out from behind the pillar. He noticed Becky and the priest seemed to be in deep conversation. Jake walked quietly down the aisle towards them, his heart beating slightly. What was he going to say?

The priest looked up with a sad smile.

'Excuse me, Father, but—' Jake attempted to explain what was happening, but the priest gave him a knowing nod and motioned him to sit down with his hand. Becky didn't seem to realise he was even there. She just sat still, talking in hushed, hurried whispers.

'I just wanted to hold her... I saw her in the coffee shop once and I was desperate to see her again, to look after her again...'

The priest sat and listened.

'Then she started to cry, so I brought her here. I know she likes the windows, you see,' the girl tried to explain, pointing upwards at the colourful stained glass.

Jake's phone bleeped with a text message, but it didn't interrupt Becky, she was totally oblivious to him.

Is she safe? Rory had texted. Jake immediately messaged him back.

> Yes. Don't worry.

'I think Poppy needs to get back home now,' Father Forbes said gently.

The girl looked up, startled. 'You know her name?'

'Yes, I know her mother too.' He smiled. 'And I'm sure she'll be glad to know you've looked after Poppy, but it's time to give her back now.' The girl nodded, accepting what he said.

Then the doors opened in the vestibule and a gust of wind whooshed down the church. Jake turned to see two police officers. The male officer was talking in hushed tones into a radio control. The priest calmly signalled to them to stay where they were by raising his palm. Then he patted Becky's shoulders.

'Come on, I'll take Poppy back.'

He stood and slowly wheeled the pram down the aisle. Jake quickly followed. Becky sat alone in her own world.

Once they had reached the police, Jake spoke in a tense voice. 'I know her. She used to go to my college. She lost a baby last year,' he said by way of explanation.

'What's her name?' asked the lady officer.

'Becky Stansfield,' Jake replied.

'She is obviously in need of help,' Father Forbes said, facing the two officers. 'I suggest you tread carefully.'

'We will. Her family will be contacted before we take her in for questioning,' assured the lady officer. 'The parents are outside.' She gestured towards the church door.

'I'll take her to them.'

Father Forbes and Jake made their way out. As soon as they appeared at the entrance, Adira and Jasper sped over to the pram.

'Poppy!' wailed Adira, scooping her baby up. Jasper's shoulders visibly relaxed. Then he looked at Jake.

'I can't thank you enough,' his voice cracked.

Rory and Cassie, standing close by and witnessing the whole thing, came over.

Cassie hugged Adira, tears running down her face, while Rory patted Jasper's back.

'You all right mate?' he asked gruffly.

Jasper blew out a huge sigh.

'I am now, thanks.' He turned from Rory to look back at Jake. 'Both of you, thanks so much,' he gulped.

'Just glad I saw her,' said Jake, a touch overwhelmed by the unexpected events and emotional outpouring.

'Good on you, Jake, well done mate,' nodded Rory.

Together they all slowly walked back to The Laurels, where Fletcher and Lilly stood waiting at the door with anxious faces. As soon as Fletcher looked into Poppy's pram and saw for himself his granddaughter was safe, tears of relief came.

'Oh, my Poppet…' he whimpered.

Jasper poured them each a stiff drink. Poppy, oblivious to all the drama, had slept peacefully once Adira had fed her. Luckily, she had slept through most of her abduction, due to the eventful morning she had had at the mother and baby group. Only once, when Poppy had woken momentarily, had she cried, then soon soothed herself at seeing the colourful beams of light through the church windows.

Jake explained how he knew Becky and her sad history, plus what he had overheard her tell the priest.

'She said she'd seen Poppy in the coffee shop and wanted to look after her again?'

Adira gasped. 'I know who she is!' she cried. 'We met in the Puddleduck Cafe.'

'How did she know Poppy liked the church windows?' asked Jasper, absorbing all the information Jake had relayed.

Adira's eyes widened in realisation.

'She was there, in the church that day I called in. I thought I sensed someone about. She must have followed me after I left the cafe.'

A chill ran up her spine. Jasper put his arm around her.

'It's all right, sweetheart. Poppy's safe now,' he tried to comfort her, although his blood had run cold too. What would have happened if Jake hadn't seen Poppy? Or if Father Forbes hadn't intervened? The very thought knocked him sick. One thing for certain, he was having security cameras installed throughout The Laurels grounds and estate.

Chapter 50

As with all small villages, the shocking news of the Hendricks' baby spread through Lilacwell like wildfire. Residents were aghast that one of their own had abducted a new-born, until learning the full facts. Hushed murmurs of cot death… broken heart… breakdown… desperation… confusion, swirled through the community.

Whilst every sympathy lay with Jasper and Adira, there was also a sense of sadness regarding the circumstances that led to Becky Stansfield taking Poppy.

Once the Hendricks family had got over the initial shock of Poppy's disappearance, they too felt a degree of compassion for the poor, young girl who needed some form of help. The police had visited them with an update and Father Forbes had also called at The Laurels to see Adira and Jasper.

'As soon as I saw the pram, I knew it was Poppy,' he told them, whilst sipping tea in the drawing room.

'Thank God, you did see it,' said Adira with a shudder.

'I'm aware of the situation surrounding the Stanfield's,' he went on. 'Becky's mother is on the church cleaning rota. She and her family were devastated at the death of Becky's baby.'

'Oh, poor girl,' Adira sympathised.

'Yes, it was an incredibly difficult time for everyone. I did the funeral.'

There was a heartbreaking silence before Jasper coughed and spoke.

'The police mentioned pressing charges.'

'Well, Becky did commit a crime, albeit with mitigating circumstances. I believe she is undergoing counselling at the moment.'

'Yes, I see,' nodded Adira pensively. She couldn't help but feel for the girl. Having experienced a glimpse of the pain of losing Poppy, she couldn't imagine how she would have coped had it been a permanent loss. It didn't bear thinking about.

'Well, we just hope Becky gets the assistance she needs,' said Jasper. He too felt saddened by the whole affair.

-

Back at The Cobbled Courtyard, Max was telling Fitz of all the events while they waited in line for their coffees. Kit and Pru had told Max everything, after hearing it from Pru's parents, who had heard it from Father Forbes, who had rather sensibly mentioned it in his sermon. There had been talk of 'compassion', 'understanding', and 'forgiveness' which, coming from a priest in a small village, would go a long way. He had hated the thought of the Stansfield's being victimised in any way.

Fitz listened and was just glad that Eva wasn't with him. He wasn't sure how she would react when hearing the news. Would it trigger something painful within her? He hoped not, especially as she had come such a long way. There was no doubt Eva would hear the story of Poppy's abduction, but it would definitely be better coming from him. So, after paying for his coffees and bacon barm cakes, he went straight back to The Potter's Bolthole. Eva was taking a telephone order when Fitz entered the shop.

'Don't you ever take a day off?' he asked, shaking his head.

'You can talk,' she said with a laugh.

'It's Sunday,' he replied, passing her coffee and barm cake.

'I know, I know.' Eva held her hands up in surrender. 'No more calls. I'm putting the answer machine on.'

'Good.' He looked warily at her, trying to figure out how to tell her the news.

Eva immediately picked up on his hesitance.

'What?' She frowned, biting into the sandwich.

Fitz cleared his throat. 'Eva, something's happened in Lilacwell,' he began, then quickly continued before she interrupted him. 'Jasper and Adira's baby went missing, only for a few hours,' he hurriedly added.

'Missing? Where? Did someone take her?' Eva's eyes were like saucers.

'A young girl from the village,' Fitz replied sombrely.

Eva was stunned. 'But why?'

'Apparently she… lost a baby last year.' He looked tentatively, gauging her response.

'Oh, right.' Eva looked down. 'How awful.' She swallowed, suddenly not wanting to finish her bacon sandwich. She put it down.

'Max just informed me, and I didn't want you to hear it from anyone else,' Fitz gently told her, hoping this wasn't about to have a negative effect on her.

'Yes, thanks,' she replied with a nod, 'very thoughtful of you.'

Fitz came and wrapped his arms around her. Instantly Eva felt better – protected in his warm embrace.

'You OK?' Fitz tipped his head back to eye her carefully.

'Yeah. I'm OK,' she sighed, then thought to ask, 'So Poppy's all right then?'

'Yeah, she's fine. Slept through most of it apparently. It was her parents that had the shock of their lives.'

'I'll bet,' agreed Eva, trying to comprehend the torture they must have suffered.

'But she's back safe and sound now.'

'Who found her?' she asked.

'A lad who works at The Harvest Barn. Jasper had alerted Cassie and Rory and they all went searching for her.'

'Blimey, what a nightmare.'

'Hmm,' Fitz replied, suddenly understanding how his own family must have felt at his disappearance.

Eva now looked at him thoughtfully. She was intuitive enough to know his thoughts.

'And are you OK?' she asked gently.

He looked up at her and gave a half smile.

'Come on, let's eat these and then…' He raised his eyebrow suggestively.

'Back to bed?' giggled Eva mischievously.

'Nope. I've something to show you,' he said, his voice hinting of surprise.

'Oh, yes?'

'Yes.'

'What?' Eva squealed; she hated it when he did this.

'You'll see,' he laughed, he loved it when she rose to the bait.

—

After finishing their breakfasts, they walked through the woods to Fitz's cottage. All the while Eva's mind was working overtime. What was he going to show her? Her curiosity was mounting. She looked sideways at Fitz, was he smirking? He was enjoying this, she thought. Instead of getting frustrated though, she began to see the funny side. Fitz was a tease, well with her he certainly was, and she was just going to have to get used to it.

As always, Eva marvelled at the surroundings that Fitz was fortunate enough to live in. Woodsman Cottage lay nestled in the trees, far away from any prying eyes. It really was a haven, in every sense. She cast her mind back to her first visit and how magical it had been. She pictured them swaying in the hammock under a starry sky, hearing the hoot of an owl and the rustle of wildlife in the forest. It had been the happiest time of her life.

Fitz was also reflecting as he held Eva's hand and strolled through the soft earth covered with russet leaves. He only hoped that Eva would be as excited as he was when he revealed his surprise. When they reached his cottage, he turned to face her.

'I want your honest opinion,' he said, sending Eva into fever pitch.

'Oh, come on Fitz, I've got to know!' She couldn't contain herself any longer.

'This way.'

He led them into the kitchen, where on the table lay drawing paper with building plans. Eva looked down at the detailed plans before her, then up at Fitz with a puzzled expression.

'I'm applying to extend the cottage,' he told her. His finger pointed to the area where a two-storey extension had been added to the house.

Eva was still a touch confused. Why had he been so secretive about extending his home?

Fitz cleared his throat. 'Eva, I want this to be *our* home.'

At this, her head darted up.

'You want me to live here, with you?'

'Yes, I do,' he laughed, leaning back against the worktop, folding his arms. 'Then, hopefully, if you can put up with me, do the whole thing.'

A smile spread across her lips. 'You mean—'

'Marriage, children, the lot.'

'Oh Fitz.' Eva's eyes filled with emotion.

'Well, what do you say?'

She laughed and looked back at the plans.

'Just how many bedrooms were you planning on?'

His face turned serious. 'There's no rush. When I originally built this place, it was for me alone. I needed to hide away, in seclusion. That's the state I was in. Then, this gorgeous girl with sea green eyes came into my life and,' he gave a deep sigh, 'I can't live without her. I love her.'

'Fitz…' A tear trickled down Eva's face. 'I'd love to live here with you.' She went to give him a hug. 'And I love you too.' She kissed his ear.

'I meant what I said about not rushing things,' he gently whispered.

'I know,' she replied. She knew what he meant, ever mindful of her past experience, but Eva had moved on. In that instant, she imagined a future of pure happiness; of children growing up in this enchanting little woodland; a family huddled together by campfire, under another starry sky; of a couple growing old and content together, hidden away in their own perfect oasis.

Chapter 51

Rory and Cassie stood over the large, padded envelope with rising anticipation. The advance copy of their book, *Life at the Harvest Barn*, had just been delivered.

'You open it,' said Cassie, shaking with nerves and excitement.

Rory's finger glided firmly under the seal opening the flap, then he slid out the hefty volume. It was heavy, bigger, and thicker than he was expecting. He placed it down on the kitchen table for them both to inspect. Cassie took a sharp breath, hardly believing her eyes. This was *their* book.

They each took in the grand, hard backed cover. The title of the book was in bold olive lettering, appearing at the top, over a sepia photograph of the smallholding with the barn in the distance. The chicken coop and goat pen were visible at the side of the field, along with the raised vegetable beds and polytunnels. The picture encapsulated what The Harvest Barn was all about. The colours were just right, all natural, earthy tones of brown and green. It smacked of an eco-lifestyle and was exactly what Rory and Cassie were at pains to achieve.

'Love the cover,' said Cassie in awe.

'Yeah, they've done a good job there,' agreed Rory.

Then he opened it to the first page where the index lay. His eyes raked over each title.

Yes, thought Rory, pleased that he had managed to persuade the editor not to have a chapter entitled, 'The Climate Warrior,' as first suggested. He really didn't want the book to become something about *him*, when it was a shared venture with Cassie. Besides, he had had enough exposure as the Climate Warrior and was afraid it might come across as milking the title to death for his own gains.

He did concede that including an introduction on his career as a barrister provided a good background to their story, as did Cassie's previous role as an assistant hotel manager to The Inn at Lilacwell. It was relevant and explained why they had started their journey in the first place. Rory was quoted:

> Being a human rights barrister had been an enjoyable and rewarding experience. However, after years of practicing the competing demands of a barristers' chambers and getting increasingly tired of the traffic,

pollution, emails, meetings, and general humdrum that defines the rat race, I decided to take stock. I knew where I wanted to be, in my home roots of Lancashire. Luckily for me, the same place where my girlfriend lived. It was a no-brainer.

Cassie was also quoted in the introduction:

When Rory first outlined his plans to live an eco, greener way of life it made me think. Swapping a hectic routine of managing a hotel, for a new, creative, and more productive existence has been the best decision ever.

The book then went on to say how the diaries of the smallholders follows the experiences and challenges of substituting the city for the country. How the roller-coaster journey involved the renovation of the old barn, acquiring ten acres of land, adjusting to a rural lifestyle, setting up a business and gradually achieving the goal of self-sufficiency and self-reliance on a fledgling small-holding. Sowing, maintaining, and reaping of crops would be explored, as would moulding lives around a new and more sustainable rhythm.

The recipes that had been added as an afterthought were a great feature, as was the chapter on the couple's elopement. A wedding photograph had been included, which Rory still had reservations about.

'I was never sure about that being added in,' he said, narrowing his eyes at the picture of him and Cassie standing by the anvil in the Blacksmith's Shop at Gretna

Green. Although it was a great shot of them both, he found it a tad intrusive. To him it didn't seem right, sharing something so personal with the general public, when their own families hadn't been there at the time to witness it.

'Oh, don't worry,' appeased Cassie. 'It's only the one photo and it does make for good reading. I mean, running away in secret to elope *is* interesting. It all adds to the marketing.'

'Hmm, I suppose so,' replied Rory, still not fully convinced.

Overall, they were delighted with the book. They felt it gave an extremely good insight to living a more sustainable lifestyle, which was their main aim.

The conclusion summed it up succinctly.

As a hectic and experimental season draws to a close, we reflect on the ups and downs and contemplate expanding The Harvest Barn business. We would really love to say we've been living the dream; however, the reality has been one of long hours, blood, sweat and tears.

From the confines of the rat race, we have progressed to a field, harvesting vegetables in glorious surroundings. We have learnt how things grow and how to sell the things we grow. We have ploughed the earth, shifted over eighty tons of compost, and harvested countless kilograms of good quality organic fruit and vegetables. We now spend days planting seeds, chasing chickens, and harvesting crops.

We have also forged good relationships with local businesses, selling our home-grown produce to the surrounding community. We're really keen to celebrate local food in the most authentic and honest way possible.

The goal of ridding our lives of the daily grind has been achieved.

They both faced each other with huge, beaming grins.

'I think it's amazing!' gushed Cassie.

Rory nodded. 'Yeah, it's pretty good.'

'Pretty good?' She laughed. 'It's bloody brilliant.'

Rory loved seeing her eyes sparkle with joy – and yes, he was chuffed with how the book had been produced. A small part of him did wonder how this would affect them, ever mindful of how the media had once hounded him, but by and large his astute business head told him it made sense.

'Just cast your mind back to this time last year,' Cassie told him, arms folded with an arched eyebrow.

Rory's lips curved at the corners. She did have a point. If he could have seen how well his life would turn out, compared to where he was twelve months ago, he'd have been elated. He recalled the punishing hours put in studying his law books, the ridiculously early morning commute, the late-night finishes and that bloody awful Head of Chambers, Nigel Kerfoot. He shuddered at the memory…

So yes, putting everything in perspective, one photograph of their wedding day in a published book which was promising to be a huge success, was indeed a small price to pay.

'You're right, as always,' he winked.

'Let's celebrate,' said Cassie, reaching for a bottle of champagne in the fridge. They had been expecting the book to arrive any day, so she had it chilled, ready to pop open.

'Let's,' replied Rory rubbing his hands together.

The cork shot out across the kitchen as they let out a cheer.

'To The Harvest Barn!' they cried in unison.

Chapter 52

'Do you think she's warm enough, Lilly?' Fletcher peered into the pram.

'I'm sure she is,' answered Lilly with an endearing smile.

They were out strolling through The Laurel's grounds with Poppy.

As Jasper had been resolute, several security cameras had been installed in strategic places around the estate. Fletcher had been keen to make sure they were all in working order, despite Jasper and Colin, the estate manager, assuring him they were.

'I'll go and test them, make sure. You can never be too careful,' he'd insisted.

Ever since Poppy had been taken, the whole family had been on high alert. Fletcher cursed himself for never having thought of security in the past; but then, ever since he'd lived at The Laurels, safekeeping had never been an issue. Now, it very much played on his mind, as it did Jasper.

The whole abduction fiasco had unnerved Fletcher. He recollected all the parties and occasions that The Laurels had hosted. Hundreds of people had stepped foot in the place, whether it be family dos, summer balls, weddings, or some sort of village event. How easy it could have been for an impostor to enter his property amongst gatherings of such people.

Jasper was even more uneasy. He'd thought of the many campers and travellers who had stayed on their glamping site. It almost seemed unbelievable that installing some form of security had never been considered.

Well now they had, as Lilly kept saying, trying to pacify them. She hated that they were all made to feel so vulnerable in their own home. Whilst she and Adira were in favour of the security cameras, they equally wished Fletcher and Jasper would calm down a little and quit being on high alert constantly. It was beginning to create a tense atmosphere, one which Adira thought Poppy was picking up on.

'Poppy cries more than she used to,' she had complained, 'and she doesn't settle as well.'

'Do you think there's something the matter with her? Does she need to see a doctor?' Jasper asked in alarm.

Adira shook her head. 'No, I think she senses us all on edge. Babies can be surprisingly alert to people's behaviour and moods.'

At this Jasper ran his hands through his hair and sighed hard.

'It's just so raw. I can't help but think, what if—'

'I know, but life goes on Jasper,' countered Adira sensibly. 'We've got to get back to normal.'

'But Adira, that girl walked up the drive and nobody knew anything about it,' he hissed impatiently, still raging inside at what the consequences could have been. Then he saw the look of utter defeat in Adira's face. He closed his eyes and took a deep breath. 'Things will settle down,' he said in a soother tone.

So, in an attempt to put Fletcher's mind at rest, Jasper had advised him to see for himself how safe The Laurels now was.

Lilly had suggested they take Poppy with them on their tour of the estate, to give Jasper and Adira some time to themselves.

'Good idea, give her some fresh air,' Adira had said, smiling at Fletcher purposely.

'Aye, let Poppet have a good look around,' he had replied, before asking, 'What will you be doing?'

This was another habit Jasper wanted Fletcher to break – continually asking them where they were going and what they were doing. It was as if he needed to know their every move and it was starting to suffocate Adira, he could tell.

'I'm going to see Cassie,' she'd said patiently.

'Lovely, dear. We'll love looking after Poppy,' Lilly had been quick to interject before Fletcher could ask anything further.

Jasper had bitten his tongue. For the first time ever, he felt torn. He understood Fletcher's anxiety and also Adira's exasperation; he was caught in the middle.

'And Jasper, what are you up to this afternoon?' continued Fletcher, oblivious to any undercurrent.

Jasper and Adira caught each other's eye, exasperation and understanding passing between them in an instant. 'I'm going to The Cobbled Courtyard.'

He refrained from telling them that he was collecting new cast iron locks for the gates, which Max had made for him.

'Don't forget to take your mobiles,' Fletcher warned.

Jasper simply sighed.

Adira was glad to get out for a breather and a change of scenery. As much as she loved Fletcher, he was beginning to grate. Then she felt guilty. He was, after all, just worried about his family and Jasper was right, things would eventually settle back down.

When she reached Cassie and Rory's, she was once again amazed at what the couple had achieved in such a short space of time. She took in the converted barn, unrecognisable from the derelict, half tumbled down outbuilding it had been. The land too, from a wide, open space to neat rows of sowed earth, raised vegetable beds, polytunnels, composts, a chicken run and goat pen.

Cassie waved up at her. She was by the front door, taking her muddy boots off. Adira smiled to herself; her friend had changed too. No longer an assistant manager at an exclusive country hotel, nowadays she was covered in muck from digging.

'Hi!' Adira called.

'Come in, I'll put the kettle on!' Cassie shouted back, glad of a break too.

Once inside the kitchen, Cassie proudly showed Adira her and Rory's book.

'Oh Cass, it's fantastic,' squealed Adira, opening the pages.

She giggled at the pictures of Cassie and Rory working the land.

'I still can't believe you've gone from pulling pints to pulling up vegetables,' she joked. Adira loved the wedding photograph towards the end of the book. 'This is lovely. It really concludes your story well,' she remarked, pointing at the picture.

'Hmm, it does,' agreed Cassie. 'Although Rory doesn't like it. He didn't want it in.'

'Why?' asked Adira.

'He thinks it's private,' shrugged Cassie. 'He doesn't like the intrusion.'

Adira sat and reflected humbly on that last comment. *Intrusion*, the very thing Fletcher and Jasper were trying to avoid.

Chapter 53

Jasper, in an attempt to lighten the tension at The Laurels, suggested he and Adira spend a night away.

'I thought it would make a nice change for us, you know, a bit of quality time together as a family.'

'Where?' she asked, head tilted to one side.

'Anywhere you want,' he replied.

He was a touch taken aback at her reaction, thinking she'd jump at the chance to get away from The Laurels at the moment. He frowned, waiting for her to respond. Why wasn't she answering him? He honestly had expected her face to light up and throw loads of suggestions at him which they could enjoy together. Instead, a rather subdued silence hung in the air. Adira didn't meet his gaze, choosing to stare out of the patio doors instead, chewing her lip.

'Adira, what's the matter?'

Jasper moved to stand directly in front of her, forcing her to look at him. It pained him to see her blue eyes look so troubled.

'I'm not sure I want to go anywhere.' Adira searched his face, willing him to understand.

'But why?'

'Poppy's only a couple of months old… I want to stay here, at home with her.'

This answer floored him. He genuinely thought Adira had had enough of the place, what with Fletcher breathing down their necks and having limited privacy. It wasn't lost on him, the way his wife had to bite her tongue at times when Fletcher, albeit with good intent, had acted too over protective about his family. He himself had found it somewhat stifling.

He had tried to speak to Fletcher, as sensitively as possible, but wondered if he'd been too subtle and not clear enough. Straight talking was what Fletcher believed in, perhaps he should be more direct, really hit the message home. Jasper couldn't help but see the irony in it, after all, what could an eighty-six-year-old man do? It was how Fletcher still saw himself that made Jasper smile, as head of the family in charge of shielding everyone.

However, times were changing. Fletcher was no longer this larger-than-life character that Jasper had worshipped and looked up to as a child growing up. *He* was now a father himself and Fletcher was an elderly man. The roles had reversed, and Jasper had to stamp his authority, as diplomatically as possible. He must make Fletcher understand that he, Adira, and Poppy were a family unit, which *he* was head of. Whilst they were all content to live together in The Laurels, boundaries must be set; lines drawn in the sand, to avoid any unwanted interference or resentment.

Jasper recollected how Fletcher and Lilly had taken themselves off on honeymoon, and rightly so, but had he contacted them daily? No, he had given them the space they deserved. Now Fletcher had to do the same.

Jasper had worried that maybe he had left it too late to reach this conclusion, but after having heard Adira's reply he somehow doubted it. If it was so bad for her here at The

Laurels, why would she choose to stay instead of having a night away? He paused before speaking.

'We don't have to go far, but I think it'll do us good to be alone, even for just a couple of days.'

Adira pursed her lips, mulling it over.

'Poppy will be fine,' he continued. 'Why wouldn't she be?'

'I just appreciate familiarity, I guess. I want everything to get back to normal, before Poppy was taken and we were all a bit more… relaxed,' she struggled to find the right words.

'But a night away isn't going to change that,' reasoned Jasper. Then an idea suddenly struck him. 'Let's go to The Inn. You could have a massage at The Bath House.' He nodded with a grin. 'I can take Poppy for a walk, and we can have a nice meal at night.'

He was relieved to see her smile, so quickly added, 'And we won't be too far away from here.'

That seemed to clinch it.

'OK, that sounds like a plan,' she half-laughed.

Actually, Adira had rather succumbed to the idea of a massage. At times of stress or strain she'd benefited many a time by her grandmother's soothing hands, which had un-knotted and relaxed her aching muscles. Edie, her gran, had not only been a naturopath, but a qualified masseur. Adira had loved visiting her in Oxford, when she'd been a student, allowing her massages to release all the pent-up pressure that studying and revising for exams had created.

'Good, I'll get it booked for tomorrow,' said Jasper, eager to strike while the iron was hot and before Adira had a chance to change her mind.

Eva certainly wasn't changing her mind. Ever since Fitz had asked her to move into Woodsman Cottage, they had done nothing but discuss their plans and future. Thrilling times, but both were keen to keep it to themselves for the moment.

For a start, Eva would need to notify Jasper as landlord that she would no longer be occupying the flat above The Potter's Bolthole. She didn't really see this as a problem, as her rent included the accommodation as well as the pottery downstairs. Eva didn't particularly want someone living above her studio though, and thought she could use the space for visitors, as well as extra storage. It would be a while before Woodsman Cottage was extended. Fitz had submitted the plans, but it would take time for the council to agree – or disagree – to his proposals. In the meantime, they whiled away the time, talking of days to come.

In typical Max style, he suspected something was in the air, especially after seeing what Eva was wearing on her finger. He'd been enjoying a drink at The Inn with Janey when Fitz had arrived with Eva, looking all loved up. When Eva's hand had reached for her glass of wine, Max had noticed what looked to be a ring, only made of wood, on her middle finger.

Eva could see Max staring at it, as could Fitz. They exchanged a knowing smile. Max, never one to stand on ceremony, came straight out with it.

'What's this?' he asked bluntly, pointing to her finger.

Janey bent forward to take a look, curious to what Max was talking about.

'This, Max, is a ring,' said Eva sarcastically with a grin, making Fitz chuckle.

'Yeah, I know that,' Max replied flatly, then narrowed his eyes to take a closer inspection.

'Oh here, have a good look,' said Eva laughing. She took off the ring and handed it to Max.

It was made of walnut, a perfect smooth circle, with the letters T and E intricately engraved into the middle.

'I made it,' supplied Fitz unnecessarily.

'You don't say,' Max replied dryly, handing the ring back to Eva. Then he asked, 'Why T and not F?'

Fitz had anticipated this question. He had considered engraving F for Fitz, then something inside stopped him. An intrinsic urge told him to use his *real* initial, T for Theo. Why? Because Eva knew him for who he *really* was. He might be known as Fitz to everyone in Lilacwell, which was absolutely fine, but Eva knew all of him – past, present and now future. The ring symbolised his full circle of life and how it had joined with Eva's. The walnut wood was from a tree branch he'd taken from Hazelgrove when they'd visited. Seeing the fallen branch in the garden, he had pocketed it, with the intention of making something personal with the wood. Though he didn't really fancy explaining all this to Max. Instead, he simply shrugged.

'Well, it is my initial, isn't it?'

'What a lovely gesture,' remarked Janey, who looked truly touched.

Not to be outdone, Max nudged her.

'I can always make you something,' he cheerfully told her.

'Like what?' mused Janey, raising an eyebrow.

'Handcuffs?' offered Max with a cheeky grin, making them all laugh out loud.

'Trust you to lower the tone,' she scolded, still giggling.

Fitz shook his head. There was nobody quite like Max. Then, on reflection, he realised there was nowhere quite like Lilacwell either. Literally stumbling upon this special place had been the best thing that had ever happened to him.

Chapter 54

'Ah, this is the life,' sighed Adira.

They had climbed up to the top of The Inn, but it was worth the hike. The bedroom Jasper had booked boasted of 'expansive views and an open fire, with plenty of space and an elegant bathroom.' Jasper had simply picked it because it was up in the rafters, where none of the other guests could hear Poppy crying in the night. He had to admit though, he'd chosen well.

'Oh, look, Jasper!'

Adira was now in the bathroom pointing at a huge, deluxe, rolled-top bath standing proudly in the centre of the room. It was inviting them to be filled with bubbles to soak their weary bodies.

'I can't wait to sink into that.' She closed her eyes with longing, unable to remember the last time she had enjoyed such luxury. Jasper cocked an eyebrow.

'Room for two?' he asked with a sexy grin.

As if on cue, Poppy started to stir.

'She's ready for a feed,' said Adira, thinking it was good timing, before her massage in an hour.

Despite her initial reluctance, Adira was pleased they had come to The Inn. It might only be in the same village where they lived, but it was more about quality time than location. Jasper was right, they did need to spend some time alone together, just the three of them.

Thankfully, Poppy seemed to be a tad calmer. As the days went by, the family were learning to live harmoniously together again, and gradually things were getting back to the status quo. She was sleeping better, not waking up as regularly and didn't cry as much. She'd also had a growing spell and was now edging into age three months clothing. Poppy was proving to be a daddy's girl. Her tiny blue eyes would follow Jasper round the room, and she'd gurgle in delight when he picked her up. Adira found this endearing and wondered if Poppy was going to take after her, who was also close to her father and labelled a daddy's girl.

Even at such an early age, there was no denying who could make her giggle the most, though. Fletcher provided endless entertainment, pulling funny faces, and making all sorts of silly noises. Poppy would chortle, kicking her arms and legs in glee, only encouraging Fletcher to continue. 'Leave the little mite be,' Lilly would say, 'you're tiring her out.'

'Nonsense, she loves it!' Fletcher would insist, tickling under Poppy's chin.

It was times such as those that made Adira and Jasper value living as an extended family. You couldn't bottle such memories, they were to be savoured in the moment, every last second, because one day… well, it didn't bear thinking about.

'I think I'll take Poppy to the stepping stones,' said Jasper as he unpacked his overnight clothes.

'Yes, it'll be pleasant by the river.'

'Not as pleasant as your massage I'll bet,' replied Jasper grinning.

He was remembering when Adira had worked at The Inn for a few months to help set up the hotel's spa treatment room, The Bath House. She had also given massages, having been trained like her gran, and Cassie, the then assistant manager, had set up Adira to give Jasper a massage for devilment. Adira suspected from the glint in his eye what was going through his mind. She gave him a playful look.

'Are you thinking what I'm thinking?' she asked saucily.

Jasper came over to kiss her lips.

'I might be,' he coaxed.

'Then I'll book you in,' she teased.

Jasper smiled and took a good look at her. That's more like it, he thought. It was as if the old Adira had returned.

Later that evening, after Adira's relaxing massage, Jasper's riverwalk and a blissful bath together, they dressed for dinner and went downstairs, carrying Poppy in her car seat. Fortunately, they had been allocated a table in a quiet corner of the restaurant, rather than the busy bar area, so Poppy would hopefully sleep through their meal. As they chatted, sipping wine over their menus, Jasper took hold of Adira' hand.

'Thank you,' he whispered, gazing into her.

'What for?' she laughed.

'For everything,' his gaze then slid over Poppy.

No more words were necessary.

—

Back at The Laurels, Fletcher was still a touch perplexed.

'Can't understand it myself,' he said, sitting down with a thud into his armchair. 'What's the point of going away for a night, if you're only going down the damn road?'

It beggared belief to him. 'Totally pointless,' he muttered, folding his arms.

Lilly put her knitting down and gave him, what Fletcher called, That Look.

'What?' he exclaimed.

'You just don't get it, do you?' replied Lilly calmly.

'Get what, woman?' asked Fletcher exasperated.

'That Jasper and Adira need time out, together, alone as a family.'

'But we're their family,' he retorted, then paused.

His memory was starting to jog now. Jasper had mentioned wanting… err what was it he called it…? Quality time, aye, that was it: *quality time*. Hmm, maybe he had a point. He then looked sheepishly at Lilly.

'Have I been a bit…you know—'

'Overbearing?' said Lilly directly.

'Well… I wouldn't say *that*.' He shifted uncomfortably in his chair.

'Interfering?' Lilly tried again.

'Now steady on—'

'Or perhaps just too overprotective?'

Out of the three descriptions, Fletcher preferred the latter.

'Aye, protective,' he nodded.

'Yes.' Lilly stared him full in the face.

'Oh, right.' Fletcher frowned. Maybe he had. But was that a sin? To want to protect?

Lilly could see the dilemma in his face and felt a level of sympathy for him.

'We all know how caring you are, Fletcher, always have been, ever since I've known you,' she smiled at him. He *was* a gentle giant, a power of strength, her rock. 'But sometimes we need to learn to let go. It's not always your job. Let Jasper look after you now,' she gently finished.

Fletcher pondered on Lilly's wise words of wisdom.

'Aye, happen you're right, lass.'

He could finally see it. It was time to pass on the baton.

Chapter 55

Today was a very special day at The Laurels. It was Poppy's christening, and the Hendricks were determined to celebrate in style. For them it was more than a baptism, it was also an occasion for the whole family and their friends to celebrate together. Adira and Jasper had always intended to plan a family gathering, but they'd decided to go bigger and extend the invites to friends and members of the village. It was as though they had recognised the family could do with a lift, a good old shindig to look forward to.

Poppy being abducted, albeit for just a few hours, had had a huge impact on them. No matter how many times Adira and Jasper tried to reassure one another that all was well now, and security was tight, they each, in their quieter moments, couldn't help but mull over what could have happened. Questions like *what if Jake hadn't found her? Where would Becky have gone if Father Forbes hadn't stepped in?* Down to the all significant question which had prayed darkly on both their minds, *had she done anything to her?*

Of course, Adira had thoroughly checked Poppy when she had been returned and found nothing at all to be alarmed about, and taken her to the doctor, but those what-ifs still plagued her.

Knowing Becky Stansfield was seeking counselling was some comfort; but the fact she had actually managed to stroll up the gravel driveway and simply wheel Poppy away was a chilling one. Not a soul had even noticed the intrusion, let alone challenged it. The more Jasper considered it, the more he blamed himself – why hadn't he installed security before? And the more Adira thought about it, the more she blamed herself – she should never have left Poppy outside alone.

In the end Fletcher had to step in on hearing the two discussing the matter, he couldn't stand by and say nothing. Bugger if they thought he was interfering, this time he had to say something. In his eyes, things could get out of hand, if the blame game continued.

'Now listen the pair of you,' he told them sternly, his tone making them stop talking and look up. 'Poppy being taken was nobody's fault. It was a disturbed lass, who seized an opportunity. That's all—'

'But…' Jasper tried to interrupt, but Fletcher forbade him, raising his hand to silence him.

'No buts, Jasper. We need to draw a line under this now. *All of us*,' he stressed the last words.

There was a quiet pause. Adira began to open her mouth then quickly shut it at seeing Fletcher's warning look. He was right. They all had to move on.

So, hosting Poppy's christening was a turning point and one which they all fully intended to enjoy to the full. The Laurels was looking splendid and dressing the bannisters with pink ribbon and gypsophila, otherwise aptly known as baby's breath, reminded Adira of how they had decorated the place for their wedding. James, The Cobbled Courtyard florist, had cleverly supplied them with false pink and cream roses too, which finished the look off beautifully.

Lilly had made an enormous christening cake, which looked very professional, standing neatly iced and ready to be cut. Fletcher, being a stickler for tradition, had wanted Jasper to delve into the attic to find the family's christening gown.

'Really?' asked Jasper, not convinced it was altogether a good idea.

'Of course! All the Hendricks babies have worn it. Including yourself,' said Fletcher vehemently.

Hmm, what state's it going to be in then? worried Jasper, not particularly relishing the thought of putting his daughter in a moth bitten, dusty old gown.

However, to his relief, once he had retrieved it, he was pleasantly surprised. The christening robe had obviously been stored carefully in an airtight bag. It was an antique ivory silk gown, fully lined in satin, with guipure lace detail on the collar cuffs and front bodice. He chuckled imagining Fletcher wearing it as a baby, as well as himself. Would his mother have been the last person to handle it? he wondered. Had she packed it away in the attic after his christening thirty-two years ago?

When he showed it to Adira, she too couldn't help but giggle, picturing Jasper in it.

'It'll need washing,' she'd told him, but rather warmed to the idea of a family heirloom, being passed down from baby to baby. It was special and much more personal than a shop bought one. Adira imagined how the ivory silk would look well on Poppy, in contrast to her dark hair. She was growing to look more and more like a Hendricks, rather than her side of the family. Although her piercing blue eyes unquestionably came from Adira, as Jasper was keen to point out. It had tickled Adira how Fletcher kept remarking on the Hendricks' traits Poppy had, like it was some kind of competition.

'Poppy is Poppy, a little person in her own right,' Lilly had shushed him, always at pains to be as tactful as possible, as opposed to her clumsy husband.

–

The Cobbled Courtyard was closed, as all its residents had received an invitation to the christening. Eva was pleased to get an invite and was going to take the sculptured praying hands she had made for baby Poppy. Once again, Eva was reminded of how village life suited her, and she was looking forward to visiting The Laurels again and seeing everyone there.

Fitz was also glad of a day off to socialise with his friends. In his mind, he was thinking of future christenings. He envisaged himself and Eva holding bouncing babies, surrounded by family, a comforting thought which made him warm inside.

Rory and Cassie, as usual, were mad busy, rushing to get all their smallholding jobs completed, before getting ready for the christening. They were chosen to be Godparents to Poppy, much to Cassie's delight. Rory had been wary, hoping this wasn't going to set her off being broody once more.

'It'll be cool having a Goddaughter to dote on,' he'd said cheerfully, whilst gauging Cassie's reaction. For fun he had bought Poppy a miniature pair of pink, sparkly Wellington boots.

'How cute!' cooed Cassie on seeing them. 'Where did you get them?'

'A farmer's market, there was a stall selling all kinds of boots in every colour and size.' He had saved them for this afternoon.

Jake was to attend the christening too, along with his mum and brothers. Jake had, after all, played a pivotal role in the return of Poppy. He had grown from strength to strength, just like the seeds he planted, and was brimming with confidence, a far cry from the shy, edgy boy, with a dodgy CV, who had been interviewed a few short months ago. Now he had firm plans and had signed up to do the next college course as advised by Rory.

Max was bringing Janey as his guest, along with his granddad, known as Old Dickie who was an old friend of Fletchers. He had sampled the Hendricks' hospitality at Jasper and Adira's wedding, so knew a good do was in store.

Fletcher had insisted the Tomkin-Jones' receive an invitation, in return for the party invite they had had for Kit's fortieth birthday party.

'Half the village will be here,' hissed Lilly, praying her cake would suffice the number of guests.

'Good. That's what we want,' Fletcher had replied jauntily. 'Fill The Laurels to the rafters, the more the merrier!'

Needless to say, security was to be in full operation for the event.

Adira had even invited the ladies from the mother and baby group, having forged good friendships with them, as well as future friends for Poppy.

As all the guests made their way to the village church of St Jude, Father Forbes greeted them with a welcoming smile. This was one baptism he had particularly prepared for. There had been a lot of talk in Lilacwell since the Hendricks' baby's abduction – some of it rather unsavoury. It was his job today to quash any ill feeling or gossip within the community. Human nature could be taxing at times, he'd come to understand, and this afternoon's service was to be very much about new life, new beginnings, and a fresh start.

All the congregation shuffled sideways into the narrow pews, whilst Adira and Jasper held Poppy at the ancient stone font. They were joined by Rory and Cassie standing as Godparents. As the priest gently trickled holy water onto a very well-behaved Poppy, whose blue eyes couldn't keep off the stained-glass windows, he baptised her.

'Poppy Grace Hendricks, I baptise you in the name of the Father, Son and Holy Spirit.'

'Still be Poppet to me,' whispered Fletcher to Lilly on the front pew.

'Shush,' murmured Lilly, hoping nobody heard him.

After the service everyone piled back to The Laurels, where glasses of champagne were waiting for them. A small band had been hired and struck up 'Blue Eyes,' as directed by Jasper.

'My baby's got blue eyes...' sang the vocalist.

Jasper looked at Adira, their gazes locked, and they smiled tenderly at each other. Fletcher, never one to miss a trick, saw the affectionate moment and grinned to himself. It was good to see them like this, relaxed and happy, instead of tormenting themselves with negative thoughts.

Lilly tapped him on the shoulder to let him know that Alice and Rufus had arrived. Jasper's parents had chosen to sit nearer the back of the church, so he hadn't noticed